THE
COLOR
WITHIN

THE COLOR WITHIN

By

K. A. M. LASHLEY

Copyright © 2021 K.A.M. Lashley

To request permissions, contact the publisher at contact@boundtobrew.com

Library of Congress Cataloging-in-Publication Data has been applied for.

ISBN 978-1-953500-06-9

Edited by Pauline Harris and Danielle Manahan

Team Publishing

9457 S University Blvd. 819 Highlands Ranch, CO 80126

Boundtobrew.com

To my Nan and her endless sacrifices for her family.

A Summer Red

WINTER WAS WOUNDED BY WAR, spring cast doubt on life, and the summer was wet with blood. Autumn could provide long-needed peace, but the Red Summer had only begun.

Corey swung his legs at the kitchen table, picking at a puff of cotton peeping from the chair arm as threads of light pierced through the seams of the blinds and wove the morning together. There was never any doubt where he'd be at this time, face down and just shy of a dozen pages into the *Messenger*, scanning for a Claude McKay poem as he got to work on a bowl of soggy cornflakes. Between shoveling mounds of wet flakes and flicking through the pages with podgy fingers, he still managed to free up his hands enough to pick at the cotton.

He knew better, but still the cotton he picked.

A newspaper swatted the back of his hand, snapping it back. "Sorry." Not even a glance up, he knew exactly what that was for.

"Don't be sorry. Be better." His father walked by, half-dressed in his favorite lounge suit.

Martin unrolled the newspaper and sighed at the finely printed headlines; there were enough words on the front page to fill a bookstore as he glossed over the uneven titles. Rubbing his square chin, he blindly fumbled for a mug to fetch himself a morning brew the same deep coffee color of his skin.

Martin took a sip and cherished the bitter burn on his thick lips as he traced the headlines with hard brown eyes. He had heard that the Northeastern Federation of Colored Women's Clubs had put forth their scorn of the rioting and burning of negroes and their homes in recent weeks and months, but he had to see it for himself. Hope, like belief, was short stocked these days. He came across nothing but morbid readings, so a dip into that short-stocked belief was the best he could manage. Still, he stretched, hoping for a mention of W. E. B. Du Bois, or the National Association for the Advancement of Colored People, but they too seemed to still be brewing up a rebuttal for the racist rapture.

So, he perused with the faint impression of déjà vu, scrutinizing the titles, which were almost a facsimile of those the day before. The only difference was the numbers. And worse, rising numbers. Bold text outlined a macabre cocktail of words, listing how many had died, the equal number of injured, garnished with whose lives still hung in the balance of a coin flip. It was sour to the thought as he took another sip from his steaming mug, which fogged up his reading glasses.

"Dad," Corey took down the last of his cereal. "Can I play outside today?"

Martin licked his lips of the heat. "Play?" He set aside the paper. His tolerance for bad news had grown as thin as the pages it was printed on. "Do you know how many people have died in the last week?" His voice was hard like polished oak.

Corey turned his round eyes to the ground. "No," he lied.

Martin knelt to meet his gaze. "Would you like to know?"

"No," Corey said. 'But you said always listen to the truth no matter how hard it is to hear.'

"Right." Martin stretched for the paper, unfolded it, and fingered the numerals in the title.

Corey feigned reading the headlines to appease whatever reassurance his father required. "I see."

Sunday, Aug. 3rd, 1919

23 DEAD, 500 HURT IN RACE RIOT

Corey had read through the paper an hour before his father awoke—the bottle by Martin's bed had sung him a whiskey lullaby the prior night.

Martin rested a calm hand on Corey's shoulder. "I won't lie to you and say things will be different soon. They may

2

not be different until you're a man, and even then, the only difference will be how much the world hat—" He paused to swallow down harsher words. "How much harder the world treats you as a black man."

Corey gave a slight nod, face pulled down by the gravity of his father's decline. He spun in his chair and fished a picture of him and his mother from his knickerbockers.

Martin rose back up to his six feet and two pennies, scooped up Corey's bowl, and dropped it in the sink with a gruff sigh. He pressed broad palms on the edge of the worktop and rolled his neck to make way for new stress the day would undoubtedly bring.

Corey noticed his father glance over the sepia-set room that lingered with the scent of pumpkin spice and the ghost of lavender. The usual domestic drudgeries always irked him; dishes, sweeping and a meal for the evening. There was never enough time in the day. The checkered floor tinted with thin dust at its edges, and Corey felt his father hold back another sigh to abstain from a waste of energy. Pressure had mounted lately with his work and the vivid violence that plagued not only his state but also scourged the heart of America.

Corey couldn't go to school. He couldn't. Martin wouldn't allow it.

His father wouldn't risk being away from him for more than a couple hours, at the absolute most, unless Corey remained at home. So he home-schooled himself while his father's time was kept occupied by work Corey was ignorant to.

The textbooks—far above his age of learning—always got blitzed first: Math, he didn't mind, and he got through it mostly before his breakfast was done; next came science, followed by the odd peek at politics and geography he never fully grasped, and lastly, English.

To say he loved it was a distortion. Corey bathed in words. He scrubbed his budding brain with a deluge of poetry and prose, from any and every source he laid hands on—even those of relative antiquity.

3

Then Corey read and wrote, read some more whenever his hand cramped, and wrote again whenever the pages inflicted paper cuts. He had favorites...well, most of the books his father brought him were his favorites, and he finished them all. Sometimes twice. On a glee-filled second read, he'd shoot for a third. Seldom any more for fear of getting bored.

Corey mined his mother's picture for glittery feelings and precious memories, but the furrow between his thick brows showed it was in vain. His mother had long since passed before the first memory he could remember. Like the rose he stretched for in the grainy photo, the soft stroke of a sweet reminiscence remained out of reach. Besides, what three-year-old would remember the brush of their mother's love? Few. Still, he tried.

"One hour." Martin glared over Corey's shoulder to view the photo.

Corey snapped his head towards his father, and his face lit up like a new bulb. "Really?!"

"Yes." Martin tightened his tie around his high collar. "But not till I get back this evening. And under *one* condition." He raised a strong finger in front of Corey.

The jitter in his legs and smile that pulled from ear to ear didn't care what stipulation his father had to offer. He'd meet it and meet it well before he got home.

"All your work must be done," Martin ordered.

Not much of a condition at all. Studying had become like breathing for Corey, and today he had laid his math to rest long before he even began his breakfast. "No problem."

"And you need to read a book."

"Any book?" A crickety tone bounced with his question.

"Any book."

That was easy. He mused the thought that his father had gone soft, but the reverie of his late wife often filed down his rougher reasoning. Corey knew exactly what book he was going to read. He hopped out the chair and scurried off with

4

a pop in his step. When he returned, in his hands he cradled a dog-eared novel.

Martin's chuckle rumbled as he caught a glimpse of the title.

The Wonderful Wizard of Oz.

Corey's most favorite book. From what his father told him, it was his mother's favorite too. She had jotted down a quote on the back page that Corey read before and after each read.

Family isn't flesh and blood. It's time and love.

The simplest way for her to capture the bond between the eclectic group of wary wanderers on their journey through Oz.

"Looks like we have a deal." Martin swung his suit jacket on, offered up a warm smile that perked up his scribble of a pencil 'stache, and careened for the door. "See you this evening."

Corey barely lifted his head from the book as his father left the house following the swoosh and snaps of locks and bolts. The sound he knew now as safety.

He had never read a book more than four times.

This was to be his fifth.

*

THE EVENING came as quickly as the morning left. Corey had done his work, kept his word. Now he waited patiently for his father to return home and hoped he had held on to his.

An aroma sailed around the kitchen on a low pressing breeze from the open window. A pot boiled with spices and tender vegetables that swished with the scents of garlic, and chili, and pepper—lots of pepper.

Corey perused over the worn cover of another novel.

Adventures of Huckleberry Finn.

He hadn't read it, but as he turned over the first page the swoosh and snaps of locks and bolts cordoned him from even a peek.

Perhaps tomorrow.

His father came in the kitchen, rubbing away the new stress from the nape of his neck, and flipped his flat cap off to reveal a low fuzzed pate.

"That looks like a long day."

Martin rubbed Corey's head. "It gets longer still, son."

Corey's face fell south, expecting a breakdown in their arrangement. His father only had that dense glare in his eye when decisions had to be made. Big ones. Corey hardly thought going outside a matter of life or death. Or perhaps it had little to do with Corey at all.

"It turns out I have to—" Martin's nose twitched when the smell of stew seized his flat nostrils. He spun to gaze at the bubbling pot, then back to Corey with a questioning finger. "Did you—" He turned back to the broth once more to make sure the day hadn't driven him to delirium. "Did you do this?"

"No." Corey set the old book down. "Oscar came back just after lunch and put it on. I guess it's his apology for being gone the last few days."

Martin blew air from his nose and gritted his teeth, "That damn kid." He pulled his tie loose, careening for the living room. "Where is he?"

"He left." Corey looked down and pouted towards his cheek. "Said he'd be by the shop tomorrow."

Martin hunkered down at the table and rubbed away the knots that had formed on his brow. It was bad enough he had to leave his only son alone daily, but the pressure of minding his own younger brother felt like the load was always doubled. And whenever Oscar opted for the opaque thrills of the street life, the load doubled again.

A silence simmered between them. Corey too afraid to ask for what he wanted.

"Did you do your work?" his father finally said.

"Yes, sir, all of it's done." He scurried to fetch his textbooks. Martin flipped through them with listless eyes. Corey wouldn't lie about his work; he loved it far too much.

"Good." He traced the veins on the back of his hand in thought. "And the book?"

Corey slid it over to him. It was, of course, impossible to check, but again, Corey wouldn't lie about reading. He loved it far too much.

Martin cracked his neck with a sigh. "*One* hour."

Corey's face jumped into animation. The playtime would seem ephemeral to some, but he was about to enjoy every brisk minute.

He slipped on the chatty black boots his father made him wear, scooped up a dilapidated tennis ball, and bolted for the door.

"Corey." Martin's voice quaked. "One hour. Stay on our street."

"Yes, dad." With a smile, he took off again.

"Corey."

He halted at the threshold.

"Stay on *our* street."

*

THE LAST strands of the dying evening light were commissioned by the sun to unstitch the day. It set the sky such a deep orange it glowed red as the evening air thrummed with unrest. There had been riots the previous day and every day since the 27th of July. Blacks had their bones and dignities picked clean—so many had lost their lives—simply because whites had nibbled pride.

Corey drew an appeased breath that came with the nasal flavors of cut grass and wood varnish—his father had just redone the porch teeth after they got knocked clean out by an assault from some stray fist-sized bricks.

For an introvert, Corey had an odd propensity for the open air and adventure. Perhaps it was being cooped up all day that teased his true temperament, or perhaps it was the auspicious tales he had read of wild forests, grand cities, and heroes sleeping under stars and silver moonlight. The best guess is that he was born of both. Parents of his better intuition, despite his obvious parental inhibition.

He bounced the tennis ball, which was split and exhausted of any real air, flipped out his mother's photo, and studied it like his favorite subject as he plodded down the street. A gust threatened to whisk it away, but he pressed it close to his heart.

The street was denuded of people. He was alone with the wind. Brown lawns piled with rubble and ruin, poised in the wake of recent riots, uneven and off-kilter, stacked like idols of carnage. Although the grass was green on his side, the question was: for how long?

The breeze blew gentle this time—unusual for the Chicago wind. It cradled his podgy face that often tempted the snipping fingers of estranged aunties. He squinted through hooded brown eyes, which were bright, and bold, and mostly pupil, until the breeze subsided. A heart-shaped birthmark stamped under his left eye, no bigger than the scale of a pinkie nail, and his nose was as broad as his lips, which blended off into his bronze complexion.

The ball bounced off into the road. Corey checked for carriages, or horses, or cars that might materialize. There were none in motion —not that many people owned cars—he could count all the motor vehicles on his street on half a hand and one sat outside his home. Although the automobile industry was experiencing a boom, they were still too expensive for the common man and his common wage. Food and shelter held priority over convenience and pleasure.

Corey dipped for the ball, clamping his eyes shut as a firm gale almost knocked him to his knees. When he opened them, his palm felt light. The ball was in hand, but in the distance, his photo had made off with the breeze.

He gave chase.

His legs revolved with unbridled abandon, to degrees he never knew his knees could bend, heart thumping in his ears as he gave pursuit. The photo fluttered low and onto a rusted yard; a brief glimmer of hope cruelly took hold before the wind whisked it away once more. His chest inflated and released like a pair of old bellows fanning the desire that burned in his chest. He darted left onto the lawn; the brittle brown grass turned to dust under his feet as he dodged one of the rubble sculptures.

The wind took it between two houses and over an unkempt hedge, jagged and divested of leaves. *No!*

Corey wheeled himself low as the hedge approached, and with all the bounce his legs could muster, launched himself over. The menacing branches nipped and slashed at his legs, tearing holes in the long socks of his knickerbockers. His father would be mad, but he didn't care. Not now. Not now.

He landed in a roll and sprung back up into full sprint, watching the photo dip and dive between curtains pinned on foreign clotheslines. Corey ducked through the maze of white garments as a gale surged passed his ears, howling and cracking the bedsheets and bloomers that sought to thwart his vision and tease his best efforts.

Efforts that were not to end, despite his chest burning like molten coals and throat locking up with a familiar strain. It'd be two more gardens, a side street that led past an old halfway house his cousin frequented—his father told him never to go there—and a ramshackle alley before the wind seized and his photo finally rested on a manicured lawn.

Chest wheezing like the screech of a broken flute, he struggled to draw full breaths. Still, he retrieved his mother's photo from the ground. Its back was faced up and the address of his father's shop was scribbled in slightly smudged ink. He flipped it and took calm in his mother's face.

Corey glanced up and around; he was many streets from his own.

The house before him had a white porch similar to his, and on that porch, sat an elder lady, un-rocking in a rocking chair. She was inanimate, limp-limbed, slack-jawed, and drooling, with a clumsily knitted cream blanket adorn with a wobbly heart over her. Corey thought the worst.

He tiptoed towards her, in case he was wrong—he hoped he was —and she was fine, the last thing he wanted was the crump of finely mowed grass to wake her to the sight of a little black boy creeping her way.

Reaching the steps, he proceeded with caution and care. The planks did not cry or complain like some overzealous alarm or wooden guard dog. They were well laid and instead remained calm under the pressure. He reached her side and the smell of lavender—his mother's scent—filled him with a warm pink feeling. It was quickly cut by the prick of whiskey—his father's scent.

Corey cocked his head in line with hers and tapped lightly on her arm. "Excuse me—"

"Ahh!" The lady jolted from her sleep, wide-eyed and heavy-lunged. She clutched him by the shoulders. "Are you all right?"

"Umm..." he said confused. "I was going to ask you that."

Bewildered, she squinted through the evening rays. "I'm fine," she moistened her mouth when the words snagged on her dry throat. "Just taking a little snooze." She recoiled when she realized she was explaining herself to a stranger. A black one at that. "You shouldn't be here, dear." She darted frantic eyes over his shoulders in search of other souls. White souls.

There were none.

Nevertheless, she ushered him towards the placid steps, in a hurry to see him leave.

Corey clamped a hand onto the railing of the porch, and he felt something tickle his palm. He thought maybe it was a splinter of varnish, some stray blades of grass or the wind. He settled on the wind. An adversity as of late. "But Miss, I'm lost. I don't know which way is home." He looked up at her through sullen brown orbs.

"Dear, it's best you leave now. I'm sorry I can't help, but you should leave." Her sour green eyes were tired and glossed over.

Corey said no more, and when he turned to leave, he saw it. A fat, furry spider crawling up his arm. He was wrong about the wind. This adversity was greater.

His eyes bulged from his head, and the familiar strain in his chest came back, invited by the fluster of panic. He froze up, his breath quickened to a hare's pace as air slammed against the brick wall of his throat.

Asthma.

His enemy.

The elder lady noticed immediately. She flicked the spider off into the lawn and set him on the steps. "All right, try to breathe." *Really? It was the only thing he wanted to do.* "I'll get you some water...and a-a banana!"

She scurried off in her red evening shoes, throwing the fly door as she bound through her home.

On the steps, Corey battled for air, lungs burning with an ache for oxygen. He dove into the tight folds of his knickerbockers searching for his mother's photo. Desperate for the calm of her face. Desperate for air. He found it, pulled it out, and stared at it unblinking.

His remedy.

There were a few more moments of affliction, but before long, the panic gave into the photo's sweet submission. His breathing evened out, and the knot in his chest loosened like a noose from around an innocent man's neck.

Neither he nor his father understood the reason for his abstruse remedy. They had been to a few unscrupulous white doctors and they presented piteous clarifications that only brought his father to derision. After consulting his grandmother, they assumed there was some psychological hypothesis behind it and left it at that.

When the lady returned, Corey was locked in on the photo, as calm as a cat's purr. She handed him a half-full

11

glass of water and the banana, from which he took a shallow sip and a nibble.

"Are you all right?" she asked; this time it was well warranted.

"Yes. Thank you."

"You have asthma?" She settled into her rocking chair.

"Yes.'

'My son has asthma."

Corey said nothing and kept his eyes fixed on the photo.

"What's your name, dear?"

"Corey."

"Well, Corey, it's nice to meet you. I'm Elizabeth."

Corey said nothing.

Elizabeth peeked over his shoulder, and the supple honey skin of some woman in a florid gown fell into eyeshot.

"Is that your mother?" She eased.

"Yes."

"Did she have asthma?"

"I don't know."

His mother didn't have asthma, but every other man on her side of the family did and was tempted to take their last breath because of it. Her mother, Hattie, long since rested and laurelled, told of times her father sought to catch his death from the dust in the granary. However, his last breath came at the dusk of an end-of-autumn day, full-bellied, half-seas-over and purring in the wake of a pile of over-salted pork chops. This was often followed by an insipid reminder of her grandfather's 'hog-chest,' and when it did, it came with passion and glower. The man brutalized his lungs with foul tobacco smoke and cradled a predilection for the taste of tar, which, as a result, tanned his teeth to a wooden quality. He was often short of breath, and after only a pair of years breathing free air, he, too, took his last breath, thanks to a maliciously tied piece of rope, some hate, and a crooked old sycamore.

"How do you not know?" Elizabeth asked. Her voice was textured with the esteem of an old wine lover. Smooth, smoky and delicate.

"Because she died when I was three."

A lump formed in Elizabeth's throat. She swallowed it down to speak. "I'm so sorry...what happened?"

"My dad says *hate*."

"It has been fatal for years. A murderer of many."

Corey turned to her, taking in the features of her face for the first time.

Elizabeth's cheeks were high and ripe like freshly picked pink ladies. Wrinkles scattered off towards the roots of her graying hair which swooped and pinned back into a tight quiff that seemed a little young for her sixty years, but she held her chin up when it was done this way. It revealed a pink scar that lined the left side of her jaw and ended at her chin with a mark that favored a little heart. The navy skirt that dropped past her knees had almost as many folds and creases as her skin.

"You have a nice voice. Were you a teacher?"

Elizabeth chuckled. "Not that I can remember, no."

Corey twisted his lip in his mouth, turning the thought over in his mind. "You must have been a singer then?"

Elizabeth's chuckle stopped short, and she rocked back in her chair with a look greased with inquisition.

Lucky guess? Or a calculated one? Either way, he had offered her a note of his intuition.

"I was," she said with a soft smile. "A long time ago."

Corey pumped the air. "Do I know anything you've sang?"

"I doubt it, dear. My career started and finished long before you were born." Elizabeth picked at her floral blouse, which was as thin and white as a ghost's breath in winter.

"You could try me?"

Elizabeth glanced side to side, fiddling with the sea pearls that shone around her neck—an old habit that poked out whenever the muse of singing filled her with untempered elation. She had no time to warm her voice with methods and rituals she was once privy to. No one was around, and the mood was mellow enough.

She cleared her throat and tidied her posture.

"*She was the best of me, made my destiny, everyone could see when the light hit Grace's Pearls.*" She brushed lightly over her pearls and shuttered her eyes. Tone mellifluous and measured. It lofted to tender falsettos and dove to soft baritones in a smooth antipodal flight. "*She gave everything, even this voice I sing, she saved this little girl*—" She held this note for a time, her hand stretching to meet the reach of her voice. "*When the light hit Grace's Pearls.*" Elizabeth finished as her eyes opened.

Corey had a broad grin on his face. "I know that song! It's beautiful."

"You do?"

"Yeah, my dad plays it sometimes, on nights he chooses wine over whiskey. He said it was my mom's favorite song...when she was still around. I think he listens to it to help him remember. To keep her alive.'

Elizabeth's cheeks rose, partly from sorrow and partly from joy. That song was born of sadness; she wrote it to help her remember. To keep Grace alive. The thought that one day someone would listen with the intent of a similar nature—although downtrodden it may be—brought her tapered delight.

The wind seemed to sing a tune of its own, blowing the antifogmatic feeling from her mind. Her face dropped, almost lost in the moment, and she hopped to her feet and ushered Corey to leave. "Corey, it has been lovely speaking to you, truly, but you must go now."

Corey clambered to his feet and tucked away his mother's photo. "I don't know my way home though, Miss Elizabeth."

She sighed. "Well, what street do you live on?"

"South Morgan Street."

14

"That's only a couple of streets away, dear," Elizabeth pointed in the direction he needed to go. "Take a left at the end of the road, and after the gated park, it'll be the second street on your left. Run along now, and be quick—"

She stiffened at the sight of an old Ford Model T mounting the curb. A slim, sinewy man of gruff disposition jumped out, draped in a loose linen shirt and dusty blue jeans. His sable hair was slicked back with snake oil, skin sun-beaten with tunnels for veins. His face was taut, exposing cheekbones sharp enough to cut the tension he created. A large black blade was clipped to his hip.

"Whadda we have here then, ma?" His voice carried an earthy element, raw and raspy like the dull shake of gravel against garden tools.

"J-Jerry, the young man was just lost. He asked for directions, that's all—"

Jerry pushed her aside, and she crashed to the ground with a whelp.

"Miss Elizabeth!" Corey dove to help her.

Jerry gripped him by the collar and flung him across the yard towards the curb. Corey crumbled into a ball.

Jerry stepped up onto the porch as the two groveled on the grass, bruised by what were two simple motions for the long man. A life of labor in the South had hardened his hand. He looked under the rocking chair and fished out a bottle of whiskey. His face pulled down like he had tasted something bitter.

"Drinking?" He ambled towards his mother with the barely opened bottle in hand. "Consorting with a nigger child?" He shook his head. "I thought you better than this, ma..."

"I wasn't drinking—" she managed before a cough caught her.

Jerry dropped the bottle beside her and walked slowly over to Corey. Elizabeth shot to her feet and motioned to pull him back, but Jerry shrugged her off without much struggle, and the back of his hand clipped her lip. She fell again.

"You see, boy, I once learned a lesson about ablution. It came from a wise man with clear ideas of purification." Jerry drew his blade that glinted with the dead-red hue of the evening, staining it the color of blood. "He explained that *darkness* is a disease, one intent on afflicting a pure mind." He stood over Corey now, glaring down his long body, knife in hand. "And before that disease festers and breeds, becomes beyond your control, you must cut it out. I was young back then and didn't understand" Jerry drew back his blade. "I *do* now."

A car screeched to a halt by Corey's head, engine ringing like a bag of busted silver bells.

Martin jumped out, some warped piece of metal in hand, face a depiction of glower. His hard brown eyes met Jerry's dead grey ones.

Corey's chest ballooned violently as he peered up at his father.

"Corey, get in the car."

He obliged and swiftly made for the door. Martin said nothing more as he edged towards the car himself.

"I hope I see y'all soon." A sardonic smile was plastered across Jerry's face.

Martin and Corey drove home, not exchanging a single word. Corey knew what usually followed an act of transgression. A strip of privileges was imminent; playing outside would soon be a faint memory, and his father would roar until his voice was hoarse.

None of that came.

And for a journey he could likely sprint faster, the silence made time tiptoe by with lead soles.

The silence scared him. He wished his father would roar.

Yet, despite time, the night fell with celerity, the day was near done. Although it sighed the relief of a winter wind, the Red Summer had only begun.

A Chalk White

OWNERSHIP was essential.

For a black man, it meant he could have something the white man couldn't take. It meant Martin had something to hone and cherish, like his well-preened office, which served as a crown for his kingdom of a grocer below. Martin, a magnate of meats and other routines he hid in deep pockets, shared it with his family. Although they weren't all bound by blood, they were all bound by love. All by his late wife.

All bound by Cora.

Vivian, his mother, had migrated further north, eager to differ from the austere echo of slave fields and plantation days, to sow seeds in the big cities. She had hauled a fine assortment of nurses to join the National Association of Colored Graduate Nurses in Boston, along with his Aunty Ada, who he was especially fond of. In his years of high voice, she often snuck him spoonfuls of boiled honey and brandy, which was an old family nostrum she claimed cured insomnia. It worked for him, but in turn, he developed a precocious predilection for the flavor of firewater.

Martin's office was ornate by intention. He had designed it himself and fell in love with the reverence it held. His desk sat back near the far wall, separated by a single step and settled on hard mahogany flooring. A depiction of burgundy. Drawers and cupboards with painted gold handles lined the walls; crystal and quartz decanters rested on the bar, stained with a bronze twinkle from the remnants of a long night, while smoky late-noon light whispered an invite of the evening through half-mast blinds.

Martin spent more time in his office than anywhere else, even the floor rug he had bought from a pinguid man in St. Louis was kept cleaner than his home carpet—it was detailed with some obscure renaissance 'masterpiece,' so the man sold him, that Martin knew nothing about.

He glanced over his desk, privy to the time ticking on his gilded clock.

Four-fifty-three P.M.

They were late.

He assumed this of Sylvester; Sylvester was Sylvester. The man was allergic to the practice of keeping time. Donald's tardiness, however, raised ample cause for concern; the elder man had many rustic talents and timekeeping served as one of his sacred persuasions. The Lord only knew where Kat was. Martin became accustomed to the law of finding her in his office before himself, settled with her feet up in one of the three leather chairs, nursing a tall glass of brandy on the rocks—it wasn't of his favor, but he kept it alongside his whiskey just for her.

Martin rose to fix himself a dark tipple. As he made his way back, the blackboard came into view. It blended into the wall behind his desk, as tall and as wide as his wingspan. On it, spread the contextually obscure anatomy of one of his better-laid plans. Circled words were strung to callow sketches—he was not the artist Sylvester was—linked by lines and chalky ligaments that guided any wandering eye along a strict path. In the bottom corner, a particularly alarming sketch was circled violently many times over. The terminus of his plot.

He went to take a sip, but before his lips hit the rim, the door burst open. Kat came first, swinging her hips in her boyish habits of a cream blouse and straight black pants. The only time a dress touched her legs were in the rare instances she wore her suffragette suit. Sly followed, hands in the wing pockets of his raven-black lounge suit, strides as nonchalant as a bird in a mid-morning flutter. Donald came last, clipping the ear of a wincing Oscar between thick flabby fingers.

"Look who we found." Sly said with a flattened grin. His voice came out almost hoarse, like he required clearing his throat with a healthy cough.

"Os here thought it'd be smart to play hide and seek in Earn's alley and the old halfway house," Kat added in her honeyed tone. She made straight for the bar and took a shot of brandy. "Clearly, he hadn't heard about me."

Donald flashed Oscar towards the desk.

"Hey, careful now," Sly spat.

"Tha' boy don' wanna lissen nobody.' Donald spat back—accidentally but literally. A wet, heavy tongue sat on his bottom lip like a pink slug. His teeth had never met; his mouth was numb to enunciation.

Oscar rubbed his ear and made a terse effort to tidy his parched gray suit. Martin glared down on him with a look cold enough to freeze.

"Marti—"

"Wait over there." Martin cut him short and pointed to the corner where a tired old stool slept by the carcass of an ivory piano. It was piled with miscellaneous objects Martin had no more use for: untouched sheet music, bottles he liked the shape of, and a decade's worth of dust. Martin took a sip of his whiskey and waved for them to sit.

Kat was already trying to make sense of the web of words and daft doodles that sprawled on the wall as she edged to take a seat.

Kat, ironically, had cat-like features and during her junior years, it often occasioned her peers to believe her name false or of her own making. However, her father named her Katherine. Something the eldest son from each generation in the May family was almost obliged to. It came from the matriarchal ancestor of the family—however many 'greats' ago that may have been. That woman named her free family: *May*. In honor of the month she gained her long-lusted liberty. Kat was the uncanny case of tradition meeting coincidence. Her black hair was pressed into neat, sleekly laid finger waves that crowned her face, which was the color of warm beach sands. As she moved to sit, her canvassing pants drew her straight—curves hidden beneath linen lines.

Sly was already sat in the leftmost chair. Her chair. She kicked at his heel, glaring down at him as she ushered him to move. "Don't act new, sit in your seat." Sylvester snarled and hopped into the center seat—which was not his either.

Sly felt Donald over him, but before the elder man could fumble words to ask him to move, Sly interjected. "I ain't moving, old man."

Donald sighed through his nose—his mouth was too full of tongue—and settled into the remaining seat. He was a distinguished man, well-made and buttoned up, with tastes tailored from a life of liquor. Salt-and-pepper stubble cradled the bell-pepper features of his shiny face, which innately fought off the advances—much to his aching—of any female attraction. The chestnut suit he wore was crisp and well taken after, save for the cuffs, which were stained with the shadow of motor oil—he never 'changed a quick gasket' in it again.

"Don, just sit, please. We haven't got the time; you know this better than them." Martin hurried the bulbous man.

"Know what better than us?" Kat looked across to Donald and then back to Martin with a raised brow.

Martin pressed his palms to the polished wood, turned to the blackboard, then back to his company. "Last night, Donald informed me that somewhere in the city, there is a cache of unmarked, unclaimed guns."

A fidgety silence tapped at the room while the two unaware digested the news.

"Enough to start a war?" Kat's jaw clenched tight in a rhythm of abhorrence.

"Enough to end one." Martin stated.

The mood quickly diminished. Donald's demeanor remained uniform. Sylvester held back a grin, but his eyes betrayed his inner guile when they glistened with the grey of gunmetal. Kat stormed over to the bar, her heels snapping against the varnished floor like gunshots as she went to pour herself a brandy smile. It was the only way she would be able to force one.

"Word is that an old war sergeant came back from Germany, ill with a fatal case of the flu. Before he passed, he told his son about an unaccounted stock of guns that came back." Martin continued after a sip of whiskey. "That same son was nabbed by some of Earn's boys, Jewels and

20

the worst sort, during a riot a couple days ago, and he begged for his life in return for some information. That's when he told them all about it."

Martin could read Kat's mind through the narrow of her eyes. The mention of Jewels sent her scowling. It was a fitting name for the man's fast finger and idolatry for picking pockets. Kat had never been fond of the local rogue's egregious facilities or his second-rate affiliation to their family.

Sly cleared his throat, finally, as elation settled behind his languid gaze. "And this son?"

"They killed him anyway. Like I said, this is a war—"

"A war you believe will end with the shedding of more blood?" Kat took a clamorous gulp of her sweet brandy, spun full flavored with the thin scent of dried vanilla, which dangled in the room.

"Not more of theirs, just less of ours. And the only way to do that is to protect ourselves. Fists, bricks, and loud voices mean nothing when the police and their *arms* are fighting for the other side." Martin rose and paced in long strides behind his desk, glancing ever so often to whoever's shuffle broke between the quiet. "We need *arms* of our own."

Donald yapped his tongue, seeming desperate for the satiation of feeling in his mouth. "He righ', they killin' negroes like ants ou' dere." His churchy infliction exposed a home long since left in the Carolinas, despite the making and unmaking of himself for decades in the Windy City.

"So, what do we do?" Sly asked. "Cause it sounds like something out of one of them books Corey be reading all the time."

"You should try it, whenever you can pull your face up long enough from the crotches of all them gals you be claiming." Kat clapped. It seemed like her daily bashing, but in truth, it was a result of Sly's proclivity towards the plan.

"You just mad 'cause they ain't you."

"Not even if you boiled it in bleach and brandy." Kat didn't even bat her stubby lashes at him and remained uninterested, like all the other times he told tales of his concubines and conquests she never believed—none of them did.

Martin cleared his throat to catch their attention. "It ain't no fairy tale," he continued with the topic. "This is for real. You're right; few people know where the guns are, but each day, more people know they exist, and more people are talking about them. Which means..."

"More people are gonna be looking for them." Sly finished, sitting up to the situation.

Martin nodded. "Lucky for us, we have friends. *Nosy* friends. Earn said he heard about the guns, but Jewels was the one who did the persuading."

Donald told him his old friend left the boy's corpse with a handful of gem-shaped cuts. Jewels' fingers were ever adorned with cheap rings.

"So, Jewels knows where the guns are?"

"Yes."

Sly perked up higher in his seat. "Well, let's go find him; it shouldn't take too long. If he ain't at the halfway house or shooting the breeze in Earn's Alley, he'll only be a street away."

Jewels possessed the flamboyant talent of being in all places at all times. He had the ill-formed frame of a neutered rooster and ran just the same. If you didn't see him at least once for the day—blazoned with his unscrupulously acquired chattels of fine silks, broken wedding bands, and foreign silver trinkets—he was either ill, in jail, or you were walking with your eyes shut. And Jewels, despite the manner of his beguiling liberty, was the picture of health and far too quick to ever be caught in jail.

"No need," Donald said. "He gon' come 'round and see Martin tonigh'."

Sly shot him a languorous glower.

"As you know," Martin's hands caressed each other behind his back, "Donald and Jewels used to be like brothers in his days on the streets, so he convinced him to come and see what we have to offer in exchange for the location of the guns."

"So, this is what we are doing now?" Kat asked petulantly after a silent session with her thinning glass. "Dealing arms? Inciting *more* violence? Putting our black brothers and sisters to war? We were meant to mend not murder, build not break. Achieve something greater than our current selves and empower our people into a brighter future. One that doesn't involve blood as a payment for life." She paused and glared at Martin, brows turned up, forehead chewed by his dogged idea, with a glint of detest in her eyes. "Cora would have been ashamed—"

"Cora's not here!" Martin stopped and thundered rough fists into his desk, quaking the dead glass, desk clock, and folders with a deep tremor. Spit flew violently from his mouth, and a hot throbbing vein formed above his wide eyes that threatened to pop under the pressure of her incendiary comment. "She lost her life for the same reason we are losing ours. The *same* way of thinking you have now. Peace and rights. Peace doesn't exist today; it may one day but not today. It didn't yesterday, and it damn sure didn't the day she was taken from us! So right now we must fight for our lives, as they took our rights, and be that by *any* means necessary because our lives are the only things we have left to fight for."

The room fell into pin-drop silence so muted you could hear the quartz in the clock ticking. Kat clenched her jaw tight and looked away, fighting back the sting of tears that welled in her eyes. Donald tucked his tongue away for the first time, and even Oscar in the corner was rattled. He had been but a boy when Cora passed and knew next to nothing of her other than the golden tales people told. Still, his brother's words moved even him. Martin straightened his tie, tidied his desk that had become undone by his dishevelment, and fetched another drink as he collected himself.

Sly pursed his lips. There was truth in what Kat said—he knew his cousin would have opted to do things differently—but they couldn't shut eyes to the maladies of their modern world solely because of the anachronistic naivety of a past promise.

A long crippling moment passed before Sly broke the silence. "What we gotta do, Martin?" he asked with docile volume.

Martin squeezed at his nape, rolled his head, and hunkered down. "Sly, I need you to gather the people. Everyone we know: The Violets, The Mad Hands, The New Night, anybody willing from Earn's Alley, and ready them for what's about to come." He turned to Donald who spread thickly in his seat. "Don, you know your role, take a few of the trucks from the shop and fit them with new torsion bars. The load from the guns is going to be pretty heavy so we need the best suspension we can get."

"If we use the trucks, how are we going to keep up with couriering goods for the store?" Kat had a point. They only had three, and given the speculative size of the load, they'd need at least...well, all of them.

"We'll take that hit." Martin explained. "Business isn't exactly booming right now."

Kat was well aware. She kept the books because, other than Martin, neither Sly nor Donald had the acumen to parent large numbers. It was because of this aptitude for long division and predisposition for algebra that she wondered how the business even remained afloat. Clientele had dwindled to a handful of regulars and that one sympathizing white lady Sly always buttered up to buy more, yet the numbers remained steady.

"Kat, I know this isn't ideal or in line with what we originally had in mind," Martin continued, "but sometimes the only option we have isn't always a moral one. If you can understand that then I *need* you with me. I *need* your help collecting, counting, and transporting the guns once we get the location."

Kat nodded gingerly after a pensive pause.

"Thank you." A smile tested his lips but failed when he saw Kat's distant gaze pass him, glaring at the alarming image circled on the blackboard they could finally decipher:

the crude, abstrusely sketched crates. "That's all then. Once we have the location, we'll meet up tomorrow evening to go over everything—"

"What about me?" A mousy voice interrupted his speech from the corner of the room. Oscar.

Martin had forgotten all about him. This was the most obedient he had been in some time, privy to a plan that didn't concern him—he likely learned the nosiness from long spells with Earn.

"What about you?" He barely honored him with a glance as he cleaned the blackboard. "You need to go home."

"You can't put me on time-out all the time." Oscar rose and teetered towards their side of the room. "You're not my father."

"No. I'm not." Without waver, Martin turned to look him dead in the eye. "I'm never going to be our dad. But I am your brother, and if you don't have any respect for me, the person who puts a roof over your head and food in your belly, then what did dad die for? Why did you beg to stay out here with me when you could have gone with Ma?"

"Because...I wanted to be like you." Oscar chewed his hefty bottom lip and turned his slanted eyes to the floor, his brother's gaze buffeting. "But you're always treating me like a child."

"You're always acting like one. You want some respect? Start giving a little to get." He resumed clearing the blackboard. "Now go home."

"Marty, gi' the chil' a break," Donald uttered after a glance at Oscar's long face. "Now I know he done messed up a whole bunch, but it's bes' he be wit' us, ratha' than runnin 'round these streets. No house ain't gon' hol' him, the boy too slick fo' that. Besides, he got his father's name, maybe he got some of his sense in 'em too."

Martin hooked his hands on his hips and pondered on Donald's words. Although indistinguishable in sections, they were wise and reasonable. The man almost raised him in his adult life in the wake of his father's untimely absence. He paced for a short while, turning the thought over many times in his mind. He thought about his father. Remembered the way those white men beat him like a dog with rabies in front of his mother and infant brother. He thought about the way the tears seared his skin and tore unrelentingly down his face, recalled the hollowing screech of his mother's cry. He thought about the way the claret seeped from his father's bloodshot and battered eyes as he lay in a pool of gore.

He thought about the way *hate* took him.

Given the times, he couldn't—no, wouldn't—resign his own family to a kindred fate.

"Fine, you can help," he finally agreed. "Who wants to take him?" Martin darted eyes over his company.

Kat set her empty glass on the desk. "I love you, Os, but you can't drive or count very well so it's pointless coming with me."

"Sorry, Wiz, I think your brother wants you off the streets, not deeper in them." Sly would have loved him to tag along but could only offer the irenic decline this time. He nicknamed him 'Wiz' with a bitter irony. Oscar ardently sought them out, whenever in need, in hopes they would acquiesce and grant him his fallacious wishes. They often denied. He was too rattle-brained and garrulous to understand their better decisions, so in turn, he often made bad ones.

"You can come wit' me son. Learn 'bout whatcha pops taught me," Donald offered—the last and only offer.

Oscar smiled, really wanting to go with Sly but wanting to be involved more than anything.

"Come here," Martin stepped from around his desk and approached his brother, towering over his meager frame. Martin straightened the boy's saggy slate-hued suit, restored his flat cap to a fitting position, and dusted his shoulders off. He picked up his brother's head to meet his eyes. "Keep your chin up. Hold steel in your eyes, ice in your veins, and fire in your belly."

"And love in your heart," Kat added.

"Right," Martin smiled and patted his shoulder. "You go with Don and do everything he says. If he says 'no,' treat it

26

like the gospel and say 'Amen.' I may not be our father, but *he* is practically mine."

"Thanks, Martin." Oscar did well to hide the glee behind his thin face.

"Now go. I'll see y'all tomorrow." They said their goodbyes and made to leave. "Oh Don, wait up, and Sly, you are forgetting something?'

Sly's face was plastered with bewilderment before it wiggled with the clarity of realization as he sauntered over to the cupboard beneath the bar. Martin tossed him a scratchy copper key from an inner pocket, and the slim man knelt to open it, silhouette shading its contents. Martin waited for him to finish before he addressed Donald.

Before the clock could tick ten times, Sly locked it up, popped the key back to Martin with a languorous behind-the-back throw, and patted down his pockets as he left.

Martin and Donald were alone.

Martin got close, enough so to inspect him and smell the wet metal and spiced rum that lingered on his breath. He tapped his nose like he had a secret. "You off that shit, right?"

Donald was taken aback. "Com' on now, I only used them cocaine drops fo' my bad teet'. I'm good."

Martin eyed over him, paying special notice to his nose. He knew how it started, but he also knew how it spiraled into a sore habit. For a time, Donald liked to play in the snow, whatever the weather.

"Good, because I need you. And I know you got Os to watch over, but we need them trucks done fast."

"Why ya think dey call me da Engine Man, huh?" Don chuckled.

Martin smirked and squeezed Don's shoulder before the man quit the room. He always wondered why Donald owned the title. Perhaps his old routines had much to do with the reason.

A Brew Black

UNDER THE BREATH of bilious lamplight, Jerry sat pensively over a pure glass of milk while Durkin's pub simmered with the din of arid arguments and old men moaning.

Visibility was low betwixt the haze of cigar smoke, save for the glint of half-finished pints, flustered blue collars, and gnarled custard-colored teeth. The scent of old alcohol seeped from the suds-soaked and swollen flooring to shake hands with the tang of lime and salted pork rinds. The ends of black brews and sour stouts settled at the bottoms of clouded glasses that were stacked in impossible towers. Hecklers molested each other's ears with erroneous ramblings, groping at their ill-burgeoned sensibilities, which were incoherent with the practice of decency or decorum. They managed to stay imperiously off-the-cuff and out-of-pocket whenever the feeling fit them, and it often came at times that—they measured—suited to the situation.

"Those spooks better simmer down and get back in line."

"They didn't fight. They don't deserve jobs."

"Goddamn good-for-nothin' niggers takin' what's ours!"

The last jeer came from a pale, foamy-mouth fellow who was mad as a March hare. It stirred a unison of 'hell yeah's!' that scoffed at harmony and winked revolution's way.

Jerry felt the same, but he was a man who kept his feelings in his thoughts, not on his sleeve like the beguiling culture his capricious company had adopted. He preferred the path of discipline, of dominance. Of action.

Discipline was the bastion by which he laid his abstinence from alcohol. He had good reason to refrain from drinking and being jingled. It was simple for him. His father didn't drink, so he didn't. And being privy to his mother's nefarious tendencies with the devil's nectar, he abstained from the foggy habit. Even in his ephemeral years of service, where most men in the gut of German trenches required a gauze more potent than ebullient propaganda and patriotism before they could rally into a resurgence, Jerry abnegated. Many—if they hadn't drowned or were shot—brought the rum routine back with them. Jerry only needed a clear head, cold steel, and the undiluted hate that coursed through his veins.

The foolish bartender chattered on about the malignant dispatches of the black man as he polished glassware with a bleach-scarred cloth. Jerry knew he had nothing of consequence to say; the barman was loud and lurid with his opinions and often went cross-eyed when the passion took him. His thin flap of deeply dyed black hair shrouded a balding crown, and his face, blotched with burn marks from stray embers, pulled at its fringes with young wrinkles. Still, Jerry lent an ear whenever he spoke on almighty topics.

"See, our Lord says that bondage was by his decree and that those blacks were made to be in chains, under the thumb of our greater race." His voice was gruff and jagged—too many frequent communions with a smoky disciple. "They should be thankful we brought them here over rough seas from their huts and ditches to serve us in good favor. But this is the thanks we get. They steal from us, take without asking, even try to kill us! Soon they are gonna start thinking they're better than us. Then what?" A preened gold crucifix dangled limply from his neck, catching the bile shine of the thin lamplight as he spun for another glass. "When it's all said and done, the Lord's way will prevail, and they will know their place, whether that be by peace and submission, or blood and broken bone." He adjourned indefinitely from logic, or any other viewpoint for that matter, nailing his flag to the mast of Christ and the opaquer teachings of his religion, ignorant to the purpose of parables.

Jerry said nothing; he only offered up a glance from his cold gray eyes between the breaks in the bowl-bellied man's cold gray speech. He, too, was a man of the Lord's word but balanced his God-fearing ways with the realities of the world, seeking not to align his faith with the likes of born sinners, denouncers of heretics, and rambunctious religious zealots. Instead, he swanned from mystic radicalism and dogma of others who thought themselves higher. He chose to employ God when sin took the reins. Heresy, on certain accounts, spoke more logic than the Good Book, and on slippery occasions, zealots became close cohorts.

He was constantly self-correcting on his path to purification.

Yet he held dear demons disguised as angels, eager to feed them with the black lies he distorted as a diet of white truths.

The bartender pressed on with his devout preaching of what was right and what was meant to be to a stubby man with browning fingertips that sat beside Jerry drinking up the words more than the beer he had barely touched. Offering questions and contradictions to the barman's verbose ramblings. Jerry had been subject to this trap once before, but he quickly decided the man was partially blind—mentally at least—as any inquiry against his word was met with an insipid rebuttal in the form of a quote from the Bible that often carried no weight or topical relevance to the conversation. So, Jerry came now only to ruminate in the presence of small minds he felt dominance over. There was a part in him that felt in control, despite not saying but half a word to anyone aside from the boor of a barkeep. He was sure that with a prudently placed speech, filled with the demeaning mentions of negroes and their fictitious deficiencies, he could rally the men to his cause by massaging their facile temperaments.

The muse of dominance kept him coming back.

Jerry looked over his shoulder to scan the crooked smiles and sour frowns that crisscrossed the dim tavern. Belligerence still held dominion over the tone of their debates and moaning. He sighed through his hooked beak of a nose, drained the pint of milk, got up without a word, and flitted out of Durkin's pub, sick of the hostilities.

*

THE MORNING was untouched by the nearing fingers of noon, and the sun snoozed under a quilt of milky clouds as it approached its zenith in the sky. The day was fervid like many had been recently. It occasioned the horizon, which was dotted with street signs, denuded storefronts, verdant oaks, and effulgent car glass, to haunt with the mirage of a waltzing heatwave that danced between the gray-brown buildings.

Patrons paraded the streets in an afternoon drift. Women in peach and periwinkle blouses floated along the sidewalk, locked in the arms of their lovers. Kids scuttled across the roads, weaving between the *chuck, chuck, chuck* of horsecars and carriages, desperate for shade from the stirring sun. The trampled stench of oil-slick manure strangled the air with a thick, burnt rubber scent. They all seemed to mind, all busy mopping sweat from their low brows, cowering at the heat and complaining. Always complaining.

Jerry pulled up his blue jeans and loosened the top button of his soot-colored shirt, exposing the stringy muscle on his chest. He was a sore thumb in a place like this; he wore clothes fit for the habits of the South and crop fields, while men around him strutted by, swimming in baggy lounge suits. He paid no notice and dove into his shallow pockets to scrape together the dregs of a vacant paycheck.

Ninety-five cents—just. That amount only assembled from a rummage in his other pockets. But this was handsome considering his unwanted intermission from employment. And perhaps pretty enough to buy the victuals he promised his family.

Across the street, a boy stood chewing a warped toothpick with his heel kicked up against the wall of a florid grocer. With the glare of the waking sun in his eyes, the boy's suspenders and knickerbockers favored the silhouette of tarnished overalls. It reminded Jerry of his prior engagement to a fiancé named 'farm life.'

The mid-July sun beat down on his bare back, reddening his pale skin to blister while persuading sweat. The heat became scrutinizing, buffeting with each effort, but his early lessons of discipline from his father made him persistent in

31

ploughing. The infant sheep complained with crooked cries as they scampered for the fringes of their pen, which was draped with the shade of fresh oaks. Jerry never dared look up during high noon; the glare would cause him to sway and faint, harvesting a crop of sweltering words from Clinton he preferred not to swallow. His young budding arm hairs curled and popped under the strain of the blaze. The air was syrup, each breath a sweet labor.

That was something to complain about. Discipline deemed he did not.

Jerry slipped back from his reminiscence as the street materialized in front of him once more. He crossed, careful of any potholes and gaps in the uneven cobblestone. He reached the other side, and the boy's cheesing round face came into view. The young man had a distinct strip of vitiligo streaking the bridge of his nose and looked no older than thirteen, yet his demeanor hinted at a disposition nurtured by a requisite to mature. Whether that be from rationed amounts of love, or being starved of it entirely, the boy seemed aged and hardened behind his hazel gaze. As Jerry passed, the boy plucked the toothpick from his mouth in a fashion that mimicked a cigarette and feigned tipping an invisible cap. Jerry usually ignored such indolent pleasantries, but he returned the gesture. After all, he was only a boy—what harm was a cordial nicety?

The jingle of the store bell announced Jerry's entrance and a chirpy voice greeted him. He didn't even peer up as he ambled through the rows of the small grocer. The voice was lost under the tin-like tick of a ceiling fan and the glacial hum of a new air-conditioning unit. It was the first time he had felt the beach-like breeze since he moved to Chicago. How he would have loved one on the farm in his youth. Pacing the store, Jerry mumbled his list to himself—best not to forget it. He scooped up a batch of lemons—his wife kept on about them, and one of her superstitions had flared up lately—eggs for breakfast, a newspaper, and a pack of cigarettes for himself. Discipline didn't extend that far.

Dropping the goods on the counter, he shelled out the totality of his pockets without calculating the sum, still not gifting the storekeeper a glance.

The clerk cleared his throat. "That'll be ninety-seven cents please, sir."

"That's all I got, can you let me off till next time?"

"I'm afraid not, sir. That'll be ninety-seven cents, thank you."

"I said—" Jerry gazed up, finally. The sight of the man's shiny black skin sent him stiff. He swallowed back the ends of his sentence and threw up a new one. "Excuse me, *boy*?" He looked daggers at the clerk, sure he was dreaming, or still reminiscing on darker days, or in one of those sadistic reveries his mind often cast negroes in.

The clerk, troubled now, reclined to call back for his co-worker. "Louis!"

A man rustled from the back of the store and came through a door behind the counter.

When his bronze complexion emerged from the darkness, Jerry's heart almost seized to beat. A chill shot down his spine, rattling bone and jarring nerves as it plummeted. This couldn't have been a dream, because it was akin to a nightmare.

Louis's eyes bulged from his head when they met the grimace that dominated Jerry's face; he turned straight around and hollered for a man named Mr. Howard.

Jerry seethed in waiting, certain there would be no more dark surprises. He decided on desolation if he was wrong. A tall primped white man emerged from the door behind the counter.

"What's all this hollerin' fo', huh?" The man glared at his employees before he turned to Jerry. "What seems to be the problem here, sir?"

Jerry darted eyes over at the two men posted by the door, his stare so intense it averted their gazes. "This *boy* denied me the purchase of these here goods." A callous finger stabbed at the counter. "I think they need to be taught some manners."

The owner looked down at the change. "Sir, it seems you don't quite have enough—"

"I'm well aware, but I asked him to make an exception given my—" He searched for the apropos word. "*Creed.* Now, if *you're* not willing to allow two cents to slide, then perhaps I'll get real noisy. How'd you like that?"

The owner swallowed hard and tugged at his collar. "No, no, sir...that's fine. Here, lemme help you with that." The owner packaged the things in a brown bag and gave a modicum of a nervous smile.

Jerry snatched it up and backed away from the counter. "Teach them the meaning of hospitality," he said as he reached the door. "Or they may learn the definition of hostility."

*

THE STREET served as no solace for his annoyance, the sun no bliss. Even the three breaths he took to chill his mind only filled him further with hot air. Jerry pulled the cigarettes from the bag and stuffed them into his breast pocket as he headed home down the street. A wind whizzed by him and the bag was snatched from his hand. "Hey!" He thought to give chase, but the culprit was brisk and feather-footed. They stopped, winked at Jerry, and feigned the tipping of an invisible cap.

The boy with the vitiligo.

Jerry clenched his jaw so tight you could see the muscles flex through his wiry beard. The boy took off around a corner and out of sight.

No money, no job—the blacks had taken them all. And now he was being robbed by his people, in such stark times of moral and racial peril? His eyes grew dark with disdain and something turned in him. Something old and poorly hidden. He had had enough. Discipline and dominance were close friends and timeless mentors from which he had learned all his egregious lessons. Now was the time for him to teach. It was time for him to do something other than brood in dingy pubs. Now was the time for a change in course.

Now was the time for action.

A Snow White

"WHO DO YOU WANT TO BE?" was the first thing Donald had said to Oscar since they settled into the garage. He didn't speak as clearly, but it was Oscar's best effort at translating the elder man's southern slur.

If Oscar were anything like his brother, Donald assumed, he'd want to be just like his old man, and at a point, so did Donald. Before he met Oscar Sr., he was busy with idle crimes and fixated on the frivolities of street life. When Donald fell on hard times and fled his roots in North Carolina in his early thirties, some thirty years prior, Oscar Sr. asked him that very same question.

Who do you want to be?

Before they met, he owned not even the stolen shirt on his back and engaged in the company of allies with unscrupulous distinctions. They'd steal and eat, do drugs, and whenever the ground was dry, sleep. At some point between it all, they'd repeat. It usually followed the drugs.

That was the crux.

Homeless and too old to learn—so the world told him—and too young to inspire piteous aid, Donald accepted his brittle fate. It was either do drugs or sell them. Commit crimes or be the victim. That was, until the day Oscar Sr. asked him: *Who do you want to be?*

Oscar hadn't conjured an answer yet; he was too busy doing nothing with his head in his hands on yet another stool in the corner. An hour had passed and the most Donald had told him to do was pass him a rusty iron wrench that was greening at the teeth.

The garage was stumpy and slim, mirroring Oscar's body if he didn't soon adopt a diet akin to that of Donald's four-course indulgence. It was three strides from the workbench to the door, and the white truck engulfed most of the space, displaying the name *Malcolm Meats* in cursive like some mobile billboard. The cold concrete flooring was stained with gobbets of dried engine grease that streaked across the slanted ground. Anything that fell started into a frantic dash for the cobwebbed confines under the workbench.

The suppressed screech of tightening bolts and Oscar's hyperbolic sighs were the only tones of resonance whenever Donald wasn't slurping at the saliva that deluged his tongue.

Donald popped his head up from the bonnet, a woolly brow raised high towards the ever-receding line of his low hair. "So, son, who ya wanna be?"

Oscar mumbled into his hands, "I'm not your son—"

"Speak up now chil', I can't hear ya."

Oscar raised his head with a listless look in his eyes. "I'm not sure, but I guess I wanna be like my pops and Martin."

"Why's that?" he pressed, cleaning the viscous oil from his wrench.

"Because of the success, I guess. I want money and fine women and a big ol' car I can ride 'round in, show off on all them street cats." The fantasy inspirited his eyes with an auspicious shine. "That way, ain't nobody gon' be able to tell me nothing when I make it. Not Martin, not you, not anybody."

"Money don't make ya a better man, it jus' make you more of what you already are." Donald knelt onto his creaky, poorly lubricated joints to tighten some spigots and tire nuts. "Ya need to find principles to live by befo' you go on an' worry about making all that money, son."

Oscar rolled his eyes, not for the first time when Donald was speaking. "Everyone on the streets seems to like me, so when I got money, they gon' love me." He tapped his feet with a ticking monotony, looking for something idle to do. His views exposed a young mind; truancy had marred his intuition with incorrigible influences.

Donald sighed through his nose and dipped into his shirt pocket to fetch a shiny red-and-white Altoids tin. It was clean; it almost appeared as if he had polished the little metal vault. He popped a mint into his mouth before concealing it again, savoring the flavor. He shut his eyes as the icy sensation of an arctic breeze modulated the climate of his mouth, each pellet mimicking the muted ting of numbness.

"Can I get one?"

Donald returned from his indulgence. "Ya ain't did nuttin' to deserve this." He laughed the request off and went back to the topic. "Ya see them cats, they love ya 'cause ya in the streets like them. 'Cause ya broke like them, ain't got no direction just like them. The moment ya summin' to be, they gon' switch on ya. And that's ya own people. Once the white man get going with those knockout punches of his, what ya gon' have then?"

"I'll have my money. That's all I'll need," Oscar answered naively while he picked blue paint from the workbench.

"I thought I needed the same thang once. Turns out I only needed love. Real love. Not the love ya get from people who don't know ya and only have a purty idea of ya, but that love ya get from a home. The kind that only exists in a place ya feel ya belong. The love ya get from a family. Yo fatha' gave me that love."

Oscar kept at the paint; it seemed more appealing. He was perhaps too juvenile still to appreciate the nuances of love and its root in life's purpose. It was far too placid a concept to placate his urge for quick thrills, even quicker cash, and the desire to be lionized.

They went quiet. Donald popped another pellet from his Altoids tin before dipping back under the hood of the car to resume maintenance. He thought about the boy's father as he worked.

Oscar Sr. was by no means on the precipice of abundant earnings when Donald met him. He owned a small stand of farm goods on an old market lane. The stoic man passed hammering judgement on produce he deemed guilty of frail quality, only opting for a jury of finer crop to stand witness to his law-abiding living. From Donald's low-angled and acute perception, the man he found himself looking up to was the apotheosis of who he wanted to be. And that was someone of auspice and ambition.

Oscar Sr. presented Donald with many phrases and pearls of euphonious wisdom from a life of self-study and espial of the modern man and his modern means. Donald had favorites; *'Everybody is self-made. Only the successful admit it.'* It struck a chord never strummed in him before; *'Intelligence is the acquisition of knowledge. Wisdom is the application.'* It was one Oscar Sr. embodied with austere standing. He had many dimes that would be seen as a mock of their human condition.

So instead of inviting contempt, Oscar Sr. offered only to share the sights from his mind's eye with those that could aptly assimilate the views. Donald was lucky enough to be one of them.

"Why they call you the Engine Man, huh?" Oscar broke the wistful silence.

Donald surfaced from the pool of oil, nuts, and bolts, face streaked with dark grease, chewing on his tongue.

"Well, ol' Jewels gave me that name." A semblance of a smile formed, exposing wizened teeth. "Said I was like an Engine wheneve' we were on a job. He used to put his head to my chest and play like he could hear the sound of horses racin'. The ol' fool." He chortled at the thought. "I love that man, but boy am I glad I met ya fatha'. Otherwise, he would have been the death of me."

He lied—mostly. It was indeed true the nickname was given to him by Jewels, who himself was known as Lightning Limbs, because of the breakneck speed his legs moved and the swiftness of his sticky fingers. Donald was called the Engine Man not because of his affinity for engineering, mechanics or any other ethical feat, but because when he was high, he never stopped going. He didn't eat, he never seized to speak, and had no real use for sleep.

Donald popped another nub from his Altoids tin and went back to work.

"Why I can't get one, Don?" Oscar cocked his head towards the man's pocket.

Donald looked at the tin, then back to Oscar with a furrow wedged between his brows. "'Cause they ain't yours, son. Ya gotta earn what ya have, no matter how small. It's what—"

"What my father taught you?" Oscar scoffed through his nose with a feigned smile. "Anyway, what work did Jewels and you do?"

"Well now," he said with a throaty chuckle, licking the wetness from his lips. "All sorts really. Not much to talk 'bout or be glorified in the eyes of the law. Let's just say we were, ahh...savants of the streets." Donald's amusement vanished when the morose memories began to materialize. All the ones that came before Oscar Sr. were recalled with a whisper of ambivalence. They almost always put an impulsive smile on his face, then wiped it clean when the reverie became too detailed. Indeed, they were part of his making but served also as beats in the process that beguiled him to reflect on unbridled pain.

"You used to be in the streets?" Oscar perked up, his eyes alight, eager to hear what Donald had to say for the first time.

"Son, we *were* the streets."

"Tell me about it!"

"Not a chance. Marty would kill me."

The days he spent on curbs and street corners had left him mentally emaciated, with methods that were malnourished and starved of any prudence. Oscar Sr. changed that, and he preferred to revel in the plump memories he was cast in.

Oscar pouted and went back to doing nothing. Donald started for his Altoids tin but Sly burst into the garage with an unusual urgency.

"Donald, Martin needs to speak with you. Now."

Donald was wise to his pressing tone and slammed the bonnet shut. He was in such a hurry he dropped his Altoids tin on the hood of the truck, scooped up his blazer, and careened for the door.

"Don't touch nuttin' till I get back, ya hear?" He wagged a finger Oscar's way.

The kid gave a nonchalant nod. As the door shut, he was alone in the garage, now bored of peeling paint from the shedding workbench. Glancing over the truck, he spotted the Altoids tin and smiled.

"He ain't my father."

*

MARTIN boiled under arrested noon light that hassled across his dim office and mumbled a grim rhyme of news. Many things served as insipid anodynes for his tranquil condition. Dereliction, without ample or just cause, always rubbed him the wrong way. His disdain for abandonment was deep-rooted and thorough. Ignorance, especially that to education, cordoned off any invites for reasoning and inspired feelings of pity. And worst of all: *surprises.*

It seemed like whatever surprise Martin received came dressed in a sordid fashion. Never one that made his efforts any easier. He lived in the gallows of America, where surprises for a man of his lineage were not surprises at all— they were prophecies. Living in the halls of the unexpected made everything he expected akin to a living hell. He knew not if there was a haven past the hate or a haven that existed in a sequestered past, but he would not be reduced by their hellfire; he'd use it to forge a future.

Donald followed Sly into the office, which exhaled the subtle ghost of sage smoke from a thorough smudging. Martin only ever burned the pale, herby bush in preparation for the divvy of lamentable news. Donald hurried to take a seat, confused as to the broody tone, and darted bulbous, low-hanging eyes over to Sly, who was still standing.

"Sly just came back from his rounds with some bad news," Martin started without any warmth in his timbre, twirling his thumbs with his hands clasped over his mouth. "I didn't want to tell you this because well, I hoped it wasn't true but..." Martin took a ponderous breath. "Jewels is dead."

Martin watched Donald swallow a large lump that formed before the words had fully left his lips.

"Ya sure?" Donald squeaked. His eyes glazed over but tears refused to fall as he blinked them well away.

Martin looked at Sly and nodded for him to explain.

"I was out in Earn's Alley doing what I do, and it crossed my mind to ask for Jewels." Sly paced, kicking his heels against the floor. "Without too much exaggeration of sentiment, he told me some crackers got rowdy and burnt a couple of homes and stores down—you know, a regular Tuesday for them. Anyway, Jewels was amongst the half a dozen that got killed."

Donald sat silent for a time, reminiscing on sapid days with his old partner. They were honeyed in sections as they always were but hardened to bitter thoughts like they always did. He could have been reduced by the same flames of hate and insurrection if not for the better sentiments he had opted to settle in. Now was not the time for mourning or grief; his ambivalent feelings could wait for a more opportune time; they had to hasten their plan because of the undue aberration.

"I'm sorry, Don," Martin consoled, his dolorous gaze barely visible through the swimming arms of sage smoke.

"Is fine. We got mo' things to worry 'bout." With the compulsion born of a sore habit, he ran his thunk of a tongue along his teeth, eager to neutralize the numbness.

"Indeed, he was the only one that knew the location of the guns."

"And now half the sour part of the city knows you're looking for them, Martin. Your name is on many tongues, white and black alike," Sly added.

Jewels had met the same end he permitted the sergeant's son to. Gone in sardonic and cyclical irony. He offered tailored information about the guns—Martin was certain to not mention the location—as the pale scourge beat him with his yellowing boots and garrote him with the shoelace till his bug-eyes bulged. Sometimes karma was lurid and fashionably late to the countless parties to which men had invited her; other times, she was acutely mannered and in a shocking hurry. For whatever reason, Jewels' invite was at the top of her list.

"I ain't worried about people knowing what I want. I'm worried that someone might get it before me." Martin swirled and took a swig from the whiskey that sat on his desk. "We need to figure this out and quick."

"Whatcha hav' in mind, Marty?"

"Well, this changes things, but we might still have the upper hand. Like I said before, we have very nosy friends."

They knew many nosy people who often told intimate stories of their neighbors like they had their heads in windows or ears hung on hat hooks. One man came to mind first though. Earn. If a cat shat in St. Louis, he could describe the scent; when snow fell in Baltimore, he knew how deep it was. His propensity for idle information made dismal sense, so the fact that there were guns sequestered in the dark of his city, you could be sure he knew all about it.

"I'm gonna send Sly back down there and see what Earn knows, and if God is on our side, we'll be back on track."

Perhaps it was God's will that Jewels had gone, along with the certainty of the bloodthirsty knowledge. Perhaps it was just that, God's will, that acts of devilment and vengeance seldom came to pass. If that were the truth, Martin would have to question the Lord's will himself. Ask him why his brothers and sisters were slain in the streets for their color and creed, by people who swore to protect them. Quiz him on the reason such a bleak and desolate conquest on black people lasted almost as long as the Qing Dynasty. He knew answers would come with the echo of a child's scream as their pregnant mother's neck snapped, leaving her swinging from a tree; the splat of blood from his brother's back as it broke like swollen pork skin after a lash from a cat-o'-nine-tails. He did not blame God for these maladies, as some time ago Martin decided the Lord had no say. And for the same reason God wasn't to blame, Martin didn't pray to him to whisk the pain away.

"Right—"

A harrowing scream split the seams of the door and sent them at ends. It jarred their nerves and sent their heads ringing with alarm. They snapped towards the door, and the raw cry cut the room again; this time it came with a hollow inhale and the tone of no hope.

They knew that cry.

It was Kat.

An Angel White

WHEN THEY SAW IT, they all froze, numb to the grim sight that lay macabre across the garage floor.

Oscar was inanimate, foaming wildly from the mouth, eyes bleach-white and rolled back. Blinded forever by a fatal decision. Kat had found him, and when the others came in, air and all the sound of sobbing fell silent on Martin's ears.

Unable to move, unwilling to believe, he looked on at his little brother's vacant, catatonic gaze. There was no semblance of life in him, not a fleck of motion to beguile hope or any sanguine temptation.

Oscar was dead.

Without doubt or sedition of the truth. The boy was gone.

An undying heat sweltered around Martin's collar and up his neck, his nose fizzed like the wick of dynamite moments from explosion. Breath hectic and shallow, the world vignetted around him. Kat's cry faded to make way for the quiet of his mind, Sly's befuddled questions lost under the thump of his heart in his ears. Even though Donald's silence was as loud as any sound he had ever heard, all he could see was his brother.

Stumbling forward, his joints turned to jelly as his knees buckled underneath him. Despite the feebleness he felt, an ethereal strength pressed him towards his brother. Anger and understanding were yet to set in; confusion still spun him off balance.

"Os?" He fell to his knees and cradled his brother's limp head, closing his agape mouth. Where there wasn't foam, a strange white substance plagued his lips. Brow and palms deluged in an occupation of sweat, Martin wiped the corner of the boy's mouth and played the substance through his fingers, sniffing it to a sharp recoil. The vignette cleared; sound returned, but it came with a choir of anger.

As Martin scanned the ground with a tight furrow jammed between his brows, white dust and partly crushed pellets lay sprawled across the ground like a burst of snow. The flurry came from the Altoid's tin that lay by Oscar's side. He plucked one from the ground and tapped it on his tongue, spitting at the bitter numb taste of cocaine.

Martin glared up, face painted with an inferno of grimace and glower in his features. A swell of tears blinded Kat as she joined her hands, desperate and dizzied, mumbling a powder prayer. Sly did what he could to console her, but he was aghast, unblinking and being assaulted by violent shivers.

Donald was silent.

"You lied to me..." Martin looked Donald in his wetting eyes.

"M-Marty n-now...ahh...I can explain-"

"You killed my brother..." Martin looked down, nonplussed at Oscar's listless gaze.

"I-I didn't mean fo'—"

"YOU KILLED MY BROTHER!" Martin yelled, his voice a raw thunderclap of grief as tears came down in torrents over his hard face. "With your lies! And your habits!" He took a shaky breath as his mouth moved to say nothing, sullen eyes turned down. "You killed my brother..."

Words were lost on Donald. He glanced over to Kat, who was too weak to see him, but Sly...Sly's eyes locked on his with the malice and intent of murder.

"Leave. Now." Martin demanded. "If I ever see your face again, be grateful I'll let you see your last day by my hands. If you're addiction doesn't kill you first."

"Marty—"

"LEAVE!"

Donald vanished.

They gathered around Oscar's body as Kat mumbled silent prayers, and they wept. They wept together till the evening came. They wept together until Sly took Kat away. Then when night fell, Martin wept alone.

*

PAIN had become familiar. Loss too frequent a feeling.

Despite all he had gained in his life, joy eluded him in a sardonic game of hide-and-seek that shrouded the bliss of brighter days. Martin had lost his father, his wife, and now his little brother. Soon, he thought, the pain would be the only thing he'd have left.

They settled into the graves of shallow church pews as the hallowed chapel rung with the ambience of a choir song, musing over the now-bittersweet memories of Oscar as the pastor went on. Corey was sat to Martin's left, consoled by the arm of Sylvester, whose face was damp from eyes that were broken faucets. Corey's face was drawn in a morose expression, too nonplussed to manage tears as of yet. Martin opted for a quick funeral, and it had been just that. Two days prior, Oscar was on everyone's mind, wondering where he had gone and hoping he'd come back.

Two days later, nothing had changed.

To Martin's right, Kat wept under a black gossamer veil, doing her best to suppress her body from shuddering as she sobbed. She patted her reddened cheeks with a khaki silk ribbon Martin had gifted her long ago at the birth of their friendship as she leaned against his firm shoulder. Still, tears continued down her cheeks as tenderly and as softly as a psalm.

The plump reverend stood stolid at his lectern waving a staccato hand to the echo of his vibrato tone as sweat bucketed down his face, plating it with a mirror-like shine. His voice was musical and melancholic like a somber song, one that held notes for long cycles and pierced through the people in a way that made their chests beat with low bass. The choir went on singing Lift Every Voice and Sing while he praised the Lord between the rests in the song. The NAACP had dubbed it the Negro national anthem just that year, and it was performed each time with undertones of dolor.

47

When the church fell to a hush, and the mellifluous words washed from their ears, the pastor began to preach after a long watchful pause and some deep pensive sighs.

"We gatha' here today, not in presence of the Lord's blessed joy," he started slowly. "But in the testing of bitter sorrow. Joy is only the answer when we are asked the question of pain. Life can only *truly* be appreciated when it is taken away. It shouldn't be the case, but it is, my brothas and sistahs." He picked up passion as the churchgoers roused him with a softened chorus of 'Amen's.'

Martin remained silent.

The pastor went on for a while in high volume and higher spirits, speaking broadly of Oscar and the six others who were being eulogized that morning. He was poignant with his prose and luminary in his delivery, coloring the precession with an effort of bright words that occasioned tears to streak cheeks with silver lines. The day was dimmed by the pathos of the moment, unlike the usual glee-bleached and almighty ebullience often synonymous with Sunday Mass. Today shrank to a bleak emaciated wallow, fasted of any hope.

After a long hour and many tears, he came to the culmination of his sermon. "We will not fold under the pressure of the devil's palm. When he comes a-knockin', tryin' to steal our souls an' sanity with his deceit an' sweet apple, we say *no, no, no*, not today!" The man's accent roused sullied memories of Donald and tears welled deep in Martin's eyes. "Ya can keep ya apple, an' even claim our bodies but ya can't take our spirit, 'cause when ya come callin', we say *no!*"

Martin's eyes broke with tears as he remembered his last words to his brother. He mumbled low and weak under his breath.

"Amen."

A Bitter Black

IT WAS A PALACE compared to the barns and outhouses Jerry grew up in during his peasant past. The house was fashioned for highbrowed moguls or corrupt tycoons who made a living off cheap promises and expensive sins. The type who fell ill and grew sallow at the utter thought of impecuniosity. For some time now, Jerry's fingers swam in pockets as shallow as street puddles, and those who lived by a similar stroke would commonly see the mansion as a blessing. Call it freedom.

Jerry saw it differently, as he often did when deterring from the rose-tinted and skewed views of the demotic. Jerry didn't view the house with effulgence. Not because it wasn't perfectly beautiful by a modern measurement but because he did not own a single blade of grass that sat on the acre of groomed lawn. For Jerry, it was not freedom.

It was a cage.

A constant reminder of his inhibiting destitution.

Jerry stormed through the front door and entered the house, which opened with an echoey, white-washed lobby hugged by the marble arms of twin spiral stairs. He slammed the door, and the opulent chandelier, which dripped with hundreds of crystal tears, shuddered faintly.

"Jerry, do *not* slam the door in my house please." A Cajun voice bounced from deep in the house. "You may be a little older, and if your ego needs to hear it, wiser, but you don't have to come in here with all that," the woman finished.

He could not see her yet as he passed the first lounge room and headed for the second, but he could be sure Flo was posted in front of a fabulously framed mirror, primping herself to look more plastic than person.

Jerry entered the room in a poorly hidden fluster, scanning to find Flo exactly where he knew she'd be, perusing vanity's favorite artwork. The room lingered with the sweet chemical stench of some sordid perfume that besieged the senses. Like the lounge, the entirety of the house was blazoned with a floral French theme. Everything from the plump tasseled cushions, to chaise chair arms and legs, to picture frames that were filled with foreign faces and someone else's memories. Even the fragile wine glass she drank from was carved with the ghost of a fluffy bouquet. Imperiously cast in colors of cream, the place dazzled in dandelion-yellows and the accent of pale ocean-blues that trimmed curtain linings and table edges.

"Where's Loretta?" Jerry demanded.

"Upstairs." Flo looked over her shoulder with askance eyes that were sharp uncut emeralds. "She's in one of her mumbo-jumbo moods." She looked back again, not crazy about his tone. "Seems like so are you, darlin'."

Jerry left the room, thundering upstairs as Flo turned back to her image on the wall. She owned a beauty many would commit crimes for and an elegant style that derived gazes from rich and poor eyes alike. A silky, satin blue dress fell down her slender figure like April rain, while a fluffy white boa caressed her neck and shoulders with a cotton touch. Her blonde hair curled with the lambent summer shine of new sunflowers and her features were all petite and fully made up.

Still in a strop, Jerry returned. His wife had been sleeping or inebriated...or sleeping because she was inebriated. Either way, he did not plan to wake her. "Where's Arthur?"

"If you could slip in a 'please' every once in a while, it'd do you nice there, Jerry." Flo sipped on some twinkling golden wine that clipped her tongue with a delicate citrus crisp, staining the glass rim red.

"Flo."

She caught his hard glare and rolled her eyes when she decided he was in one of his sour moods. "He's in the kitchen." She wet her heart-shaped lips again. "But get out of that funk. It's warm today, and I've got a little friend of mine coming by. Can't have you all grizzly and scary now, it might fright the poor thing."

Jerry quit the room again as Flo descended into one of the yellow chaise chairs that surrounded a glass-topped coffee table. She plucked a little green vial from her breast pocket and tipped out fine white powder onto the surface, hoovering it up in a swift line, catching new life. She tucked it away and finished off her ritual with a tipple of gold wine.

Flo, or Florence—the name given by parents she never knew—was accustomed to the rare pleasures and higher decencies often feigned by mortal men. She played in the snow in the summer many times. Had brown sugar without tea only once—she didn't take well to the raw flavor of that inebriation—and slept in clouds that had been lofted from green roots. Despite all her frolicking and follies when under the impression of angel dust and devil's nectar, Flo's disposition carried a touch of ambivalence. There was a sense that her care-free living was a product of a hard-fought and well-shaded past.

Jerry returned from his kitchen excursion, this time with Arthur, who swaggered behind in fitted brown suit pants and an off-white shirt that was tucked in and rolled to his angular elbows—he had made more of an effort to assimilate to the northern foppery than his elder brother. He was carrying the broad sprawl of a newspaper, reading listlessly as they trickled in.

Jerry seemed simmered—Arthur's mellow demeanor often balanced his fervent soul—but by no means was he placated from his broiling state.

Flo barely looked up as she gazed languidly into a stagnant ceiling fan. "Arthur, is your brother feeling a little less lousy yet? It'd make a girl feel mighty fine about doing nothing in her own home." She spent the years that made her in New Orleans, so her tongue could only flick words in that musical cadence the way Southern folk often spoke. The French décor of her home likely took inspiration from similar sources.

"You're in a mood?" Arthur asked Jerry, surprised, his voice close to a whisper.

"One that's appropriate for how my day has been." Jerry thumped over to a long firm couch, settled into it the best he could, and swooped his hair back.

Flo looked his way, amused. "Since y'all moved up here, all these days been *appropriate* for your mood, darlin'. You should have a drink; it'll take that edge off," she mocked. She knew full well how he felt about drinking; he reminded her almost every time *she* did. With a smile, she rose and left the room to go and change for the third time of the day.

Arthur moseyed over to join Jerry round the coffee table, which propped up a dead rose in a cracked jade bowl. He was much shorter than his brother, whose head dared to graze the tops of door frames, and thinner too. Arthur's presence was eternally undercut by Jerry's stoic persistence. Forever subject to an insipid fraternal comparison. He held no discord in being the 'gentler' of the Lynch brothers, because his mind flexed more muscle. Growing up in the South, where children and their tempers were as hot as the hellish weather, Jerry acquainted himself with discipline and dominance, while Arthur, took books and Bibles as best friends instead of boys and girls.

"So, I've found a few places that are hiring," Arthur said, looking up at Jerry. His eyes were green on most days, but in this light, they were the same stoned-washed blue of a cloudless sky, lucent and earnest. "Some preliminary training is required for about half, but I think we got a good shot if we get in there early."

"It's not about getting *a* job; it's about getting any job we desire and not having to fill in the gaps left by them spooks."

"But Jerry—"

"But nothing, Art, it's the principle of the matter."

Arthur cleared his throat; it always shook him whenever Jerry cut him off. "What choice do we have? We need to eat. We need to live. We must find a job so we can help ourselves, despite the riots and everything going on. It's not like we can drag them out of their jobs."

Jerry sat up and glared deeply at the wizened petals of the dead rose. "Who says we can't? The law? Pfft, they've killed just as many negroes as civilians. The police, the judges, the lawyers, and every white man in between has a brother or cousin or uncle just like us. On the brink of poverty. You think they don't want those blacks out in the streets so their sons and kin can take their place?"

Arthur tucked a stray lock behind his ear, his hair tied at his nape in a flaccid bun, bright and long like noon sunlight. "It's not right though, Jerry. The world ain't like that no more. We already survived *one* war; do you want to fight another?"

"Do you know what happened to me today?" Jerry ignored the question. "I went to buy them provisions y'all asked of me, and when I went into the store, two niggers were working the damn thing. Taking up two jobs we could have had. On my way out, a little white boy, young enough to be my son, robbed me. He was no more than a few years older than Rose was." His words wobbled at the mention of his late daughter. "You think that's okay? No. You're right, however, we did both go out there, fight for our country and survived the Great War. Now, my dear brother, we must fight the *real* one." There was an intensity in Jerry's tone, and a smolder sparked a fleck of fire into his grey eyes.

They went back and forth for a while, displaying the points that favored peace and the adverse conjectures that molded the idolatry of more war. Jerry honored a credence in the idea that, without action, they would be reduced to nothing but cogs in their society instead of being the ones turning them, and he did not favor the thought. Arthur's ideals were naïve by Jerry's measurement, and the majority of their exchange saw Jerry just waiting for his turn to speak. Arthur tried to sway his brother's opinion, but before long, they sat in an undecided silence.

The doorbell rang, and from the lounge, they could hear Flo flitter down the stairs in little fairy steps.

"Hey, Bo, long time no see, honey," Flo's muffled voice greeted her expected guest.

Jerry and Arthur watched the room door as snappy footsteps neared.

"I gotcha some stuff you might like, Miss Flo." The guest's voice sounded squeaky and younger than Jerry assumed. Flo entered first, followed by her guest, who cradled a brown paper bag, which peeked the contents of eggs, lemons, a newspaper, and other foreign chattels.

Jerry's eyes widened with rage.

The boy with the vitiligo.

Jerry's bitter-black mood rushed back as he charged across the white marble. Clutching the boy by the throat, he hoisted him into the air. The bag fell and split across the ground, sending silver trinkets and large lemons racing for the walls. The boy gasped for air, and Flo smacked Jerry's arm in a befuddled fury.

"Jerry! What on God's green earth are you doing?! Put him down!" she demanded, but it left her stalky brother-in-law unfazed.

"This boy stole from me."

The boy kicked for freedom on imaginary pedals as his small palms clawed at Jerry's sinewy forearm.

"I-I'm sorry—" the boy squeaked.

"Let the kid down, Jerry." Arthur pleaded.

"This boy didn't mean no harm by what he did," Flo hurried as the boy grew blue. "He's homeless, with no family or no set place to stay at night. He doesn't even know a dinner time. He takes because there is no other option. Sometimes, he comes around to trade what he's got. Please, put him down."

Jerry pondered for a moment; he couldn't deny that the boy's plights mirrored his own. Discarded, cast aside and forgotten. All his talk and belief of the *real* war was being tested. The boy was not the enemy; he was just mistreated and misguided. Scourging the youth for the fallible diminutions the world had set upon their lives was exactly the reason he had to let him go. Jerry released the boy.

The kid plummeted to the ground, panting for air as he rubbed the red palm print from his sore neck.

"You ain't getting off that easy." Jerry gripped him by the back of his dilapidated knickerbockers and plonked him on the chair. "You gotta make this up to me," he sighed. "What's your name?"

"Bo," the young man croaked.

"Just...Bo?"

"Boston Rind, but 'Bo' is enough."

"Arthur, get Bo here some water."

His brother acquiesced and left for the kitchen.

"I can't believe you, Jerry, treating this young boy like a grown man. Do you have no restraint?" Flo berated him as she soothed Bo with the stroke of his hair.

"Now, Bo." Jerry's tone was a touch rueful in wake of his realization of the boy's abjection. 'Being often in the streets and all, you must hear a lot of things from a lot of different people, huh?' he asked as Bo nodded gingerly, his little opal eyes shrinking to slits. "You think you could help me *know* a little more, and in return, I could help you?"

Bo rubbed his palm-tanned neck and coughed to clear his throat of the soreness. "How you gonna help me if I tell you stuff?"

Jerry leaned back and smiled for the first time since entering the house, pasteurizing his sour value. "You like to be warm, don't you?"

"Yeah."

"And full-bellied, right?"

"Uh-huh."

Jerry's smile grew larger but more sinister. "Well, why wouldn't you like to stay here with us?"

"Excuse me!" Flo was perturbed; she stiffened to the plastic state she had often desired and ceased soothing Bo's head. "Quit offering my house out like it's yours!"

"You've got enough rooms that you don't use. Why, one of them is full of clothes you wouldn't dare wear again. I'm sure you could spare some space for *our* friend whose parents couldn't." He pressed on hard, alarming buttons that he knew ardently inveigled swells of anxiety and nether memories from Flo. He was privy now to the root of her fondness for the boy. Flo, like the young man, had to grow well past her years as a child to survive and provide for herself. Survival would have been enough in most cases, but Flo had dreams and ambitions that laid next to stars she'd goggle at on hungry, wet-scalped, and sleepless nights. So, when her elder sister would cry, she decided many times over to thrive.

Flo gazed into the starry twinkle of Bo's blue eyes, which told the plaintive stories she once lived. It took only a moment for her to cave. "Perhaps we have some room for you, honey."

Jerry's eyes were benighted by a grey shade, his grin gilded in manipulation. "Well, son," he guided Bo's face to meet his intense unblinking eyes, 'how'd you like that?'

Bo nodded with a smile.

Arthur came back with a half-empty glass of water, and Jerry took it from him to give Bo.

"Arthur, Bo's gonna be staying with us for a while, so why don't we make him feel at home? Fetch him some food, ahh..." he thought for a moment about their lack of food. "A sandwich or something." He did well to limit his suggestion.

"Nice to have you with us, Bo." Arthur left to get him some food.

Jerry took the glass from Bo, and set it on the coffee table. "So, what you got for me son?"

Bo twisted his mouth and looked up in thought. "Umm, I've been hearing about this Capone guy and those Italian's planning to sell alcohol and such when that pro-pro-pro-"

"Prohibition hits? Yeah, son, I know. We all know that. I need something that people don't know."

Bo lingered for a while, training his mind for any latent information he didn't care for that others may find useful. "I heard something about some darkies looking for guns, but I doubt you care about what them spooks are doing."

Jerry perked up at the mention of firearms. "Guns?"

"Apparently. My guess is it's just some niggers looking for something to look forward too."

"Tell me about it."

Bo looked unsure if Jerry was certain, but he wasn't fond of the idea of being hoisted by the throat again. "Well, I was running with some guys in this riot the other day who caught this black guy. Begged for his life and all, started talking about guns somewhere in the city. He seemed high, so I thought he was just kidding or whatever. He didn't say where but kept repeating this one name I forget."

Jerry grabbed Bo by the shoulders and shook him. "You need to remember that name if nothing else, son."

An electric feeling bloomed through Jerry's chest as adrenaline seeped from delighted glands. Intense and ponderous, his glare showered over the boy, heavy like lead rain. Jerry didn't need everything, he just needed something. Something to help see whatever light he was looking for through his dark eyes. Something to shine forth in this moral night. It had been so long since he saw a means of substitution for his dispirit, even if that meant swapping his blue views for red ones.

"You have to remember that name." He shook him again, hoping to jerk it out.

Bo closed his eyes and scanned for the latent memory. It took him a while, but his eyes shot open after half a minute of thought.

"Martin," he said proudly. "The name was Martin."

A Paper White

TWO THINGS governed the sanctions against Martin's rules of engagement.

Lying never reached the stretch of his intention. He only did it that one time to surprise Cora for their first anniversary, and he startled himself by how good he was at it, despite having only a modicum of practice.

Begging was a fallacy for any semblance of acceptance or approval, and he made sure to never commit to that reduction. Since his father's death, not once had he retracted from those conditions, certain that any dilution of his integrity was a mar on the man's memory. It had been a tribulation of many long, pain-ingrained days since then. Today, however, was different. Today he'd leave his two sanctions at the door.

Through divested avenues and dust-claimed boulevards, Martin and Corey had driven for some time after visiting Cora's grave. They reached an open stretch of land where pale buildings cowered in fetal positions on the purple horizon as the sun headed to rest. They drove over the battered brown teeth of long-laid train tracks, and after a few left turns, pulled into the tidy parking lot of a small groomed building.

They hopped out and went up the stairs, which looked like they had been recently cleaned. Corey stayed close, following the footsteps of his father like a lion cub. The sign on the door was shaded by a white awning and read: *May's Institute of Home and Higher Education.*

Corey loved it here, but Martin rarely let him come for the sake of his blatant fears. Kat's younger sister, Nina, had opened the small organization about half a decade ago, just before the war started, and hadn't realized its true purpose would be fulfilled when the war had finally ended.

Although she had balanced the act of teaching black youth and returning negro veterans who had austere cases of PTSD and other mental erosion, from the views of his higher cause, Martin considered the damaged men as most valuable.

They entered the building and into a hallway that had new white walls and a snappy checkered vinyl floor. A lady in pearl-rimmed glasses sat at a paper-plagued desk, tapping away at a chatty typewriter.

"Excuse me." Reserved, Martin pulled the flat cap from his head. "Could you tell me which class Miss May is currently in?"

The lady pulled down the thick lenses of her spectacles, scanning Martin's frame while she bit her lip. "She's in class four, honey. If you need anything, I mean anything, just let me know. I'll be here all evening."

Martin, often oblivious to the enamor he invoked, gave gratitude, "Thank you, ma'am."

He and Corey made way down a thin hallway that trailed the smell of collard greens, freshly baked macaroni and cheese, and some form of pie that floated from somewhere distant. Unfortunately for their stomachs, which recognized the waft of dinner time, the fourth classroom door materialized before the side scent of gravy thickened.

From the seams of the mangled spruce door rang the muffled cacophony of childlike laughter. Martin noticed Corey's cheeks grow high at the jubilant hum. They crept in, careful not to alarm the class of brown faces that recited an orchestra of their nine-times-tables, with Nina conducting the symphony. The class fell silent when Martin and Corey entered, and Nina spun, surprised to see the pair.

"All right guys." She waved a cane over the class. "Let's take a break before dinner, then call it a night." Her voice was rich and motherly in tone. The class shifted their tables to the walls in a set of swift screeches and settled at the base of a bulging bookcase, pulling novels from the shelves with pleasure.

Nina was the complete antipode of her elder sister: Instead of finger waves, her hair was a puff of well-greased silky curls. Instead of pants, she wore a grey dress with ruby kitten heels. Rather than brandy, Martin recalled her bias for wine.

She gave Martin a hard glance as she flicked through papers on her desk. "Martin."

"How you doing, Nina?" He wrung his cap nervously in his hands.

She ignored the question, and her face brightened when she caught a glimpse of Corey's smile. "Hey, Corey! How you doing, baby?" She squeezed him tight, and they exchanged pleasantries. "Why don't you go hang with the guys over there?" They were all his age, more or less, and Corey was overjoyed at the suggestion.

"It's best you stay here," Martin said.

Nina pursed her lips, raising a pencil brow. "If your daddy wants to speak to me, then I'm certain it's fine for you to go read and play with the kids." She said it to Corey but was speaking to Martin.

Martin gave a nod for Corey to go and he jogged off to the other end of the room, which simmered with chuckles and humble chatter.

"Whatever it is Martin, I can't help *you*, or whatever mad plan you have. I've got responsibilities now," she looked over to the horde of bright-eyed children. "These kids need me." She turned and took a seat at her desk, which was dotted with gifts of shiny apples. The students had pinched them from the kitchen she stocked, but the gesture of appreciation was one that ameliorated any stress and reminded her of her mission.

"Nina, please, just hear me out for a minute." Martin edged forward. "This is nothing like before."

"The last time I helped you—" She felt her voice raising and modulated her volume. "The last time I helped you, people *died*."

It was true. The prior time she lent him aid, Martin had an egregious plan that involved things of a pointy nature. Nothing in the prosperous class of pens and pencils. He described it, ironically, as 'higher education' when really, Martin just wanted to teach some people a lesson. Back then, Martin was younger, more uncouth, with pain-propelled methods and far angrier in the wake of Cora's late departure. It was his point to convince her things were different.

I won't help you this time," she declared.

Martin took a breath to compose himself. "Oscar's dead."

She sat up with wide eyes. "What?"

"He's dead. Happened a few days ago." The lump in his throat was like a billiard ball, an utter strain to swallow. "And Donald...Well, he's no longer with the family."

Martin explained the saturnine situation. How Donald had been responsible and caused the attrition of better sentiment. How they were on the brink of being humbled by hard times and all the sullen mentions the recent week had brought. He told her everything, everything he could to make her believe that this favor was not like the last, and the only way to do that was to omit the guns.

The only way was to lie.

While Nina and Kat were different in many ways, their beliefs resided in the same home, just on different floors. She would scold Martin worse than her sister did if she knew the truth. Given their former experience with doomed favors, he was prudent to keep portions of the past and present under hush.

"See, without Donald," Martin moved onto his new favor. "The trucks can't get serviced, and without proper service, we can't courier produce. Before long, the business will fall and all our livelihood with it. You know full well I can't let that happen, for Corey's sake, and Kat's, and Sly's. I won't let that happen, but I need your help. Please." The glimmer in his eye was not as stony as it usually was, exposing the fractures in his soul.

"What could I possibly do about that? I don't know a thing about cars."

"But you know people who do, right? How many brothers have you helped get on their feet after the war, huh? A few dozen? Maybe more? You must have helped someone into mechanics." His estimation was broad but one rooted firmly in the zeitgeist. Motor vehicles were a new and attractive option for people looking to switch fields; he was certain she knew at least one.

Nina ruminated on the thought. Perhaps she did know someone in the field, but there had been so many of late, the right one failed to surface with ease. On her left hand, a heavy garnet-set silver ring gave off a great radiance. She was denuded of any other clamorous glitz, but the overladen ring was a gift from the first man she helped get a job, and after a few hard-earned paychecks, he bought it for her as glamorous thanks. Nina wore it as a symbol of her, however minute, success.

She owned many tokens of gratitude from the many men she made. The gilt Indian elephant on the shelf behind her desk came from a young medic who returned distraught over the sight of dismembered friends. She managed to turn his trauma into a tool that now saw him aiding injured animals in South Asia. An eloquently painted tapestry hung on the far wall, depicting the woes of a lonely lion weeping over the bones of an eagle. It was designed by a man from the front line whose hands were so tremulous with fear, he couldn't be trusted with grenades. How ironic that the skin-splitting explosions would allow him, with his scattered nerves, to create art in the stippling effect it was composed. Then she saw the pencil holder that was crafted from regrettable cast iron and a crude adornment of scuffed rivets. It surfaced the one person in her mind that could likely help.

"I know a guy." She paused and looked Martin dead in the eye. "But by God, you better promise me this is the truth and you don't get that man in no mess."

"I promise." The words were like daggers to his soul, and he could almost hear his father sigh from the afterlife. He knew it was wrong to proceed like this but hoped this particular transgression would pay off.

Nina scribbled an address on a piece of paper. "His name is Joseph Moore—goes by "Jumpy Joe" these days though. Any loud sound could trigger war reveries and send him into a panicked frenzy."

When Nina met Joe, just after the wounded winter, his mind and mannerisms put on a shaky show. She thought he was a case even her self-taught expertise couldn't amend, but she had come far; she had learned many men to new lives and burgeoned broken souls that once sighed broken breaths. It was maybe the promises she made under an anachronistic oath that kept her going, or the fact that she felt obliged to do her part as she garnered the innate talent to mend, while others cradled a cause to maim. While Kat—before Cora died—focused on correcting the world's physical woes, Nina found discipline in curing the mind. Not with hyperbolic psychoanalysis or magic blacker than devils' skin, but with the ascension of knowledge and holy regiment—although the latter had dwindled the darker and redder the summer became.

She was about to hand Martin the piece of paper when Corey's laugh halted her, and she pulled back. "Let Corey stay a little while, and this," she wagged the paper favor, "is all yours."

"What? That wasn't what you said earlier."

"Well, I've changed my mind a touch." Nina cocked her head to one side. "If you let Corey stay and play with the kids for an hour or so, I'll drive him home before the sun is fully down." She sighed. "Martin, Corey needs to be around those his age; he needs to be a boy. You didn't miss out on your childhood, and it made you the man you are today. I know the world is scary right now, especially for *us*, but you can't let him miss out on his."

Grimace battled to the surface of Martin's face. "I don't know..."

"Listen, stop worrying about losing him. It'll be the first thing that happens if you don't let him find himself. You can't hide him from the world forever."

Martin drew a deep breath and called Corey over to put forth the idea of him staying with Nina for a while. Corey punched the air in elation before hugging Nina and rejoining his peers.

"All right?" she asked with a smile.

"All right."

Nina handed him the address. "I'll have him home in about a week." she chuckled. "I'm kidding. He'll be home before you know it."

A Bullet Black

THE SKY WAS MELLOW and wine-looking. Jerry—with Arthur and their mother—drove in a dispassion along a parched dirt road, void of any real destination. Half hoping whoever, or whatever, he was looking for, would show up and announce themselves as the night switched sides with the day.

Jerry had smuggled a pistol back from Europe with a keen election of manipulation and charm. The Colt 1911 lived under the seat of the car Flo had let him run around in, because she never had the ambition to manage a motor vehicle. He preferred the intimacy of a knife and the engagement required to fully wield it and break skin. Only two people—and countless cattle—had felt the sting of his black blade named 'Willie.' For Jerry, it was ceremonious and almost spiritual to bless someone with such a cold, detailed end. Each of the two people that fell victim to the finality of Willie's touch altered Jerry with surgical substitution.

One traded trust for his life; the other traded hate for his daughter's.

After paying their respects to her grave, Jerry often drove around with empty aim, dulled by the somber occasion. Arthur, at times, recited Psalms from the Bible as they cruised—he was certain the one he spoke first was always the twenty-third—and Elizabeth remained eternally forlorn during these trips, humming the melody of her granddaughter's favorite lullaby.

This time, they were silent.

It had been a decade to the day since her death.

The ghost of rosebuds haunted the car with a prematurely picked scent, one bereft of the damask texture, fruity notes, or musk acquired from matured ones.

Jerry ignored Arthur the first three times he asked where they were going, partly because his mind was far suspended and festooned with the dark, dangling décor that changed him. Partly because he had no idea. An hour had passed of disengaged travel, while the same hour, a decade prior, crossed through his mind in a trudge of ire that seemed to last a lifetime.

They passed over the battered brown teeth of a long-limbed train line, and Jerry peered out the window to seethe for a moment. Evening was drawing in; the few people he managed to view were so far away, he could have mistaken them for the shadows of pigeons cast on walls or the silhouettes of mangled streetlights. They came to a stop sign, engine ticking its tinny tune as he gazed out into the bare street. A car pulled up beside them, and Jerry hadn't even taken in the passenger's nonplussed face until it turned from black to a phantom white. The boy's eyes were wide and cold with terror, and a raw moment of realization came over Jerry as the young man's petrified expression came into focus.

The negro child from his mother's house.

Corey.

The boy was visibly panicked, ushering the woman driving to move quickly. She stared at him, confused and a touch alarmed by his timorous display.

She should have listened.

Jerry slammed the car into motion, rearing for Corey in a heedless collision. The screech of the impact was seismic and skin-splitting. Their hoods popped off, along with a racket of gaskets like a chorus of fireworks, leaving plumes of incessant black smoke in its wake. The mouths of the vehicles kissed gruesomely; wheels warped together in a deathly embrace.

Jerry jumped out the car and reached under the seat for the gun he handled with a familiar tenure. Arthur tumbled out with Elizabeth, both stricken with a flustered stupor, panting for air as the world wobbled around them.

Storming over to the boy's vehicle, Jerry pried the door open and flung Corey to the dusty ground. "Looks like the Lord has plans for us yet, boy." A mad smile grew on him.

The woman flopped from the car and rushed to Corey's side, breathless, with a glower in frameable form. "Who the hell are you?! Leave us alone!"

Jerry let the hilt of his gun reply, clattering it into her nose, which sounded with a muffled crack. She crashed to the ground holding her gushing face.

Pain was the answer.

"Now, boy, Mommy's here." He looked over the lady who was groaning in anguish. "Where's that riptide daddy of yours?"

"She's not my mother," Corey spat with the frail amounts of anger his shaken voice could manage.

"That's too bad. What I'm gonna do to her won't hurt you as much then."

"What the hell has Martin got to do with this?" she groaned.

Jerry stood in sudden awakening as the wild grin wiped from his face. It all came together in an alarming hurry. He wanted to find Corey's father, simply due to the man's blazon aberration days prior, and he wanted to find the guns and whoever this Martin character was who sought them.

Now, they were the same person.

The mad smile returned as he wondered awhile over the new entanglement of his intention. He thought it divine and attributed God for the way his ambitions convened in such an ingratiating manner.

"Martin has *everything* to do with this." Gun raised, Jerry crept towards her. "He's seeking out some of these old things." He wagged the Colt in an unnervingly playful fashion. "Likely to arm *your* kind."

The woman looked absent for a moment. Whatever she had realized put her in more pain than her broken nose. "W-what?"

"I knew y'all were hard to understanding," Jerry sighed as he stood over her, baring the abyss of the barrel at her chest. "Now tell me where Martin is."

"I-I don't know where he is and wouldn't tell you if I did," she spat through gritted teeth.

Elizabeth came from around the other side of the car with Arthur following close. "Jerry, leave these people be!" Her heart fluttered when she saw Corey on the ground. "No!" She went to charge for Jerry, but Arthur held her in a tight grip.

"Ma, stay yourself out of this. You still think you have a say in things?" Jerry asked rhetorically, turning back to the woman. "If you won't tell me, that's fine, but you can be sure Martin's gonna come looking for his son, and when he does, he'll find me and a corpse."

A harrowing air filled the space around them, and the wine tone of the sky bled from the fiery horizon to meet violent vermilion clouds. The only sound was silence.

Jerry didn't need her to acquiesce; she was surplus at that point. He only needed a clear head, cold steel, and the undiluted hate that coursed through his veins. The trigger pulled, and a black bullet crashed through the woman's chest, leaving her gaze vacant and aghast at the dimming heavens. Nearby birds scattered off into the sky. The lights left her eyes, and as the blood pooled around her lifeless body, tears left Corey's.

There was no way to save himself. There was no one to save him.

He was next.

A Fire Red

THE BARREL OF THE GUN was a passage of hellish despair. Corey had heard and read of the phenomenon of one's life flashing before their eyes when at the crux of fatality, but no reel of his short life began to roll. Not the faint angelic remembrances of his mother not the sequestered devilment his father fought with and against, on late nights with long bottles; not even the mementos he worshipped of acquainted peers whose names he so sorely forgot. As Corey glared wide-eyed with wobbly pupils, he couldn't see where the barrel ended, but if a light flashed at the end of the tunnel, he'd be sure he'd meet his.

"I hoped we'd see each other again, boy," Jerry said, deep and hollow. "Now, I can purify this world a little more."

The southern man's voice sent a shrill through Corey that snagged against his spirit.

"Jerry, no!" Elizabeth struggled in Arthur's arms, her mesh of a blouse pulling every which way.

Jerry ignored her cries and bared the gun down over Corey's head as the banal whistle of a train in the distance seemed to cruelly signal Corey's last stop. He peered up at death's gangly silhouette with his heart knocking a harrowed tune on the drums in his ears. Jerry's arms were bone without the detail of his sinewy muscle showing, face gaunt with scared shadows hidden in the hollows of his cheekbones and sunken eye sockets—the impression of a disrobed grim reaper.

Corey couldn't avert his eyes, they flitted between the barrel of the gun and the barrel of the southern man's grey gaze. Jerry's emaciated-looking finger settled hungrily on the warm trigger, thirsty for the spill of more blood.

Corey saw something flash before Jerry's eyes.

The mad smile he wore was replaced with a look of melancholy as his hand shook with a rhythm of inhibition. The ailment of hesitation.

Elizabeth saw it too.

She wiggled free from Arthur's grip, tearing her blouse as she charged for Jerry with wrecking speed, slamming her shoulder into his ribs, which threatened to crack under the force. Stunned, Jerry squeezed the trigger with piercing pressure, but Elizabeth's ram knocked his hand away from the path of Corey's head and into the engine of Nina's totaled car. A torrid eruption exploded their senses with a sonorous clamor, sending a wave of disorientation over them as flames bloomed from the engine like a fervid red flower, lashing the broiling air with hot clicks.

Corey was low enough to escape the brunt of the sonic blow, but Jerry was still collecting himself as Elizabeth scooped Corey up and the two bolted for the horizon. Panic still writhing, their limbs were feeble and tremulous from the sudden ordeal. Still, they ran. They ran knowing Jerry had a gun and there was only open air and a vibrating train line before them. A sharp whistle grew loud in their ears.

Corey decided it was a bullet.

But as he gritted his teeth for the bullet's bite, the elephantine horn of a trudging locomotive blared by in its metal skin like a rusted herd. Slow enough to count the lumps of coal and bales of hay that rested in the open carriages.

Elizabeth glanced back. Jerry and Arthur were rooted; their figures shrunk with every scuttled stride she took. Arthur had a pacifying palm on Jerry's gun arm, and she took solace in knowing that he wasn't going to shoot. Despite the maternal friction that had become the implicit nature of their relationship, he wouldn't fire at his mother. So she hoped.

She looked down at Corey, whose eyes were dimmed with dread, and spoke between the heaps of her violent pants. "Corey," she started, heels stifling her strides. "We have to get on this train. I know it sounds mad, but we have no choice, dear."

Corey was flushed of color, skin as pale as paper. He was unsure if she hadn't realized the train was moving, but it had almost passed them and despite the trepidation, he acquiesced. "O-okay," he agreed in a haggard voice. The copper dust the locomotive kicked up only further imperiled his scourged chest.

They fled faster now across the baked dirt with the desultory intent of boarding the train, desperate to escape. They knew not where the train was headed, but in this case, it was better the devil they didn't know than the feculent one they did.

Corey went first. The sliding door of the cargo hold was open and inviting with the promise of a strawy haven. He clamped on to match the trains meandering speed and with the count of three, jumped as Elizabeth helped hoist him onto the carriage. He made it and stumbled in.

Corey rose and hung onto the door's railing, stretching his arm out the car for Elizabeth. "Miss Elizabeth, c'mon, you can do this!" he yelled over the roar of the steam engine.

Bronze dirt cast a misty wall of worry between her and Corey; her stunted strides made it seemed like she was running in reverse. The distance grew, as did the sting of leather sawing at her heels. Legs burning, she realized.

The shoes.

She'd never reach him with the hindrances of gilt heels holding her back.

Elizabeth kicked off her pumps and began to pick up speed, light filled her green eyes to a neon shine, reflecting the thought that she might make it. Sharp stray stones lacerated the soles of her feet, and she cried out in echoey pulses. Her pace was crippled by the bite of shallow cuts that marred the gristle between her toes, and her face grimaced as she tried to maintain her diminished speed. She was in trouble: That split second of anguish had caused Corey to slip further away. Glancing back, her son's figures were two faded marks in the smoky distance. Looking ahead, Corey's pained face and outstretched arm called for her.

"Please, you can make it!" he cried.

From somewhere deep, a forgotten spirit was roused with a zealous admission. Whether she'd regret giving up or that spirit that slept for a decade was awake now to amend the dicey transgressions of her past principles, she was unsure. But if she didn't try, she would never know. Elizabeth wouldn't know if regret was a hard-to-view virtue or a collection of ailed decisions that mingled with cardinal sins. Ones misshapen and mangled by pride and the envy of prior times.

She couldn't leave him. Let him ride away somewhere unknown, scared and lost.

She couldn't leave him alone.

Teeth gritted through the pain, she remained privy to any stones laid to endanger her path and accelerated with an intense abandon, leaving warped red footprints in her wake.

Elizabeth was close. Corey's hand was only a fingernail away, and when their palms embraced, he pulled with all his might as she wrestled onto the carriage, collapsing into the enclosure.

They were safe. They didn't know for how long, but for now, it was a black and rusty heaven in comparison.

On the cold flooring of the open carriage, Corey and Elizabeth looked at each other with glares of relief. She shuffled over to cradle his head as his chest ballooned. "Are you all right?"

"Yeah," he wheezed, still shaken from the desperate sprint.

Elizabeth looked around, the car was about six feet wide and thrice as long, with hay at both ends hidden mostly in heavy shadows. A dark middle-aged man with ripe cheeks and a kind face popped his head out from the strawy shade. He was drenched in thick folds of clothes that were frayed and way too insulating for the sweltering summer they were having. Even the patchy fingerless gloves and split leather boots seemed more like a poverty statement than a fashion one.

"Don't be startled lady," he warned with surrendering hands and a hoggish burble that hinted at a predilection for raw bourbon.

Elizabeth jumped nonetheless and pulled Corey close to her.

"W-what are you doing in here?" she asked, ignorant to her hypocrisy.

"Me?" He picked his burnished teeth with a jagged dagger of a pinky nail. "Hitching a ride. Just like y'all peoples." He smiled a big smile that was missing a myriad of teeth. "The name's Skip—"

Corey began to draw haggard breaths, ones that locked up his little chest. Ones the signaled an attack. His lungs grew small and seized as he fumbled into his knickerbockers for his mother's photo. In the panic, the wind took advantage of his weakness and whisked the photo out the carriage.

His remedy. Gone.

"No!" He lurched for it, but Elizabeth pulled him back.

"Corey, you have to relax." She grabbed him by the shoulders; she knew his pain was mounting, and without his solution, she wasn't sure what would happen.

The hyperventilation sharpened and vacuum-like daggers dug deep into his chest. The world vignetted around him, and before long, his eyes shut. His head went limp.

"Corey!" Panicked, Elizabeth laid him down with quivering hands. "C'mon, c'mon, Corey!"

"I wouldn't do that if I were you, lady."

"What? He's just fainted; what else am I to do?!"

"Hmm," Skip pondered and scratched at the patchy beard that plagued his chin. "Perhaps loosen that shirt of his and sit him up."

Elizabeth looked at him, nonplussed and despondent with upturned eyes. She reached to check Corey's pulse. It was still there. Then she hovered a finger under his nose, and the faintest squirt of air passed through. She scooped his limp body up and lugged him to sit upright against a bale of hay, loosening his tight shirt before erecting his head. A few pensive moments passed of waiting for Skip's elementary nostrum to take effect before she checked his pulse again. It was stronger. Then she was thawed of worry when a firm stream of air flowed through his nose. Tingles radiated from her spine to her toes as she hung her head back in relief.

"Thank you," Elizabeth swallowed down dry air.

"No problem, lady." Skip settled onto a pile of hay on the other side of the carriage. He kicked his feet up, pulled his dilapidated flat cap over his face, and chewed on a strip of straw.

Elizabeth peeked outside and wondered where the train was headed. "Excuse me, where is the next stop?"

"Lady...this is a one-way to Dallas."

A Lens Black

AFTER THE YOUNG DAYS he spent shrouded in a peppery Southern gloom—the days Elizabeth's maternal inhibitions were the reason for his precocious enmity—Jerry developed rancor for his mother. Now, she was headed somewhere distant on a slow locomotive—like he once did, and she was the reason—shame accompanied that same rancorous feeling as she headed away, and he was the reason. It was one of his sole purposes to diverge from the neurotic distinctions he carved his mother in, as any kindred thinking could lead to kindred pain.

Although he knew pain, he seldom sought to acquire any more.

Jerry fanned the flames to quell their rebellious temper, finger scarred with a pink pressure-formed tan line as he flashed off his brother's calming arm.

"We need to find out where that train is going." Jerry puffed hot steam through his hooked snout and seethed beside the thirsty fire.

Arthur looked around and caught sight of a bony station in the distance despite the dimming daylight. "I might be able to get something from the station if anyone's there." He pointed to the emaciated shed that was clothed in cork boards, all adorned with cereal advertisements, vague notices, and a wizened propaganda poster of Uncle Sam in his patriotic habits, stabbing an indicting finger of moral responsibility directly at them. They had done their time, served their country; now that pointing finger felt just as obligating but of a more sordid edition.

As Arthur went off, Jerry brooded over the innumerable destinations his mother could end up. There was a stark distinction between the places he thought she'd land in and those he hoped she would. Perhaps she and the boy would end up somewhere unforgiving to his kind like Hattiesburg, Mississippi, where riots crippled peace from walking the streets. Or perhaps they would pull into a station where, with the grace of the good Lord, he was waiting —a slumberous thought that even he understood was best put to rest. Then the idea that they'd stop somewhere close enough for him to walk to took hold. Along with the grasp of his other inordinate predictions, it was the one he favored the most, as Flo's car had been reduced to ruin after the capricious collision. A further encumbrance.

Jerry stood persistently, watching the train as it vanished into the horizon, blending into quivering black hills. He wondered no more of their fate. Tt was not his place to institute direction or destination; that was the purpose of abstruse higher powers. Instead, a proverb his father preached to him crawled through his mind with a reverberant speed: *The heart of man plans his way, but the Lord establishes his steps.*

With that truth, a peace humbled him. The Lord would surely establish those steps, and Jerry would take them with grace, despite the prospect of damnation.

From the direction of the fleeing train, a white page fluttered from the sky like a letter from heaven. It fell silent and lucent, like an angel had shed a feather, and as he stepped towards it, his foot hit something fleshy.

The woman.

His brows knitted together in a perplexed weave as he stepped back, searching her vacant, blood-drooling face with a look of bewilderment like he had forgotten who she was. Like he had forgotten he had killed her. He crouched with sharp elbows slung across his knees and cocked his head to the side to match the angle of hers as he mumbled something unholy.

Jerry had seen those sodden eyes before, pictured in the same frame under smoke and hate. Despite the rueful results of his ritual executions, he evaded the mark of bitter infamy with beguiling interjections. Though he, and others of his creed, need not speak too sweetly in explanations upon the lobes of lawmen. As the reason for a black corpse could at worst be a complacent mock of that person's actions with a jovial chide, like when a father has to scold his son for fighting to appease their mother but in truth is overjoyed. And at best: the remaining emancipated with reparations for their trauma and time.

He could leave her where she lay, caked in drying blood and copper dust, rigid in her extinguished mortality, and no one who mattered to Jerry would even care.

The Southern man rose with a sigh and stepped over her with exorbitant dispassion, his indifference for her lost life harrowing. The woman's road had reached an eternal dead end. For Jerry, she was just a pebble on his path.

The white page had landed some twenty feet ahead of him, his boots crushing more brittle stones as he homed in. He scooped up the paper to see it was a photo, squinting as he inspected it. The boy's lens-washed face was distinguishable only by the heart-shaped birthmark that stamped under his left eye—he was at least a decade younger there. Jerry's heart thumped with a nauseating pace when the woman in the picture's round face fell into view. He was perturbed by her broad nose, full lips, and the angelic gaze she held in her slanted brown eyes as she clipped the wizened petals of a rose to preserve the flower's budding life. Jerry stared at her with an ambivalent sensation for a long pensive moment. Indigestible reproach swelled in his stomach before it broke down into shame and piteous emotions, for who he was still unsure.

The photo felt heavy, like it was printed in lead. He turned over the picture to avoid the gravity of their faces and smiled to see the gift of direction and destination before him. Not the one he wanted or wondered over moments ago, but the one he needed. It was scribbled in cursive.

If found, please return to Martin at,
Malcolm Meats
S. Wentworth Ave.

"Looks like the Lord has plans for us yet, boy."

A Moldy Green

TO SAY HE LOATHED WHITES was a redundancy. Their presence alone disturbed his deeper peace and brought about only feelings of glower and derision. Sly was not fond of their ways, which he ardently described as *nefarious*. There was a time when Sly wondered—better yet, illustrated—a world where love undercut hate to a richer, but cheaper, degree. A more affordable form of latent human expression. He once saw life through lucent eyes, where the only dark lines visible came from the ends of lead pencils he had put down long ago. His fingers were no longer stained with black grain, only black skin, which the white man hated because of the hateful way that his image was painted.

The cold air of the delivery bay spoke with the smells of rotting pork and slaughter. The wet stone floor was treachery to stable footing and dotted with patches of macabre red spillage that looked like the faded hide of the disrobed cows that hung in the cold room. A heavy evening fell, and Sly had shed the wings of his raven suit for the drab of an apron daubed crudely in pig's blood. Upstairs, meetings came first; downstairs, the meats came first.

He jotted down the residual indifference of the late stock that trickled in on a parched clipboard, hoping mildly for the interest of complication. The loyal butcher, August, came from around the corner of a truck lugging a cloaked palette of squealing wood with the help of Dumbo and the man's gelatinous arms.

August had run the place for the better part of a decade whenever Martin or Sylvester's presence was required by more lively allegiances. He tended the slaughter and produce and counted the tills—after Kat taught him the basics of arithmetic a few years back. He even worked under Oscar Sr. in the infantile days of the business. His senile obscurities were ones that occasionally offered the odd wise word and under-the-breath speech that was so poignant, it left those subject to it to ruminate over his phrases for days.

As they came in, so did the turbulent wind of the early evening. Dumbo's face was masked in the infinite perplexity of slack-jaw stupor as he licked the placid glaze from his rubber lips.

"Hey, Sly, h-how you doing?" Dumbo tipped off his flat cap. His words splashed from his mouth like water from a ring float.

"What's up, Dumbo," Sly looked straight past the heavyset man and his twisted lounge suit to gaze at the robed parcel he most certainly did not order.

"Uhh, me and August got somethin' real good to show ya." Dumbo took the rear up the slope towards the storage room where Sly was stood.

August was a small man, frail in physicality but fervent in spirit; if Dumbo didn't take the bulk of the weight, they wouldn't get the thing up there. As the pair reached the top, Sly's curiosity grew, and he became a touch anxious for the revelation. He thought it may be another dead thing they weren't going to sell or something exciting enough to wash away the dullness of the day. Dumbo slipped on a rogue strip of lettuce and slammed into the ground, dropping the palette as he quaked the concrete. He wasn't called Dumbo for his lack of cognitive power—although, for him, knowledge was a novelty—rather because of his clamorous and cumbersome disposition that people knew him for. He made sure to steady that intimate stereotype.

From under the tarp tumbled a sappy white arm. Sly's eyes glimmered with shock and a feculent sensation at the sight of the pale palm.

"Dumbo! You damn fool!" August scurried up the rest of the slope, with a hunchback higher than his head, and tucked the dead man's arm back under the sheet.

There was little left for Sly's grinning imagination.

"M-my bad, August," Dumbo picked himself up and dusted the dirt and stray veg from his musty grey suit. "You know my knees be getting in my way sometimes."

"Damn fool." August shook his head as he looked the thunk of a man up and down.

The suit Dumbo wore carried a hint of garlic from weeks without a wash or full removal. It pulled in every which way. The collar button was missing, the blade of his tie was strung low like someone without care had tugged down heavily on it—likely himself—and it was mauled by creases and lines enough to rival that of a railroad map.

"Take that thing inside," the old gray man hissed through gritted ivory dentures.

As Dumbo tugged the palette into the back of the store, Sly watched it with eagle eyes. "So, Aug, you gonna explain?"

August ambled over to Sly's side, and his mushy leather skin, which sheathed crumpled features in thick wrinkles, caught the sulphury sputter of a waking streetlamp. "You know 'bout what them boys and Jewels done did not so long ago, right?"

"Of course."

"Well, that's one of the white boys they killed. His face is all jacked with little gem-shaped cuts." August spoke with the rhythm and solemn of an untuned lute. "It turns out it's Mrs. Pennymore's boy. She gon' be real sad if she finds out."

Sly's brow furrowed as he wandered the small reserve of white faces he remembered. "The lady that always comes in to buy that moldy ass meat like it's gonna atone for her people's past transgressions?"

August nodded. "Indeed."

"You gotta be kidding me..."

A strange smile crept across Sly's lips, one he hid the meaning of from August as he clipped a stroking hand onto his chin to ruminate the dynamic of the situation.

"What you want us to do with it? Tell Martin?" August scratched at his flaky scalp.

"No," Sly popped.

"Well, we could just burn it in the furnace after hours. Rid all evidence."

Sly pondered for a moment, pulling at the tuft of hair below his dry lips. He didn't expect a complication as interesting as this, and although he was right in part about it being another dead thing, he was wrong in thinking he couldn't sell it. "Grind him up."

"What?" August's head clicked back, and he raised his ruffled brows to reveal asking eyes. "You *serious*, Sly?"

"Yeah," he added without hesitation. "And pack him."

August didn't dispute any further; he was in charge whenever Sly wasn't present, but now that Sly was, the ancient butcher relented from transgression. He tightened the apron around his slither of a waist, marred the color of war and made for the store, mumbling something senile as he went.

It was an indignant practice on any moral account to do what Sly had planned. But for this exception, he had the perfect customer in mind.

*

AN IDLE HOUR had passed since Sly had been back behind the glass counter that displayed monuments of cold meat, and another would have to pass before the store shut. They had remained open late in recent months to sell to all the customers that only existed in Martin's mind. Sly knew it was a gimmick. A gesture by Martin to disguise the sinking ship his father set sail on many years before his end.

Only one man sat in the store with Sly, Gold Moe. In all his years, Sly had never heard the man's voice, not even seen his teeth, which were allegedly replaced with solid gold nuggets. Some say he didn't speak because his voice was ruined after his windpipe got crushed from an encounter with some lethal members of the Klan. They were said to have dragged him half a mile naked with a noose around his neck, clubbing him with stones whenever he wept. Others say that he didn't want the gold knocked out of his mouth, so in turn, didn't open it.

Despite the speculation, Sly knew two things: Moe ordered the same thing every day, which Sly never forgot—how could he when Moe was the only customer for hours on a good day—a brisket sandwich with hot mustard, extra cheese, and the kicker: grated beetroot. The other thing was Gold Moe was quiet. Extremely quiet. Sly reveled in the serenity of his esoteric company's silence.

Kicked back behind the counter, nibbling nuts from a thinning bowl, Sly sketched in his mind the fantasy of people flocking in from the streets through the glass facade. The instinctive sentiment to doodle in vacant times like these was initially hard to resist, but he made an internal oath to put the pen behind him in the pursuit of more despondent habits. The last time he drew anything, other than letters to form words, was a decade ago. He had finished the portrait Cora had begged for since the days he and his three cousins were bungled together in one room.

She died days before he intended it as a gift.

Today he had gifts for someone that came in hateful portions.

Below the counter, on bastions of depressed mahogany shelves, sat chilled piles of meat. The two leftmost sets of shelves were labelled *Blacks*, which cradled prime cut cow rump and chunky chicken breast. The rightmost shelves were labelled *Whites* and sunk with a scarce question of moldy meat that August—when he was fantastically bored, Sly cut away the green to resell to any whites that came in the store. And on that shelf was a rather ripe package with a tag that said: *For Mrs. Pennymore.*

He knew she'd be in just before they shut, and as the time crept by, a cynical smile slid across his face in anticipation of her obligatory arrival.

The doorbell chimed, and on cue, a lady shaped like a Matryoshka doll entered in a polka-dot green gown and a pearl-toned cloche hat to match. As she set her woven basket upon the counter, Sly could see the sadness in her eyes, and he had better than a guess for the reason why.

"How you doing, Mrs. Pennymore?" He rose to meet her sodden eyes, which were slick from a passing of tears. "You don't look so great. Something wrong?"

The lady flicked away the damp brown curls that bounced in front of her face. "Nothing to worry you," she murmured. "It's just my son. He's been missing for a few days, and with all these godforsaken riots, who knows what's happened to my boy."

"Hey, hey, now." Sly warmly ordered her to look at him as his voice simmered to a consoling tone. "I know this summer has been wild with all the carnage that's going on, but if we all gave into fear and disorder, we would already have a second world war on our hands. It's people like you, the people that say *no* to chaos in favor of order and integrity that makes the difference in this world that warrants revolt." Sly stroked her hand. "Keep hoping and keep your integrity. Your *son* and *everything* will be fine."

Mrs. Pennymore looked up at him with a touch of brightness in her eyes and the hint of a smile that tempted to part the dense flesh of her face. "Thank you, Sylvester. You done made me feel a whole lot better."

"That's not a problem. With what's going on we need to remain true to our principles and maintain that integrity I mentioned."

Sly was all too familiar with the specific definition of the word *integrity*; Martin used to throw it around like a toddler with a baseball when he first met him. Sly preferred to remember it as: *Doing the right thing, even when no one was looking.*

"So, what can I get you this evening?" he grinned, lips creased with hypocrisy. "The usual?"

"Of course, you know me," she chuckled through her rue.

Sly collected her regular provisions from the white shelf and whatever cheese he knew was coming to the end of its edible life, before packing them into her basket as she went on about her son's roguish anecdotes.

"I got a special blend of mince for you today, ma'am. Might take your mind off your son." He relented his attention from the plump broad, simply due to the apathy for any more ramblings. He swung his arm behind the counter, tapping the chilled wood selves and crackling wrappers of packed flesh to fetch the special victual. His intent reflected a facsimile of that moral insurrection he only just inspired her against.

When she saw the tag with her name in curly cursive, her eyes gleamed with surprise. "For me?"

"For you." He handed it off to her. "It's the least I could do since you feeling down about your boy."

"You're too good to me." She rummaged the purse she kept tucked in the corner of her basket to retrieve his payment. "Thank you ever so much."

Sly raised his hand in protest. "No need. It's just a pleasure to put a smile on your face."

The round woman's face fell, almost offended by his blatant refusal. "I will do no such thing as not pay." Her voice dropped from its high chirp to a detesting bellow.

"Ma'am, I can't take your money this time."

"What happened to all that of principle and integrity?"

"Integrity is doing the right thing even when no one is looking. But it is up to us to determine what the *right* thing is." Sly elaborated on his prior dictum.

She smirked and dropped the money on the counter. "Well, this is me deciding what the right thing is."

"Thank you, Mrs. Pennymore. Have a good evening, and I'm sure you and your boy will be reunited sooner than you think."

The thick woman flitted out the store with the ting of the bell, and Sly laughed till his eyes welled. She was none the wiser to the morbid reality that she had just bought her son.

To say he loathed whites was indeed a redundancy, and a sardonic smile pulled the dark corners of his mouth high into his cheeks. He took pride in knowing he treated them all the same. Gave them all an equal opportunity to repay through the same subtle hate so many of them once and still displayed.

It may have been wrong to hold them all in contempt for the sins of their ancestors, but when those elaborate sins delivered their descendants' privilege and majestic blessings, Sly saw a problem with them all. He hadn't time to sort the grass snakes from the vipers.

To him, they were all snakes. Past and present alike.

The phone rang, and he ambled over to his prior position to answer. He was slightly shocked at the sound of Martin's voice, then his smile dissolved when he heard the words, "Corey's missing."

A Ghost White

BROKEN GLASS GLINTED ACROSS THE GRAVEL, catching
the harrowing sulphur-yellow of a shattered bulb interspersed
with the spray of blood.

Her blood.

A wound flooded the rubber-scarred floor around them,
gushing freely from her gut. She was already gone. He
called out for help, but the people just stared, uneasy with
the act of aiding a black man. They watched as she died, a
part of him with her. A wreath of smoke passed over him
and through her languid body. It was soft, ethereal, and a
haunting ghost white.

Martin snapped from the spectral reverie as his office
door knocked with a peppery passion. "Come in."

When Sly entered in a flustered heap, panting from the
torrid sprint up the wheezing flight of stairs, he was met first
by a dense wall of sage smoke that submerged the room
with musky menthol notes. Then he saw Martin brooding
under a heavy evening shadow cast by the half-mast blinds.

"What happened?"

"There was a car crash."

The words crawled onto Sly's lobes like a hellish
earworm, turning the thin man to stone. Each syllable interspersed
with the echo of crude and unwelcome remembrances.

Martin glanced around the muted disorder of his office,
searching for a place to set his eyes so his mind didn't
wander.

Everything reminded him of Cora.

The burgundy varnish of the furniture appeared matted
and gray like the gravel she died on. The golden cabinet's
handles submitted all their shine to the voided regions of his
mind and reflected now only the sickly sulphur hue of the
busted headlights that beamed her copper skin sallow. The
chalice that smashed across his desk the moment he heard
about Corey, sprawled in a painful pattern that mimicked the

broken glass that tangled within the kinks of her hair. Even the smoke from the sage, although sweet-smelling, was the idyllic canvas for the indignant memory to loop.

Everything reminded him of Cora. Now, the fear that an assimilate memory might be married to his last of Corey, harrowed him with an insipid affliction.

It took even Sly a moment to shake his reserve of uncensored scenes from thought.

Martin went on to explain that a car crash got reported not long ago, with Nina being the sole fatality in the ordeal. Some eyewitnesses claimed they saw a boy and a lady fleeing from the scene onto a train, but the area was shrouded in a cloak of black smoke, so why they were running was unknown. Sly quizzed him on where they were going and got the obvious response that Martin was unacquainted with the answer. Although he did have a clue.

"The train was headed south. Some cargo locomotive on a long haul headed for Dallas." That far south, whites had racial jurisdiction that translated, in their minds, to racial reign and slavery was only abolished in name. The thought of Corey in that environment was daubed with regret.

"Dallas?" Sly was notably rocked, incensed by the mention of the Deep South. "How the hell we gonna find him?"

"I don't know. He could be anywhere from here to St. Louis by now, there's no telling where he could get off."

"So, what's the plan?"

Martin rose and paced the lane behind his desk with clamorous steps. "I'm going to go look for Corey."

"What?!" Sly popped as he scuttled through the smoke towards Martin with a pleading tone.

"I need to go find my son, Sly."

"Of course, we need Corey back, but we need to find the guns."

Martin shot a splitting glance at him; the mention of guns in the same sentence as his missing son called his nerves to attention.

Sly felt the heat and retreated his plea. "I'm sorry."

Martin paced in silence for a while as Sly picked a stubborn speck of blood from the torso of his shirt.

"How about I go?" he offered.

"Huh?" Martin ceased his stride.

"It only makes sense. We need to get Corey back, but you know more than I that we need to fight so that things like this don't happen, and if they do, then we can do something about it. So let me go find him." Sly put forth the proposition. "We both know you're the one with the best chance of finding what we need, so let me go find Corey instead."

Martin edged over to the bar and poured himself another drink —a sign of consideration. He took two habitual shallow sips and offered Sly a drink, which he gently declined. "All right, but what about business?"

"August won't struggle without me, plus I can manage the main source on the road. I can handle this. Ain't we been doing things long enough?" Sly further buttered his proposal for Martin's digestion. "I'll even bring Dumbo for a little help on the way. He may be clumsy, but he's as loyal and trustworthy as an old hound."

Martin took an apprehensive third shallow sip—a sign of hesitation. He swirled his drink around in deliberation. The next sip would determine his decision. A big one meant he'd acquiesce to the notion; another shallow one meant there was no chance. Martin locked eyes with Sly over the glistening rim of his glass and guzzled a wholesome gulp of whiskey.

"Fine." He rested his drink on the glass-scarred desk. "I want you to check every stop from here to St. Louis. Corey's smart, if he gets the chance to get off the train close to home, he will, and we don't want to miss him."

"Right," Sly nodded. "If not, we'll keep going till we hit the gulf."

"One more thing," Martin added. "If you see—" He wavered with the clench of his jaw and a shallow uncertain sip. "If you see Donald, bring him back."

Sly almost stumbled at the sound of the man's name. He never thought he would hear it again, and especially not so soon after his lapse took the life of someone they loved. "Excuse me, did you say, *Donald*?"

Martin rubbed a knot from his brows. "I know what you want to say, but don't. Given our situation, we might need him. The things he did, he didn't do on purpose, although I know the pain is still sailing steadily through us. Grudges won't ease things or bring anyone back, it just makes living with them a lot harder"

Sly dug his nails into his palms so deep they threatened to break skin, hands tremulous with reproach. "What could we possibly need him for? Ain't you got someone else to help with the trucks?"

"Nina only gave me a name and an address. Who knows if that'll payout. Meanwhile, we can't take any chances and lose any more time, so having Donald back will be great insurance for our cause."

Sly seethed over the thought. The conjecture that Nina's information could prove null for one reason or the other was sound, but the bitter thought of seeing Donald again swelled inextinguishable flames of loathing within him. He nodded without a word.

It was an uneven aberration but a necessary one. If anything happened to Donald after all that had occurred, for some obscure reason, it'd add to Martin's stack of self-censured guilt that had begun to take the shape of a traumatic-looking tower.

They spoke about Kat and how torn she was over her sister being taken by hate. Sly asked how she was doing after he hurdled the idea of inviting Donald back into the family. Martin explained that she shouldn't be alone, not tonight of all nights. But first thing in the morning, they'd get everything underway. Perhaps he too needed the company of misery to breathe a breath of sanity.

"What do you plan to do?" Sly inquired as he gathered his bloodied apron.

Martin drained the last of his drink and ambled over to the lone window, peering out through the blinds to the moonlit street below. "How do you think I knew about Corey so quickly? We have friends. *Nosy friends.*"

With Jewels departed and the other dubious ears he had in the city likely full with the cacophony of riot, Earn was due a visit.

A Book Red

THE WORLD WHIPPED BY like a stream of postcards. Corey and Elizabeth had accepted their fate as the purple night was falling. He had come back around an hour before the silver moon had risen, flustered by a hypnic jerk, head thrumming with delirium.

Elizabeth felt a similar strain. Her mind swayed with indigestion as the teeth of their destination sunk deep into reality.

Dallas.

They were headed south without any means for measuring time other than the frequent urge to sleep, the glitter of stars that took their first breaths and the shifting company of eclectic, in-a-rush scenery. Low-flowing tributaries of the Illinois River scattered off with blue fingers into a wild bog that still awaited conservation and frowned with the dark splintered brows of driftwood. The moonlight that danced with twinkled toes across the great river caught even Corey's tired eyes as they passed by the town of Browning. He tried with almighty efforts to stay awake and soak up the vista, although fear sat beside him as a spectral fourth member of their travelling party. Corey had never been this far from home or seen anything of such spectacle, save for in his imagination inspired by countless novels. It failed to live up to the palpability of the real thing.

Elizabeth's yawns were part of the night's soundtrack, along with Skip gnawing on straw and sputtering butter-colored pulp each time he asked Corey something—the same thing. Crickets and any other chatty critters were mostly drowned out by the howling wind that was indigenous to Chicago nights but seemed to follow them south. The sonorous engine caused the aching metal container to hum with a long incessant moan, rumbling their chests despite the hay that cushioned their backs. It added to the nauseating chuck of the train tracks that undulated below and made it feel like an auditory form of Chinese water torture. Elizabeth resisted sleep as she didn't want to take her eye off of Skip for more than a brief moment to gaze out the carriage door or take her arm from around Corey. When she did look, those moments trudged by with a reflective deliberation.

Between the drape of the night, Elizabeth managed to weave her eyes through the silver-washed wilderness to spot some awkward, battered-looking buildings—likely wizened from weather abuse. The cobblestone cottages that slept on mossy lawns tempted her with the misplaced sensation of déjà vu. It was uncanny how the homes looked like her childhood one, but the town she grew up in was long since a myth—at least the one she remembered.

This town didn't have the same pink Stargazer lilies that lined every path with the scent of forgotten heavens. Instead, from where she sat, she could only smell coal smoke that slapped through the open door with harsh grey hands, sour and raw like a meatless barbecue.

The glimpse of a tangled garden gifted her with the overgrown memory of her father pushing her in a tree swing. The chuck of the train warped in her reverie to sound almost the same as the clang of his boots stomping up the path to their house with a rhythm she cherished, as it seldom filled her ears. Without any doubt, he'd be carrying a brown bag teeming with fresh fruit: strawberries, grapes, melons, and apples, which she loved the most. They would laugh, eat on the grass with her mother and Grace and sing all Elizabeth's favorite songs.

That was before the war.

Before the Union took on the Confederacy for the freedom and rights of the colored, her father, Arthur—for whom she named her second son—fought for the side of love.

That was before he never returned.

Only six at the time, the age when most lucid memories began to adhere to one's psyche, her father was gone. She saw little of him for years when he was alive as he was so often serving, and his best lessons were victim to the common curse of childhood amnesia. The missed memories sat like unloved souvenirs on the shelf of a store that was forever closed, Elizabeth eternally staring.

Her mother said *hate* took him. Grace, her negro help, who she insisted was her other mother, elaborated by explaining that that particular hate had cold white hands.

"So what do you say, young blood?" Skip's raspy voice asked for the umpteenth time. He had spent the last hour of the trudging journey trying to coerce Corey out of the few dollars he exposed when he removed his shirt to cover Elizabeth.

"I don't know," Corey said with a mousy tone. "Miss Elizabeth says I shouldn't."

"She's not your mother, is she?" An insensitive attempt at rhetoric.

"No, but—"

"Well, c'mon, young blood, help a man out." Skip pulled a pack of ruined cards from one of his jacket pockets. "How about we play some poker? That's fun and fair, right?"

Elizabeth straightened from her slouched position, careful not to rattle her feet, which were bandaged in the shreds of her blouse sleeves, too much. "And *you* are not his father. We don't even know who *you* are. You should be ashamed of yourself, asking the young man for money. Then trying to swindle him out of his cash with gambling."

"All right lady, didn't mean nothing by it. I was just hoping for a little help is all." He slumped back into the pile of hay across the carriage and fetched a fresh piece of straw to nibble at. "Maybe get a little something other than straw to eat when I get off this thing..." His voice descending with the demand of pity.

"Sorry..." Corey picked at his cuticles, feeling bad for the impecunious-looking man.

For a while, the silence resumed. They all went back to their idle activities, but before they cleared the next prairie, Skip broke into one of his musical hums, which were soulful like church praise on Sunday. Then he lurched up with the spriteliness that an idea had taken him.

93

"What about this, young blood?" Skip pulled back the first two jacket flaps to reach the third and slipped a red book and pencil from his pocket. "You ever heard that knowledge is power?" Skip uncurled the edges of the thin notepad. "Well, imagination empowers one to seek knowledge."

Corey wasn't sure where he was going with his esoteric speech. "I don't understand."

"Neither do I...It was something I overheard back in Boston. The point is," he slid over his ignorance, "I'll trade you this here pencil and pad for a dollar."

"Ridiculous. Corey, don't listen to him."

It was a steep price for a half-worn pencil and a red notebook with but a dozen pages in it, but Corey's eyes lit up a little. He could write his own tales on this hazardous journey, fill the small notebook with colorful details of the places he passed and people he met, then show his father when he got back home. Produce poems with an ever-changing muse—his mind even reached the fantasy that one of his works could sit beside a poem of Claude McKay's in the *Messenger* one day. Be like the many people that daubed his heart with wonder and hope to do the same for someone else one day.

"I know it's a bit much, but I promise I'll make up the difference—"

"It's a deal."

"Corey!"

"Miss Elizabeth," he looked up at her perplexed face. "I know it's a lot, but I want to write. Plus, it's only money. I have more, and he needs it more than me."

Elizabeth's face softened when she saw the childlike plea behind his eyes. The gravity of the situation had convoluted the principal truth that Corey was still a boy and he wanted to do the things that boys did. She was not going to take that from him.

"You," she turned to Skip. "You better make up the difference to him when we get off this train."

Skip smiled. "You got it, ma'am." He shuffled over to Corey, and they made their exchange, not before Skip shook his hand so ardently Corey's body quaked. "Thank you, young blood."

After some time, the train's pace evened out from its rocky ripple. The hum of the engine sung like a lullaby and persuaded their eyes to shut with a sleepy opinion. Elizabeth rubbed her pearls as she drifted away. Skip nodded off with a smile and flat cap covering his face.

Corey began writing.

*

NEW HEAT riding on the admonishing rays of the morning stirred them from their slumber. Little rivers ran in the creases of their necks, dampening their collars. Corey woke only a few moments before Elizabeth. Breaking the sleep from his eye, he tidied himself the best he could and inveigled her to rise as the train had come to a halt.

Dallas. They were here.

Elizabeth yapped her mouth, cracked her neck, and yawned with a musical delicacy—exhaustion had made the sleep sweet. "You all right, dear?"

Corey nodded.

She turned to look for Skip, but they were alone.

He had gone.

"Son of a—" She caught herself when Corey's head snapped back at her tone. Puffing through her nose and sufficiently irked, she took a breath, as now was not the time for 'I told you so's. "Let's go."

They exited the train to be greeted by a cluttered rail yard filled with the husks of lifeless locomotives, gazing for a sign of human life.

"What do we do?" Corey asked.

Stood on the tracks, Elizabeth had no reasonable answer for her worried partner. "I'm not sure, dear," she swallowed hard. "But my ex-husband lives in Dallas."

A Bush Red

BY THE TIME THEY WALKED THE DISTANCE from the station to Ross Avenue, Elizabeth's feet and cheeks were as red as the wild bushes that hummed a flaming hue, huddling under and around the mountainous homes. They, too, cowered from the fierce Texan fervor.

It was the type of heat that made Corey's ears ring with each futile glance up at the nude sky, in hopes of an imaginary cloud offering some ephemeral salvation.

They moved quickly with staccato steps and a careless discretion as Elizabeth glanced over her shoulder with erratic swivels. The odd pair occasioned a few meddlesome glances, as a white woman with a black boy in the South was as rare as a cloud in the sky. She wanted to be sure not to arouse any deplorable attention.

A riot had just passed through Texarkana near the northern border of the state, some many miles from them, but it left the entirety of Texas ringing with a racial alarm. Reports of the black lives lost—perhaps 'purged' was a better word from more hateful points of view—had come in only through dispassionate rumor and word of mouth the two had overheard outside the rail yard, encouraging an emboldened urgency.

Corey removed the socks of his knickerbockers after the first sweltering minutes and gave one to Elizabeth to mop the sweat that dripped from their chins like broken faucets. He understood why Chicago had been dubbed the Windy City; it was a banal yet apropos name thanks to the city's tempest attitude. If he could name Dallas himself, from the half-hour he had been subject to an onslaught of fiery whips, he would brand it the *City Without Sympathy*—crude from his young mind, but the relentless sun proved it true. He wrote it down with sweaty fingers.

When they were out of the sight of prying eyes, Elizabeth thawed from her frigid state but not enough to unclench her balled fists.

Relaxation was not in order. She still had to look Henry in the eye.

The lawn they halted at was as long, and wide, and green as a small football field, with enough room for Corey to play with all the friends he wished for. Grasshoppers popped across the yard with their six-legged acrobatics, pitching on dandelions and daisies while they rested from graceful leaps. Red bushes surrounded the grass, hugging it with crimson arms.

In sheer awe at the building before him, Corey looked on slack-jawed, able to compare what he could see before him only to the whimsical descriptors L. Frank Baum had used to explain the wonder of Oz's palace. However, all the emerald greens were substituted for ivories and eggshell. He also suspected whoever lived behind the white pillars that propped up the house's facade like giant polished bones, was one of less wisdom and certainly little wonder.

Elizabeth crouched and grabbed Corey firmly by the shoulders, and she took a breath. "I don't know how long it's going to take for us to get home. I don't know you, and you don't know me, but if we're going to get back in one piece, then we're going to have to trust each other." Her grasp was tender. She glanced over and around the elephantine home. "Do you trust me?"

"Yeah," Corey nodded with solid affirmation.

"Then I need you to hide behind the bushes until I'm done talking to him."

"How come?"

Elizabeth sighed through her nose. "You see, Henry isn't the most welcoming of hosts and seeing me after such a long time isn't going to put him in the highest of spirits." She stroked his arm. "And I'm afraid if he sees *you*, we'll have no chance of him helping us." The words not spoken were bitter.

Corey turned his eyes to the ground. "I understand." He scurried off for refuge behind a bush beside the house.

Elizabeth reached the door, and a pressure formed in her chest that left her lungs stranded of any air. The last time she felt anxiety with such a black intensity was two and a half decades prior, when the same man she was about to face left her stranded.

She knocked, and an old, muffled moan came through the door before it opened.

"Henry."

"What on God's green earth are you doing here?" His voice coarse and tangled in disbelief.

"It's good to see you too."

Henry grunted in response, chewing the air. His cheeks were saggy and wrinkled like dried teabags. The comb-over that struggled atop his melting pate was so thin you could see his sun-spotted scalp even through the sable strands. No amount of dye could hide the truth of his age. He wasn't the type for suits; instead, his sappy frame drowned in unwashed folds of off-white cloth and starchy overalls, stiff enough to match his attitude. "The hell do you want?"

Elizabeth cleared her throat. "I've run into a spot of trouble, and I know I wasn't exactly what you expected—"

"You're damn right you weren't." His mouth barely parted when he spoke, jaw stiff; the arthritis that had deformed and swelled his knuckles had also set into his remaining teeth.

Startled by his interruption, she continued. "I need your help."

His wrinkle-masked eyes shrank to slits, readying for the brightness of her request. "Lemme guess, you thirsty?" A sardonic grin bared the scatter of his oily teeth. Jerry had inherited a facsimile of that smile built from hereditary cynicism.

Elizabeth despised it.

A lump formed in her throat that the drink he spoke of would have not washed down. She swallowed hard, her collar hot with verbal rebate. "I don't drink alone," Elizabeth glanced over the frontage of his echoey-looking home with piteous eyes. "I'm sure you know more than enough about loneliness."

"Only a little less than yourself."

"Seems you still have trouble keeping the family together."

"I think there are those that would beg to differ."

"And I think there are those who wouldn't need to beg if you had handled things better."

They exchanged stilted words with blazon amounts of malignant subtext. Warring with the weapons of the unsaid.

Henry grunted. "That bone box of yours just talked you right out of your favor." He went to shut the door.

"Wait!" Elizabeth lurched to the door. "I'm sorry...I'm sorry, please just wait," Her desperation demanding his attention. "I don't drink any more, you know this, and I seriously do need your help..."

Henry looked her desolate demeanor up and down. Chewing on air, his eyes said continue.

"I'm stranded down here with no money." She released her grip from the door. "And I need a little cash for a couple of train tickets back to Chicago."

"Whatcha need a *couple* tickets for?"

"Umm." Elizabeth's ears burned. "You know them riots have made it hell to get a straight shot out of here. So I'm going to need to switch over once I get to St. Louis."

"Unfortunately for you, I ain't got two nickels to rub together. Just 'cause you see this big ol' house, don't mean I got anything to give." Henry knocked the frame of the door with swollen knuckles. "After me and the boys sold the farm, all the money went to putting this roof over my head. I can't help you." He turned to teeter indoors.

"Henry, please, there must be something you can do to help. We need to get home."

"*We?*" He paused and spun around with a venomous look on his face. "Who the hell are you with?"

"Uhh...nobody—"

He stiff-armed her out the way to get a look in his yard. The sight of Corey's black face bobbing behind the red bush embittered the senile old gruff. "You nigger-loving drunk..." "Henry, he's just a boy!" "That's gonna grew into a heathenish man." He sounded almost disappointed. "I wouldn't help you even if I could." He turned and slammed his door.

"Henry!" There was no answer, and her tone was rocked by the failure. "Henry, I know you can hear me. I carried two of your children, gave all the love I had, and never disrespected you even when you deserved disrespect. All your late nights weren't spent planning business with Clinton, some of them were spent planning futures with other women. I know I hurt our home and could have done more, but you can at least help me for the sake of all the good times and not just punish me for all the bad." Her speech was poignant enough to shiver the leaves on the bush Corey hid behind with a deep-rooted penitence. "You can at least tell me where my car is. I know Jerry brought it down here after—" Her throat grew dry. "After Rose died. Give me at least that."

Silence ruled the air. She waited, hoping, half-praying, and wishing he would respond. Then the door creaked open.

"It's in the only garage in town. Ask for Ray."

Elizabeth let out an invite of shuddered sighs that awaited the RSVP of tears. "Thank you." She spun, but before she could get to the lawn, Henry's haggard voice called out.

"Elizabeth, I'd very much like to never see you again." The door slammed tight.

Henry wasn't always this way. He had charm when they met and a subtle stoicism in his spirit that came from tales of his forefathers and the bliss of not knowing. All those decades ago when Elizabeth's mother suggested him as a suitor, Elizabeth saw only those shining qualities in him. Her mother had expressed, "You have tried your dreams, now it is time to try reality."

To her, Henry was a glass half full, but she had all the intention of pouring. A mere three months went by before they turned from acquaintances to wedded, and only three more before Elizabeth was expecting their first child.

Henry wasn't hateful; he showed no signs, or perhaps she was just blind. When everyone around him was the same hue, who was there to resent for those ostensible reasons? It wasn't till they moved to Chicago that Henry's glass began to look half empty, and Elizabeth was too busy pouring everything into rekindling her career.

"Corey, let's go."

The young man followed timorously by her side as they ambled down the street. "I'm sorry," he mumbled.

Elizabeth skidded to a halt. "Sorry? For what?"

"I mean if I wasn't blac—"

She grabbed him by the shoulders again. "You never do that all right? Never apologize for who you are." A tear broke from her eye. "It's not your fault people hate you for less than a millimeter of skin. You're great just the way you are. Don't let any of those hateful souls tell or make you feel otherwise. Do you hear me?"

"Yes."

There was much of Grace in her words, soft and pragmatic but hopeful in intent. Truly understanding half of what Corey might feel would be an achievement, but the crucial element was in *trying*. She tried hard to assimilate the plights of a black man, but their worlds were so antipodal, it often occasioned swells of imperious frustration that reduced her to hot tears on many moments. Grace would have had better words. Grace would have been able to understand. But like her patience for hate, Grace was gone.

They walked in silence towards the town's center. Corey decided he might be right with naming Dallas the City Without Sympathy.

He hoped he was wrong.

A Powder White

EACH TIME HE FOLDED THE PAPER, his fingers seemed to burn him with an abhorrent feeling of regret. Martin strolled down a bustling South State Street, fiddling pensively with the location Nina had left him, ruminating over his ill-burgeoned agenda as he wove through the smoke-spangled crowd.

The ting of tram bells pinged off the wires of power lines that sprouted along the street like rusted iron oaks. Patrons, black and white, read papers that still honored a frontage of hateful headlines. The same headlines Martin had the dishonor of reading just days ago. Tension grew as the crowd thickened; the sidewalk was packed. The violent clash of tobacco ash, shoe polish, and the corrosive snap of cheap lady fragrance was almost as intense as the showdown occurring between black and white eyes. Hostility was incrementally high.

Martin stopped to glance at a newspaper, eager for some political advancement regarding the matters that plagued the country, but even their commander-in-chief was tight-lipped.

President Wilson, despite the fancy pince-nez spectacles that seemed almost invisible, yet fused to his face, turned a blind eye to the priority of indignation. Two years prior, when riots saw the loss of around two hundred black lives in East St. Louis, the man remained silent. Nothing had changed today except for the slight minutia of obligation.

Whites, with impunity for their actions, garnered an attitude of invincibility. You could see it on their scowls, the cut of theirs gazes, and their gaudy, abrasive dispositions. Blacks thought to test how inviolable they truly felt. Martin could see it throughout the morning swarm. Not all white people carried their weight as such, but enough for him to feel the stares pierce his skin. He felt it because he, too, carried that same weight, frolicked with a similar temperament. It took one to know one, and fighting fire with fire, he decided, was the only way to burn the blight from the forest.

After passing through the meat of the crowd, he took a route down a few streets till he was alone with the echo of his shoes. With all the misfortune he had encountered in the last few days, he hoped a stroke of luck was inbound, and it came in coy form. Both his desired locations were within spitting distance of each other.

Earn's Alley was first.

A few feet into the street he turned into the alley, ducking a half-strung tarp to enter.

"How you doin', Martin?" A man with a bourbon voice and glassy eyes greeted. That was Randall, aged and crooked in his battered linen suit. He had a home at the mouth of the alley and always met Martin with pleasantries before anyone else.

Berta, the self-designated cook, was drenched in her ratty summer gown just a little further up the alley past a handful of other homeless. Martin crouched, greeted, and gave them furtive handshakes as he moved through. She always welcomed Martin with a firm nod and, before anything else, began to complain about the those in the alley complaining about the lack of food. "What do they expect, ay, Martin? Steak and collards? Child o' mine..." She kissed her teeth and resumed stirring her pot after Martin pacified her by slipping something in her pocket. She thanked him.

Gus was young, no older than twenty-five judging from the youthful exuberance in his eyes that had been quelled in most of the others. He made even Martin feel small when he stood up. Broad as a bulwark, the young man never stopped working out and loved to see Martin. "Hey, Marty The Great!" he insisted on calling him despite Martin's efforts to placate his enthusiasm.

"You need something today, Gus?"

"Not this time Marty. Gotta train." He returned to lifting a trash can filled with rubble and broken bricks, working in untidy reps. "Dreams work off of steam."

Gus strived to be a boxer, even given the conditions of his existence. He lionized Jack Johnson and his feats—the first black world heavyweight boxing champion. Gus wanted to be the second.

Martin proceeded, giving the same furtive handshakes to those he passed before he reached another of the alley's names, Mary Lou-Mae. The gentlewoman was the sedentary matriarch of the alley—even Earn recognized her as such—and her husband passed sometime in the last winter from a stringent affliction of the flu. It left her mothering six, no, seven kids, judging by the depth of the bags under her eyes, as well as the others in the alley. Martin knelt and graced her with a bright smile. He held her leathery hand in his and cocked his head to her half dozen and one, who scampered through the alley like freshly fed guinea pigs. The children locked away a glee behind their thin, mud-scuffed faces, which were ignorant to the curse of their liberty. Freedom came at the price of poverty.

Unlike their ancestors, who bled through cuts deeper than knee grazes, they were indeed as free as they could be. Martin slipped something in her cracked cup, and she offered up silent thanks with a warm squeeze of his palm as the sting of tears tempted her.

A dozen more homeless lay hopeless against ash-stained trash cans that had growled with fire bellies the night before. Draped in a question of gray, they sat on pedestals of plywood caked in layers of dated newspaper that only answered with the creak of abjection.

All thankful to see Martin.

At the alley's end, fiddling with some abstruse contraption, Earn sat on a depressed cream couch under noon light that filtered through a stitching of washing lines.

"H-hey Martin, I thought you weren't coming no more."

"Earn, it's eleven a.m."

"It is?' The man looked up, confused, hair floppy and thin like trampled cabbage. "My bad. You want something to drink?" He reached for a rusty cup and a jug that bore an alarming 'XXX' marking—likely dubiously brewed moonshine.

"I'm good, Earn. You got something for me?"

"That depends, you got something for *me*?" Earnest—an ironic name, as he only held endearment for those things insincere—rolled up his white sleeves and loosened one of his suspenders for further tinkering. He was a little older than Martin but forever subject to his intellect and ideas.

Martin wasn't fond of the feeling of paying dues after he had already done so in his destitution, but Corey was missing, Oscar was gone, and everything seemed a thin line away from falling apart. Martin pulled a green bottle from his breast pocket no bigger than a pinky finger and handed it over with another furtive handshake.

"My man." Earn tucked it away. "Take a seat." He patted the couch, which sighed some fishy-smelling dust. "Don't act new."

This was what he hated the most. Martin could deal with Earn feeling in control, the white man's foot on his neck, and even the crippling pain of his recent losses. But not this. Not what he had to witness every time he sat on that couch and stared into the vein of the alley. It gave him the sensation of falling—from grace, he thought, in his father's eyes.

As Martin looked on, each one of the people he greeted, sat gleefully uncorking little green bottles and hoovering up lines of white powder. Some bumped it, using their nails as crude measurements. Others tested if it went cold against their teeth and sent their tongue numb. They were all high by the time he sat next to Earn.

They were all high, thanks to Martin.

Chills took hold of him as he watched. Earn was rambling something beside him but he could only hear the screech of hungry sniffs. This was the reason the books were always balanced. If Kat knew, he could guarantee he and Sly would be the only ones left in the family. Martin turned away as his heart beat the beat of retrogression.

Earn fell into eyeshot, nose decorated the shade of attrition. He was so fair-skinned and trim-featured, his own mistook him on many accounts for a white man, especially when his hair was done the right way. This paved the avenue for his haphazard curiosity to wander down. Whenever the middle-aged man was bored, which was inordinately often, he would adorn the apropos attire, slip into the dark resonant corners of white diners, pubs, and dives, hook on his elephant ears and listen for the tidings they wished to hide. From duplicitous gossip to indignant plots of a violent persuasion, Earn knew it all. Even the odd misdemeanors of adultery were not excluded from his *Guess-what-I-heard* reserve. And now, what Martin was there for: the guns.

"Martin, you know some things are best left alone, right?"

"This isn't the time to take some moral high ground Earn." Tired and disinterested in anything but the guns, Martin tapped away at his knee.

"Just trying to look out for you is all. Times like these, I don't want to see you of all people get hurt. I thought you might reconsider and remain neutral about everything." Earn put down the contraption—the guts of some timeless clock—to focus on his company.

"Neutrality is a negative word." Martin remembered hearing President Wilson say something similar at the crux of deciding whether to join the war, and it was likely the only thing he agreed with. Poetic irony tiptoed around the words. "Nothing of purpose comes from its exercise." Those were his additions.

Earn sighed through his nose and scribbled something on a piece of paper he fetched from the crease of the couch. "Here." He passed it to Martin. "It's gonna be more trouble than it's worth. Look what happened to Jewels."

Martin folded it in his fingers. It held the emboldened feeling of fruition, unlike the one Nina gave, and he tucked it into a thin band of five-dollar bills. "That's your opinion. Opinion has caused more trouble than any bullet or blade. I haven't got time for opinions." His tone was cold and detailed with bitter inflections.

Earn had a look on his face like he didn't recognize the man that walked away from him. He mumbled a muted prayer as

Martin made his way down the alley. "Hey." He took a breath for some volume. "I'm sorry about Oscar..."

Martin didn't flinch. He was done with that pain.

As he glanced over the address Earn had written down, the alley was jittery and in high spirit, under the gauze Martin provided for their strain. The drugs, the racial enmity, the spiritual taxation of dead-end daily rhythms—they were all conducive to their impoverished reality. Wounds heal, but scars never quite vanish. Even if they did, the reverie of past perils their people endured would echo into future history and hopefully serve as an edifice for their descendants.

Martin sighed and left with a leaden heart.

*

JUMPY JOE. What a name.

Martin was eager to see the severity of the man's tremulous inclination. He hoped it didn't impede his hands.

When he reached the factory, the pale foreman questioned the intent of his visit with a lyrical suspicion. Behind his nasally inquisition blared the cadence of beating iron and the song of metal quenching.

Martin conjured some lie that he was looking for his cousin by the name of Joseph, because the man's mother was sick. All simple fiction. The man left the door slightly ajar as he went off to check the day's work roster. Black men, mostly, hammered away at heat-warped car parts, churning springs and molding tires from scrap rubber as Martin waited. In fact, he'd have an easier time counting the white faces. He smiled. This is what he was fighting for, the right for his brothers to work freely without threat or the oppression from bigots. To provide for their families and have equality in some reserved semblance. But he knew it would have to be taken, as one thing remained true.

Equality felt like oppression to the privileged.

A metal clank thundered through the foundry, and from the corner of his eye, a fidgety gentleman manned a lathe that was caked in white powder.

The foreman returned.

"We got four Josephs on record today. You got a surname for your cousin, sir?"

The man's surname missed him; he knew Nina had mentioned it, but he was having such a hard time dealing with lying that his focus only latched onto the poignant nickname. "Uhh, unfortunately not, we just met not long ago when he moved here after the war. See, his father left before he was born and his mother, well...it'll only be the third time he's seen her since they reunited. So not even he knows his true surname. Couldn't begin to guess which one he told y'all."

The foreman scratched his belly that pressured the buttons of his shirt, unimpressed with the desperate effort. "Sir, I'm afraid if you don't know his full name, I can't authorize any contact." The man turned to shut the door.

"Wait, wait," Martin clutched the man's oily forearm. Another metal clank rumbled the air, the person manning the lathe was notably shaken by the loud noise. Nina's report on Joe's relationship with loud noises sat up in his mind. "That's him."

"Who, Jumpy Joe?" They both locked eyes on the lanky, balding man in the black apron. "Why didn't you just say so?"

After the foreman whistled for him to come over, Joe arrived jittering like a bag of grasshoppers. His sunken eyes were puffy, skin shiny and soaked, covered in sweat and soot, but his eyelashes were dusted with white residue.

"I'll leave you two." The foreman departed.

"Joe." Martin shook his hand. "I'm Martin."

Martin told him about Nina and regrettably, her end. He explained he had a job for him, one that inspired a gentle environment with more euphonious acoustics.

Joe was hesitant but knew even in his shaky state that work came day by day. He could arrive at the factory doors a few seconds late and be a day's wage out of pocket. So he listened to the stipulation.

"How much you get paid a day, brother?"

"Uh, about three dollars." Joe wiped muck from his pink lips.

"I'll pay you six, plus a bonus if you do a good job."

Joe's eyes widened at the proposition of double pay. "S-six? How long you gone need me for?"

"Not sure, that depends on you really, but I was thinking about a week. And just to show you I ain't playing," Martin shelled out a crisp five-dollar bill from his pocket that stamped with a wistful portrait of Benjamin Harrison. "That's the first day's wage right there.'

"W-when y-you want me to start?" He couldn't hide the excitement in his voice, and it broke the start of his words more than usual.

"Tomorrow, if you can."

"Of course."

"You know where South Wentworth Avenue is?"

"Sure do."

"Good, my store Malcolm Meats is on the corner. I'll see you in the morning."

Joe shook his palm with both hands, thanking him profusely. Martin left with the tint of a grin, musing over the day's successes.

Outside, the crowd from the early morning had thinned as Martin strolled with an esteemed air. A young white boy with a strip of vitiligo across his nose bumped into him.

"Watch out, nigger."

Martin flexed to grab and scold the boy but the sight of two policemen swinging long blackjacks caused him to recoil. He let the disheveled child be. The boy looked no older than Corey.

No matter the respect or praise he gained, there he stood, a black man in a white world.

A Paint Red

TOWN AT THIS HOUR was free of wandering souls. Anyone with the courtesy or reverence for the midday sun wouldn't dare tempt its perpetual punishment. Elizabeth hadn't been south in more years than Corey was alive.

They walked, wondering how far a half-mile was—as the last sign lied—resisting the sun's demand for genuflection.

Blood and blouse thread scabbed the soles of Elizabeth's feet, yet she didn't wince a single time during the journey from Henry's house. A strange focus quelled the pain.

Corey noticed but said nothing.

They passed a bar with open doors and the salvation of shade. White men in damp white shirts drank merrily and played dice games on the stained floorboards, shading even their truckled beer from the heat. Though their stale gazes tracked the pair as they walked by—half confused as to why they were out in the sun, the other half bewildered as to why they were together—Corey locked eyes with the young black man behind the bar who served them all with a face glazed in sweat and a thin coat of what Corey assumed was shame. How was he safe? How could he stand amongst them, even in service, and remain tame? Maybe his service was the crux of his safety. Perhaps the bitter echo of some anachronistic obedience placated the white men and neutered the man of any proposed threat. As he looked on, a smile peaked from the corners of the man's mouth when a particularly gaunt patron asked for another. Corey's brow furrowed. He couldn't understand what level of glee a black man could feel this far from the, albeit diluted, liberty of the North. The bar laughed when the black man cracked something wise and resumed its games.

It skewed what Henry had made him believe.

He felt ashamed to assume each white man in the South was of rancorous diminutions. They weren't all the same;

they weren't all redacted to the lowest denominator of human misery that was hate.

He kept up with Elizabeth, and they passed several more bars, a dilapidated looking grocer and a small clothes store that displayed a pair of Keds sneakers in the window. He had longed for a pair but the ones on display were for women.

A rickety blue-roofed building appeared after the last bar they passed. It was a strange place for a garage. There weren't many cars around, but it was shaped like all the other buildings they happened by. All crouched low, huddled together as if telling each other wooden secrets. If you were tall enough and jumped, you could likely see onto the next unpaved street.

The place was shaped like an L; the end of the shorter leg faced the street and the end of the other stuck out the metal tongue of a ramp. Inside was nearly deserted; a few nude bulbs hung across the cracked ceiling next to the dominion of a pull string and mangled spider webs. Corey shuffled closer to Elizabeth at the sight of the treacherous things. The concrete was monopolized by pools of motor oil, dried grease, and some unidentifiable stains that caused Elizabeth to watch her bare-footed steps. Several half-dressed cars filled the room—some draped in brown tarps—along with the misplaced stench of ammonia that likely sprung from the unidentifiable stains. A menagerie of mildew poked ugly green heads from between the workbenches along the walls.

Elizabeth called out, and at first, there was no answer. The second time, a stringy fellow came from deeper in the building, rubbing sleep from his eyes and drool from his lips.

"How can I help, ma'am?" he said, feigning interest. The man was spindly in his browning overalls, with a picky horseshoe moustache, lazy eyes, and an attitude of half-baked servility, seeming seldom enthused to strike with initiative.

Elizabeth offered up pleasantries before getting to the meat of the meal. "I'm looking for my car." Her eyes wandered in hopes she'd recognize it if she saw it. "A man named Henry dropped it off some time ago, told me to mention his name."

"Henry who?"

"Henry Lynch."

The sun-scarred mechanic asked for her patience as he plodded off to find a file. Elizabeth felt Corey leave her side but was too focused on scoping out the vehicle. Any of the vehicles could have been the car she once owned. So many were covered, it was impossible to know if any of them were the wounded heap she remembered. She racked her brain for the number plate.

The mechanic returned. "Henry Lynch." His long, emaciated fingers traced over the clipboard. "Intersection crash." He travelled further across the page. "Chicago, 1909." He puffed air from his cheeks and looked her in the eye. "Sheesh, I remember this; it was one of the first cars to come through." The man tapped at the board with a rhythm of nostalgia. "That's a long way and a long time ago. The hell's it doing down here?"

"It's a long story." One she'd rather not tell.

"Okay, well, what you want with the thing?"

"I'm here to claim it."

His brow raised, and he went back to his clipboard. "Looks like it's paid for so that's all fine. I just need to see some paperwork."

Elizabeth stiffened. Henry had given none, and this was likely the sadistic part of his last-ditch manipulation. She peered down to his name tag and readied herself to blab.

"Ray, is it?" She said rhetorically. "I haven't got a lot of time."

He chuckled. "Boy, I've heard that one before." A gapped grin peaked through his cracked lips.

Elizabeth straight-faced the unnecessary humor. "I have no paperwork, Ray. What can I do to prove the car is mine?"

"No paperwork, no car."

"I can tell you the contents of the glove box, exactly as it is."

"Nope."

She couldn't remember that anyway. All memory of the car was parked in a bay of her mind long since taped off and shaded in regret. It was clear the man wasn't going to make allowances.

"W-what about the plate? That has to be worth something."

"No, ma'am."

Desperation kicked in.

"No, no, please." She pressed her fingers to her temple, then darted around the garage when her memory shifted into gear, muttering the numerals. "9-6-1-5, 9-6-1-5." She tore a tarp from one of the shrouded vehicles, exposing the off-blue body of a Buick Six. It wasn't even the right car. Another sheet flew to the ground in her frenzy as Ray made tame efforts to stop her. Two more went, and none of them revealed a car with a matching number plate. Still, she mumbled the numbers, "9-6-1-5, 9-6-1-5."

Elizabeth turned the corner, deeper into the building, the wall at the far end opened up into the street via a ramp, but her head was on a swivel search. Beside the gut of a tall pinguid man, who was silent and chomping on a sandwich that dripped with stale ham, a lone car was covered and caked in forgotten dust. She substituted the numbers for a calculated prayer and dashed over to the vehicle. With a breath, Elizabeth peeled back the tarp and peeked at the number plate.

9-6-1-5.

This was it.

Gooseflesh ran thick across her arms in the relief that she had found it. "See! I told you." She was lightly panting from her burst of desperation. The corpulent man next the car had a breath that gave away his jingled state. She held back a gag.

"Always wondered who'd leave a car this nice in the shop so long..." Flecks of pork tumbled from the stranger's mouth as he licked dried mustard from his lips.

Cletus, the burly fellow who ravaged away at his bread and stale meat, sat a few feet away from them and didn't bother to introduce himself. Instead, he carried on about his seemingly undying adoration for the vehicle. He settled back in a moaning chair with lionizing eyes that Elizabeth was uncertain were for her or the car.

"It's an old thing, but I bet she has a lot of spirit left in her." The man licked his lips again.

This time, Elizabeth was certain he was looking at her.

Elizabeth was almost twenty years his senior, and he was three, maybe four, times her weight wet. The man's shoes were bruised and swollen and leaned forward like he was in a perennial state of tiptoeing down a steep flight of stairs. His thinning pate suggested him older than he was, but with a hoggish diet that was conducive to quickened ageing, not much more was to be expected. Each time he sniffed, it rung like the squeal of a wild boar, his back built hunched and heavy like a shrugging bison.

"Lady," Ray came around the corner to her. "I still can't let you take it."

Elizabeth didn't hear him; she was too busy conjuring ways to further convince. The car wasn't how she remembered it: the wheels were not warped like once before, the windscreen wasn't in pieces and mingling with gravel, the red paint was still the same, but someone had given it a fresh coat, and the leather seating looked brand new. Impossible. She ambled over to the window for a closer look inside. "There should be a rip on the passenger's seat from some broken glass—"

There was no rip. No remnants of any damage or evidence of harm.

Elizabeth felt cold.

Her hands trembled without her wanting, and her slack-jaw expression in the reflection cruelly emphasized the pink scar under her chin. She brushed over it faintly, and scenes began to replay as if the scar were the play button for the pernicious memento she couldn't pause.

Ray moseyed over, chuckling to himself before peering through the window as Elizabeth stumbled back.

What on heaven or earth could be funny? She didn't know.

"I'll be goddamned; looks like it is your car after all."

Elizabeth's cheeked twitched. "What?"

"You see," Ray scratched the back of his head, a touch embarrassed. "Like I said, this was one of the first cars we got. I can't forget the night it came in; it was messed up real good. I had to replace the windows with this here cover." He flicked at the bouncy clear film. "Changed the wheel frame which gave me a kink in my back for a week after, and even got it painted again. Anyway, my wife saw it and offered to sew up all the torn leather—amongst cleaning all the...let's just say 'gore.' The rip you mentioned was real nasty, the only ones that could have known about it were me, my wife, Henry, and the owner."

"Thank God," Elizabeth let out a heavy sigh of relief and a wave of calm washed over her. Perhaps the city had sympathy after all.

"I'll be right back with the key." Ray vanished through some back door.

"Corey," she turned to find him missing.

Panic kicked in.

Her eyes shot from their sockets as she snapped through the building calling his name. "Corey!" She got to the entrance; he was nowhere to be seen. She cried out into the street for him. "Corey!" The world spun when she stumbled into the road, not entirely sure if it was from the fierce heat or her unbridled alarm.

Shielding her eyes from the daze of the sun, she peered down the empty street from which they had come. In the distance, a short silhouette grew towards her from the mirage on the horizon.

Corey.

She took off after him with little regard for her bare feet. The hot dirt was more afflicting than any pebble or stone.

When she reached him, he was shaken by her rattled face, wobbled eyes, and quivering lip, but her hands were firmly on his shoulders. "What do you think you are doing?" She checked over him for any injuries. "You can't just leave like that! Dear, it's not safe down here for you." The words were cyanide. She swallowed to kill any more that remained.

Corey pursed his lips, "I'm sorry, I just thought you could use these." In his hands were a new pair of Keds sneakers, the ones from the store window. Since Chicago, Elizabeth had been barefooted with only the amateurishly wrapped blouse scraps for protection. Her discomfort wasn't a fond scene.

She hugged him tight. "My God, thank you..." She pecked him on the cheek, feeling guilty for her premature admonishing. "This is very kind. You should have told me you wanted to buy them; we would have gone together."

Corey grinned wide. "I wanted it to be a surprise." His voice captured a rare childish charm. The truth was he didn't want her to know he spent the last of his money on them.

Back in the garage, Ray was waiting by the car with the key. Cletus nearly choked when he saw Corey, but he swallowed down the bigoted reflex.

They hopped in after their goodbyes, and as Elizabeth clutched the steering wheel, she seized up. Her palms were wet rags, and her knees, noodles. A feeling so fibrillating pulsed through her; the phantom motion of driving made her almost throw up. She was paralyzed by her fear of the past. Corey tapped her shoulder, because she didn't hear when he called. Ears pounding with the thunder of her heart. It made little difference; her skin was numb. Elizabeth burst out the car and heaved for air as her senses returned.

"You alright there, miss?"

"Y-Yes," she lied. "Do you know anyone that could drive us?"

Ray shrugged, "I don't think many people around these parts will be willing to take you with the boy anywhere. Sorry."

Cletus rose, dusting the crumbs from his patchy beard. "I'll take y'all," he spoke with plebeian prose that was hard to grasp the first few times he offered up any burble. "For a price."

"I don't have any money, but I can pay you when we arrive."

"Keep your money. I want the car."

Not much consideration was needed. "Deal."

Cletus smiled through brown teeth and glazed eyes. "Where y'all headed?"

"Chicago."

A Rum Red

LOUISIANA MADE THEM FORGET they were hundreds of miles from home.

It was divergent from the concrete monuments that populated the North and its obelisk-inspired cities, but it was a change that lulled their minds from their precarious position.

Their fleshy chauffeur was a stranger by the most punctual definition. Cletus claimed they needed to go through the Pelican State to avoid the blockages and hiccups the recent riots had aroused in Arkansas. They didn't dispute; they were tired. Instead, they just took in the views while they cruised through the rural scenery.

Drizzly hills tumbled from the horizon into the sway of waterlogged pastures. In the distance, in the palm of a still bayou, skeletal trees stood rooted in watery graves. Corey imagined how many of those trees were tombstones for runaways of the past. Perhaps few, perhaps all. Perhaps there weren't enough to mark them all. The lake on the driver's side was a mirror reflecting the frosted black cake of the night sky.

Cletus had swapped his overalls for a shirt, which he rolled halfway up his elbow-less arms, and some lounge pants that were tight and stained with mustard. It made his body look like a pinched raw sausage, tinting his face blue— likely from a lack of oxygen that he struggled to get down the folds of fat that noosed his neck.

Quiet ruled the car for the first leg of the journey, but when they crossed the western border into Louisiana, Cletus couldn't stop his bird box from talking about himself. Family was the topic of his first ramblings. He spoke about the uneven wagers, regarding respect, he often engaged in with his father when he was a boy, invariably leading to domestic affliction. He described his father's hands as iron ingots. An uncle, whose name he didn't have the poise to mention, filled in when his pops took a turn on his mother, and although his hands weren't iron, bronze was still an apropos comparison. His mother gave up by the time he could walk to school on his own and preferred to be an ornament hung from their garden tree than live a life of grievous reductions. "Family is no good, best to keep 'em far or not at all," he said at the crux of the conversation he had by himself, swigging hungrily from his flask. Which poetically led into his second topic. Alcohol. And the principal objection he felt toward the impending prohibition.

The first day he drank was the day his mother took her life. Just nine years of age, he guzzled down half a bottle of rum as if it were the hot chocolate she used to feed him, and he threw up all over the kitchen floor. On that occasion, his father beat him with a learned brutality. Each blow a metal lesson. The second time was when his father had been jailed and his same nameless uncle fell from the window of his home, paralyzing the man. Blame was left at Cletus' feet by daft cousins and aunties he hadn't seen in long terms, who were eager for a reason to exhaust their unattended trauma on some scapegoat. He was the chosen one.

Drinking was everyday past that point. Whatever he could get his hands on, he'd consume in copious amounts. Whiskey, brandy, bourbon, gin—which was a more recent flavor—and his favorite of the bunch, rum.

Whatever Cletus had brought with him in his aluminum flask invaded the car with an aroma of inebriation. Elizabeth did her best to stay as far from him as she could, but the man was likely jingled enough to set fire to his sweat.

The troubling stories ordered up empathy from Corey. Although he had ideals instilled in him that subverted his father's thirsty cycles, he listened to the man's misery, ears keen to the indistinguishable. "My dad says you shouldn't drink." His father exercised a *do-as-I-say* liberty when expounding that particular lesson.

"Hush up, boy," Cletus snapped. "Ain't nobody care what yo daddy think. Besides, I think the lady here would disagree."

He wafted the flask under Elizabeth's nose that she waved away. "What's the matter with you?' his barely visible brow scrunched up. "You some type of uptight prude or something?"

The scent gave her a decrepit reminiscence. Elizabeth said nothing and shuffled closer to Corey. It was a while before anyone spoke again; without surprise, it was Cletus in his rummy slubber.

"We should find a hotel to pitch in for the night; don't wanna get caught alone in the dark down here." He glanced glazed eyes over Corey. "Especially with this one."

"We don't have any money," Elizabeth said.

"No need to worry about that," Cletus licked his lips as he looked at her. "It's all on me."

They came to a dimly lit hotel around half a mile down the road they were on. Before they got to the room, Cletus had to pay a special fee for Corey to be allowed in the establishment, which inveigled him to a specific bitterness. He had every intention of being paid back.

In some form or another.

*

SHADES OF FOOL'S GOLD, to strangled greens and streaky clay-colored paint that made the walls feel like they were closing in, cast the entire décor in gaud. The bathroom, which was dark and peaked through a cracked door, had a display of mosaic-style hex tiles that caught the moonlight cutting between the dust-drenched curtains. A double bed monopolized the room, laced with a starchy lattice top sheet, while the sickly-sweet odor of mothballs was infused in the fabric. Other than that, only a baroque highchair that was tucked close to a vanity table lived in the room. On it, sat a radio that favored a shrunken jukebox with nobs of military precision.

Corey's face lit up.

He'd only heard about them from Sly when his fancy teachings came in flamboyant abundance. *'Magic,'* was one of the words he used to describe it. *'A weapon,'* was the comparison Corey didn't understand until his cousin explained that with the power of radio, soldiers and infantry were able to transfer key information—it was evolutionary in war. It was only a matter of time before it was used for further information and entertainment—revolutionary in society.

Corey hurried over to the thing—it was heavier than he thought —and set it next to the wall by the table, laying on his stomach in awe.

"You can have the bed," Elizabeth offered to Cletus. "We'll just take a couple of pillows and sheets for the floor." Her tone was flat and mirrored the cadence of mistrust, not nearly sold on the man's selfless amity.

"What? All by myself?" He thumped onto the bed, which moaned under the punishment.

"Corey," Elizabeth turned to him. "Go wash yourself up before you play with that thing."

"But Miss Elizabeth, I haven't seen one before. Can I just have five minutes first?" He twisted a few knobs and aimlessly prodded a few buttons before static started to play. Between the black and white tussle, only the occasional word popped through.

"Corey," Her voice a touch stern. "Go now, please."

Like some ethereal emission of his disciplined conscience, the word 'listen' popped from the radio with peerless timing. They caught each other's eyes, and without a word Corey scampered to the bathroom to clean himself.

Elizabeth sat at the vanity table with her head down, too ashamed of her dishevelment to look at herself in the mirror. Her feet were blistered when she took off the sneakers Corey had bought her. The blouse that hung loosely from her shoulders was an outstretched arm away from falling apart and her hair had been styled by a vicious Chicago wind. They had barely slept or let water touch their lips since the abrupt train journey. Corey seemed to be coping, but Elizabeth was uninspired to let her guard down.

"How about I fix you something to drink?" Cletus said from the bed that his wide body covered, wagging his flask with a chipped smile.

121

"No, thank you," Elizabeth declined. "I don't drink. Been dry ten years now."

"I bet you ain't," Cletus mumbled. "You see, this prohibition baloney got me all mixed up. How they gonna take away drink from the hard-working man because the rouse of some good-for-nobody Temperance—" The phrase eluded him.

"Temperance Movement."

"Uh-huh, that's the one. A load of humbug if you ask me. I'm getting my fill before they take it all away. You should do the same." He winked her way.

"I think it's good. It'll test to see if the country has the discipline of abstention. Hopefully lead us away from future wars and ways of oppression."

A picture came to mind following Cletus' failed effort to coerce her to the bottle: *The Drunkard's Progress*. It was an illustration by a since-passed lithographer named Nathaniel Currier. It depicted the undulating degradation of alcoholism and the rather patented steps one took towards their end. Even the tagline underneath the image was vivid and highly presumptuous: *From the first glass to the grave*. Right above the phrase—under the bridge that propped up the so-called path to desolation—was a lady in a red dress wiping her tears as she dragged along her daughter. The first step on the stair-like overpass featured a well-to-do gentleman simply indulging in a tipple he likely deserved after a hard day's work. The next few escalated the intensity of the degenerate concept, ranging from a drink being necessary to a drunk and disorderliness being commonplace. The bridge's apex peaked with an image of three aristocrats, half-seas-overs with cigarettes, loose and languid in demeanor. On the way down the other side of the bridge, the impression of poverty began the descent. A fleabag fellow continued the fall with shame in his eyes before desperation and crime led ultimately to the finality of a self-dealt bullet to the brain.

The idea was fallacious and awfully sullen but captured a snapshot at some of the country's reasons for prohibiting alcohol. Elizabeth believed Cletus to be firmly on the descent, somewhere between desperation and death. She hoped they would part ways before the latter occurred.

Corey came back into the room drying his face with a hand towel, avoiding the spots of mold around the edges. He plodded down beside the radio and fiddled with the knobs to tune it. But only the pop of random words flew from the crackly speakers. "—soon—" The day was still in the future when he'd be able to turn on a radio and hear the sounds of the world.

Right now, the only sound audible other than the gentle breeze knocking at the window and growl of rusted steam pipes, was the licentious cacophony coming from the room over. Muffled grunts and groans – louder than the unsettled pipes – beat against the walls with a carnal inflexion. It sounded like perhaps three people were engaged in the coital activity by the frequency and volume of their moans. Corey did his best to ignore it but had a juvenile smirk on his face.

"—love—" the radio spouted with ironic timing.

"When was the last time you had any action like that, huh?" Cletus' gaze was unbuttoning and invasive.

Taken aback, Elizabeth huffed. "That isn't exactly an appropriate conversation." She eyed Corey, who continued to pretend he was deaf. "Nor with someone... I don't know." *Stranger* was the word she wanted, but she couldn't afford any angst from the man.

Cletus rose and trudged over to her, flicking a wisp of hair out of her face.

Elizabeth pulled away.

"Everyone else seems to be having fun tonight." He raised the flask in offering once more. "We should be doing the same."

"I'd just like to get some rest." Elizabeth suppressed a gag when his fermented breath caused her to purse her lips.

"Darling, rest is for the dead."

"—stop—" the radio popped.

Cletus backed away a touch and sighed through the hollows of his nose. "Turn that thing down, boy!"

Corey peered at him before his eyes flitted to Elizabeth, who nodded. Anything to deter complication was permitted. He turned down the radio and flicked out his notebook, writing down the words that came out and using them as prompts for flash poems—four or six lines at the most. When he got bored with that, he turned his attention back to the poem he had begun on the train.

Cletus drank listlessly at the edge of the bed, eyeing Elizabeth as his head sailed on a rummy wave. "It's the fault of women like you." He wiped liquor from his lips. "The suffragettes and such, that seek to ruin the living of hard-working American men."

"It must be hard work ruining the lives of American men, given all the privileges granted at birth. I'm not sure even American men could ruin the lives of American men."

"—truth—"

Corey kept his head down whenever the radio had something to say.

"What you tryna say?" Cletus spat.

"All that you aren't."

Cletus looked riled, and his flabby collar grew to a maddened red when the radio popped again.

"—loser—"

He stormed over to Corey, draped him by his neck, and smacked him across the face with an indignant ferocity.

Pain exploded in Corey's cheek as his eyes brimmed with searing tears. Cletus had inherited his father's hands.

"Corey!" Elizabeth rushed to his side. "What the hell is your problem!" Elizabeth screamed at the towering man.

"I just had enough of his shit!" Cletus stood over them like the shadow of some wild black bear. He grabbed Elizabeth by the hair and dragged her towards the bathroom. She screamed and kicked out as the carpet burned her knees. "And I've had enough of yours too. Either *we're* having fun." He flung her over the edge of the bath. "Or *I* am."

Elizabeth squirmed for freedom, crying out in harrowed wails for Corey. It was futile. Cletus was too heavy for her to break away. When she heard his belt unbuckle, panic bestowed her a second wind. Her heart pounded like the boom of African war drums, and her struggle made it hard for Cletus to proceed with his violation.

In the room, on the floor, fighting the unconsciousness, Corey wriggled, clutching the side of his skull, which bloomed like an afflicted flower. Through tears that blurred his vision and the static from the radio, which felt as though it lived at the center of his head, he saw the warped image of Cletus bending Elizabeth over the bath.

"—quick—"the radio popped.

Corey stumbled to his feet, room spinning and senses pinging as if rattled by firecrackers.

Elizabeth's screams injected him with urgency, but his head was too frazzled for rational thinking. He couldn't move Cletus, not even with his best effort, and if he could, then what? Another swift strike from the man's paw would certainly render him catatonic.

Her screams grew. He had to think. Fast.

There was nothing around the room that could aid him. The chair was too cumbersome for him to use effectively; all the toiletries on the vanity table were much too dainty and minute to allow any moving force. He put together some choking contraption in his mind involving a curtain but quickly got rid of the idea when he decided endurance was a losing battle.

"—weapon—" the radio seemed to taunt him.

Corey dove down to look under the bed, head still ringing the same static as the radio. Nothing but families of lint, a bottle cap, and a stranded sweet wrapper populated the darkness. At the other side of the bed, he could see the light from the bathroom flicker with their frantic movements. His chest ballooned in fear as Elizabeth's cries were becoming strained. She was close to giving up. Corey turned from the light and the radio fell into eyeshot.

A weapon.

Pulling himself from under the bed, he hurried to the clunky thing. Head singing from the bruise Cletus dealt, he hoisted the radio into the air. Sly said it was a weapon, but with a metaphorical logic.

Corey was about to understand it by a literal logic.

He pelted full force at Cletus, slamming the radio into the back of his balding skull. A loud crack severed the struggle in the room, and blood hissed from the man's head all over the walls and into the tub. Cletus' body fell inanimate over the edge of the bath as Elizabeth slipped from under his crushing frame.

Unkempt and wide-eyed, she panted with tremors writhing through her body. "Corey..." She couldn't keep her hands still when she reached out for him, and tears massacred her eyes. Corey dropped the radio, and she embraced him, trembling with arctic proportions. "W-We have to leave." She glanced over Cletus' body. "We have to leave now."

They got themselves together in a hurry. Elizabeth slipped on her sneakers and fished the key from Cletus' pocket while trying her best to calm herself.

Corey watched the man, hoping he wasn't dead. They quit the room as the radio popped one last time.

"—fatal—"

*

A WAR-mangled decade had passed since Elizabeth had last driven a car. People said it was impossible to forget, like swimming or the bipedal balance of riding a bike. What they fail to expound was that anything is easy to forget when one has the desperate intention to. She had no food for these thoughts or need to reflect on the ingredients that had produced her dereliction of the practice. She'd sooner starve herself of ever thinking again than chew on the heavy fat of morose, indigestible trauma.

But if she wanted to carry on thinking in any capacity, if she wanted Corey to continue thinking, she'd have to think about those things she hadn't thought about for ten years.

Under the cloak of the night, they hurried to the vehicle. Elizabeth turned it over, and anxiety fizzed to the end of her nose. Adrenaline-infused delusions flashed before her eyes in the hellish red scars of the past, projecting grandiose and malignant memories of dank smoke, shattered glass, and claret palms.

"Miss Elizabeth."

Corey's voice shot her into motion. Still quivering from the ordeal, she cranked the clutch and flicked the accelerator. Somewhere between him asking, "What do we do?" and "Where are we going?" the adrenaline wore off. Her flight instinct had run dry of fuel.

When she realized she was driving, memories returned in an assault that turned her face pale. A wooziness pulsed from the back of her head like she was imagining the thump of the radio upon her skull. But it wasn't unease for Cletus' life; it was for another.

"Corey...I-I need to stop...I-I can't—" The car sped up as the world dizzied before her. She veered off the road, and Corey's warning was too late by the time they slammed into the pole.

A Hand Black

9-6-1-5. IT WAS WHAT HE SAW FIRST amidst the sour, burnt-black smoke and the sting of tinnitus before he caught sight of her body lying at the edge of life.

The world rendered an alarm to all his senses; he was at odds with balance. The ground was turbulent, as if walking through a rushing tide. Knees the consistency of jelly, he fought to stay upright. Fought for stolid strides. Fought to reach his daughter.

9-6-1-5. Four numbers that were the code to his past.

The first step was the hardest.

His legs were numb, and tendons clicked a brittle sound against bone. The last time his body felt this way was moments after he took his first life. Hunkered in a deep trench along the Western Front, when the guns went quiet and the stars were loud, a German soldier attempted an ambush on his platoon with nothing but a Stielhandgranate and madness in his mind. Jerry dealt him his end with a broken bottle and knee-jerk reflexes, disposing swiftly of the stick grenade. Nausea held him close that night.

He never thought the bottle would save his life, but he feared it may take hers.

Now, however, stars were exchanged for shattered glass, guts for car parts, but there was just as much blood. At least France had the decency to hide it in the mud.

The second step was accompanied by a new pain.

When he stumbled at the sight of smoke clearing from his daughter's face, agony in his arm sent him weak again. Blood gushed from a gash that ran the length of his forearm, dripping onto the hilt of his blade as he looked around for something to help his balance. Only his mother's unconscious and bleeding face, sat in their ruined vehicle, came into view. A rancorous feeling spread in his chest. "Illness is more than physical symptoms," he recalled Clinton saying when being taught the man's illusory opinions on purification. He knew his mother needed purification from her undertow of illness.

After the third step, he was used to the ache. The moment before he reached his daughter, a black, bloodied hand reached through the smoke—the devil coming to collect her, he thought.

"I'm a nurse," they said.

"I'm a curse," he heard.

Panic sequestered his rationale in morbid hollows as he lunged for them through the haze...

*

A ROSE, a reason, and resentment.

Jerry gazed onto the sepia-flushed photo, whose edges were a vignette of bleach and forgotten pigments, with the glisten of a ghost behind his eyes. He saw the boy, he saw the boy's mother, but the rose, despite its two-toned nature, seemed to bloom the same color as his beating heart. He had been studying it, unblinking, for more moments than some of his longer memories as smoke from a dying cigarette snaked over the monochrome portal to the past.

The furniture in the room stood staring at him from mangled brown shadows, haunting and gaudy with a macabre affinity. Tobacco and myrrh tangled in white whispers around the room, seeking refuge between the dark and demented tension.

"Jerry..." The voice was muffled, and distant, and calling from downstairs. It was his wife by the melancholic music of her words. Tipping the last of his cigarette into the eggshell china ashtray that was gilded along the rim, he rose to leave the room.

9-6-1-5. Four numbers that were the code to his past.

It took nine steps to get to his daughter that day, six labored breaths that roused his asthma with brutal increments, one decision that would walk with him in this life and the next, and five minutes of chaos that took his Rose away.

A Face Red

SMOKE WRAPPED THE VEHICLE in a white squeeze, strangling them of hope with each tightening second. Louisiana teased them with peace, but Louisiana was to make them remember all the reasons they were so desperate to get home.

When Corey came around, it was like the last time. The same ping played in his ears like the end of an unconscious song; his head beat louder than when Cletus performed a hand along his face, but fear did not sit beside him like it did on the train.

It sat in his lap and forced his breath.

He pushed through the daze as the crackle of flames danced outside like demented figures in the night. Beside him, Elizabeth dripped over the steering wheel in a slumberous slouch, mumbling indistinguishable pleas for remission. Lament tumbled from her split lips, but she was half comatose from where Corey was sitting, and he wasn't sure if she knew what year she was in. Judging by the names she murmured, it wasn't this one.

"Miss Elizabeth," his voice croaked from the heat and his half breaths. Corey had no idea how long they'd been out; guessing from the alarming choreography of the fire it was safe to say it was too long.

After a few shoves, Elizabeth awoke with a frightened gasp, latching onto Corey with wide eyes. She saw the fire as smoke knocked on the windows and tempted her eyes to tears. "Are you all right?"

He wasn't sure. An inspection was in order. Corey checked over his body for injuries. Other than the thrum in his head, there were none. A slight split lip seemed to be the only damage Elizabeth sustained.

Luck also appeared to ride with them.

"Dear, we need to get out of the car!"

"I think the doors are jammed." He tried the handle, but nothing. Even a shoulder barge seemed to leave it unmoved.

"Okay, we'll have to *make* it open." Elizabeth licked the blood from her lips and spun so her back was facing Corey and her feet were planted on the door. "Put your back to mine." She caught a scare when the engine popped, adding new fiery figures outside. "Then kick against the door as hard as you can. I'll push too to support your back."

Corey nodded. He got into position, and on three, they heaved to no avail. Again. Nothing. Again. And the door only squeaked.

"Dammit!"

Corey sat up and an idea came to him. "I'm going to try something else." Another pop that sounded like a firework sent Elizabeth jumping. He pulled the laces from his boots, tied it around the handle and got back into position. Tugging on the lace to release the latch, they pushed again; this time the door creaked with more hope. Corey drew back his knees to his chest, and with a gritted roar slammed his heels into it with all the force he could manage.

Nothing.

Hope burned away.

But as they sat there watching the fiery fingers prod against the plastic windows, Corey spotted a reason to believe they could break free.

The heat had stretched and warped the film, weakening the clear window with stretch marks. Drawing the pencil from his pocket he mumbled to himself, "I hope this works."

Corey thrust the pencil towards the window with all his might and the window popped open. Cool air blasted in through the hole as he widened the opening.

"My goodness, Corey..." Elizabeth was wonderstruck by his quick thinking and helped him stretch the gap.

They climbed through the smoke and into the blackness of the night.

Corey flimsily laced back up his boot, leaving them half loose in his haste. "What do we do?" He glared around; it was hard to see much in the darkness, and the only source of light other than the bloom of the car on fire was the red glint from that same fire on broken glass.

"I don't know, dear." Elizabeth looked around; to their right was a naked lot filled with some lonely trees and an abandoned-looking building that seemed to stretch for miles. To their left, a reed field as tall and towering as Jerry, stood swaying in the night.

Then they heard it. The hollering of a posse and the bark of maddened bloodhounds. Elizabeth's face was rattled when she looked at Corey's. How did they find them? How could they know where they were? By all accounts it was impossible. But it wasn't.

"Corey, run!"

They dashed into the reeds; Corey's nerves clattered like sharpened knives as the bipedal stomp of siren bells thundered their way. Tearing through the sea of tall grass, they couldn't know which way was safe and which way was to the dogs. Corey's chest tightened, but he took long breaths to prevent an asthma attack.

The moments that followed were madness.

The sound of the inbound posse undulated with their frantic twists and turns. The lefts looked the same as the rights, and backwards mirrored forwards. Cornhusk appeared on the floor and made their steps crunch with an unwanted call. Somewhere between the fear and the frenzy, the reeds braided into cornrows.

Turning from the cornfield and back into the reeds, they ran the direction adjacent to it, and as it came to an end, they clattered into something, crashing to the ground. Corey thought it the dogs. Elizabeth thought it the end.

Confusion brewed when they sat up to see a dark-skinned man and a little red-faced boy.

"What's y'all doing out here?" the man's voice was raspy from running. The posse had grown closer. "Best follow us, them peoples gon' be here in no time."

Without hesitation, Corey followed them, but Elizabeth was apprehensive to the stranger's aid, as recent history had a rancorous record.

"Miss Elizabeth, come on!" he hurried her.

The dogs were getting closer. She had no choice.

A few moments passed before the cornhusk materialized again. Elizabeth was sure they were running in circles.

"This way." The dark-skinned man called from the front. She noticed him following the husk and then it hit.

The cornhusk wasn't random.

It was a trail.

They came to a chain-link fence with a small creek on the other side and the thin man squeezed himself and his son through the gap first. Corey and Elizabeth went through together and as Elizabeth emerged on the other side, Corey didn't. On the ground, his lace had caught on the fence as he tried to get through. The barks were louder now. Bites moments away.

"Corey!" Elizabeth pulled on him with a panicked vigor, desperate to release him from the jaws of damnation. She tugged, but he didn't budge.

The stranger, their unlikely aid, pushed passed Elizabeth and shot his hand under the fence to pull Corey's laces loose, freeing him from the ensnarement. He rolled a thick lug of timber by the hole and the dogs arrived as they reached the creek's bank. Saliva and rabid foam glazed their teeth as they gnawed at the fence with futility, growling with a deranged hunger.

The four of them slashed through the water, battling against the foil of a testy undertow to reach the salvation of a thick forest on the other side. On the opposite bank, they were exhausted, but rest would have to wait. "This way," the straw-hatted man called. His husky voice hushed under the *shhhhh* of tree leaves. They cut through the tightly packed oaks, and after a few minutes, emerged onto a clearing that murmured relief.

Elizabeth went to speak. It felt like the first eased breath she'd had taken since the hotel. "Thank you." She held Corey close.

In the calm the prairie offered, they exchanged names. Jeremiah was the man's name. Mud-scuffed overalls swathed his thin body, and a frayed straw hat made his head appear the same way as a sunflower whenever he tilted it back. He had skin like polished onyx and bloodshot, yellowing eyes from heaving heavy tools with empty stomachs on cloudless noons—his lack of nourishment was evident from his emaciated limbs.

Isaac, his red-faced son, had the build and article of a pickaninny. Like a pocket edition of his rustic father, the boy had overalls that were too big for him and covering a lemon-toned corduroy shirt. He ran his fingers along his sleeve that clipped the cloth ribs like some fabric guitar—it was as close as he'd get to play a real one.

Jeremiah explained that a lynching party was after him and his boy. He refrained from the details as there was still a note of alacrity in his disposition. Simply put, he thought to help when they ran into each other. Elizabeth thanked him again.

Isaac was about three or four years Corey's junior, with a coherence even younger and less educated than that. The South didn't inspire blacks to nurture speaking skills or logistics, only blood and hard labor. A thin bony voice escaped when he spoke, one that clinked against bigger words with the same sound as his knocking knees.

"Just up ahead, there's a car," Jeremiah said. "A friend is here to pick me and my boy up. You're welcome to come along till we get somewhere safe."

Elizabeth thanked him again despite her lingering disquiet.

The sable truck materialized after some walking and an elder man with a round face, thick snowy beard, and silver hair popped his head from the window.

"Didn't expect to see no white folk with you."

Jeremiah looked at Elizabeth through the side of his eye. "Neither did I."

*

OLD MEN tended to whistle on long drives, strolls, or in conjunction with any autonomous task for that matter. The driver was very old and managed to whistle even when he was talking at times. He whistled the tune of "Wade in the Water." Corey recognized it.

Before the war, his grandma used to come down on weekends and cook her famous collard greens, candied yams, and his favorite afters: pumpkin pie. She'd sing that and other songs he felt in places deeper than his ears. There were many, but this one had the rhythm of a long battle march. The drums stomped at an increasing pace led by a pained voice, followed by an army of echoes that ranged towards freedom. Many viewed the song in different frames; some more ignorant folk only saw it as upliftment. Others, who had flagrant intentions, according to the colonizer, knew the song as instructions for their path to liberty. The great Harriet Tubman used the song to implore slaves to wade through creeks, and rivers, and streams to purge themselves of their scent, throwing their trail from the hunting dogs. Corey understood now.

He had an idea of the way slaves functioned in times of fear. Down bad, splintered hands from ragged tools, bloodied soles from kicking rocks, and battered souls from being worth less than the crop they cut. Spirituals seemed to be the only decency offered to their lives. And when they sang, they sang like they were free. The infectious vibration of their cadence rumbled against waves, across fields, and ultimately, through time.

Straw cordoned their skin from the scabby rust of the Mack AB pickup truck that was enclosed with what looked like the ribs of a garden fence crafted by an inept carpenter. It was rickety, but it kept them in the red wagon.

"So, what had y'all running from them people back there?" Elizabeth asked.

"Ya see," Jeremiah hiccupped and cleared his throat. "Them people want nothing but trouble. I don't want no trouble." The slack-jawed look after some of his words testified for an unfortunate lack of knowledge. "I's a sharecropper. No more, no less. I worked at Mr. Mckinley's farm almost all my life, paying my dues, minding my business. Ain't never been in no trouble."

"They were just chasing you both for sport?" Elizabeth looked disgusted.

"Not exactly. See, after some time I be realizing that being a sharecropper is just a, ahh..." he hiccupped and scratched the dry kinks of hair peeking from his hat. "Sy-syn-o-"

"Synonym," Corey helped.

"That's the one!" His miseducation was the thief of larger words. "I ain't no freer than the pigs in the pen. I can't be who I wanna, where I wanna, with who I wanna be with."

"Of course you can. You could have left, taken your son and your partner and found a new life in the North."

Jeremiah hiccupped and looked down at his son beside him who was stripping a piece of straw. "Ma'am, that's the thing, I can't be with who I wanna. I have my son, but his mother I can't have, and neither can he."

"What happened? Did she pass?"

"No, but she might as well be to us as we ain't never gon' see her again..."

"Whys that?"

Jeremiah sighed after a violent hiccup. "Isaac here was born on a night like this. Soft, starry, and just the right temperature for cheer. I could hear his screams even from the barn house but couldn't be there to see him take his first breath. McKinley was in-incen-"

"Incensed." Corey could see him struggling.

"Thank you, son."

"What's your son being born got to do the with the owner?" Elizabeth nudged the story back on track.

"McKinley is Isaac's grandfather."

Elizabeth went strawberry-red. In the haste of the getaway, she hadn't digested the fact that the boy's mulatto complexion was testament to his half-Caucasic heritage. The reason for their fleeing started to settle in bitter increments.

Jeremiah hiccupped. "They say you don't choose who you love, you just love." Turning his head to the sky, he spoke like he was confessing the truth to his ancestors. "The first time I saw her, all I saw was her smile. Like the brightest set of pearls or stars you ever seen. Then her eyes, brown and warm like Mama Esther's hugs, like there was a home there for me."

Isaac's eyes had the same hold as his mother's whenever he cared to look up.

"A few years after secret meetings and late nights in the woods," Jeremiah threw his arm around his boy, 'our loved made him. McKinley gave the child to Mama Esther to raise with the rest of us farmhands but didn't know who the pappy was. No one truly knew except Mama Esther, and she let me see him every Sunday for a few hours. I'm not sure how McKinley got to know, but I guess that Hector, the scalawag, was spying and wanted a raise."

"That's terrible."

"Who knew ol' McKinley had been wondering who the pappy was even after all this time?" He claimed the ranch master had gotten really good at tying a rope he liked to call "The Last Gasp." The boss-eyed devil's means of discipline had a disparaging sting. "He sent a posse of his nephews after us tonight."

Elizabeth's silence said more than her words could.

Thirty years of Lynching in the United States. About as far back and accurate as the NAACP could record when they published the booklet earlier in the year. Over three-thousand people had been the target of lynching mobs since 1889, nearly eighty per cent of whom were negroes. The South owned a staggering, but not surprising, portion of the said lynchings. Georgia and Mississippi led the count, with Texas and Louisiana close behind. Lies of fictitious rapes were often the grounds on which white men predicated for their lurid executions. It was no shock Jeremiah chose to flee; they'd hang him from one of their favorite trees, then proceed to have afternoon tea. The whites of the South still communicated with an unholy parlance despite the fact of abolition.

"Enough about us. What y'all doing running in fields?"

Elizabeth explained their situation, with the ad-lib of Jeremiah's hiccups that seemed to sound whenever the man was shocked or fighting the urge of bouncy nerves. She omitted the egregious intermission at the hotel—it was far too raw—replacing it with a small, yet fitting, lie.

Jeremiah puffed aired from his cheeks. "That's quite a pre-predi-"

"Prediction." Corey thought it was a strange choice of words.

"Not that one." Jeremiah's lips began sounding the letter M.

"Predicament?" Corey asked, unsure this time.

"You's a smart man, huh?" Jeremiah smiled. "Looks like yous both in luck. We're headed to a secret Mardi Gras party to meet a friend of mine who's headed North tomorrow night up the Mississippi, then we gonna stop off in a place called *The Bleach Barrel*. There's more than enough space for two more; if you want, you're welcome to come along."

Elizabeth's brow furrowed. "Why would you do that for us?"

"You don't choose the people you love, but you can choose the people you help. And I choose to help you."

Thanks lodged in her throat before she offered profuse amounts of it when she could get it free. "I don't know how we can repay you."

"How's about having a good time in New Orleans before y'all head home?" Jeremiah chuckled without the hindrance of hiccups this time.

Heading south to head north embodied a sort of irregular bow-and-arrow motif. One the white man would seldom expect.

*

THE NIGHT WAS COOL, fresh with the pull of every breath as they settled under the hush of muted stars. The hum of the tired engine and trudge of rubber wheels seemed almost like a snore along the quilt turf, drowned out by the hoot of barn owls and the chorus of crickets that hid on the fringes of the wilderness. A band of fireflies swirled over the truck, tracing the constellations in an untidy flow like little neon comets.

Bumps in the field were rhythmic and calming. It had already tempted Isaac to a cheek-shivering slumber as his father softly sang "Follow the Drinking Gourd" with the timbre of a husky lullaby. That song too had more conspicuous lyrics of freedom than the spiritual the driver whistled earlier. It spoke of the Big Dipper constellation, which resembled a cosmic drinking gourd in motion to scoop up the North Star. *Polaris*, to a science mind.

Martin told Corey of the star when he was young and afraid of the dark. He refrained from tainting his innocence by not telling Corey the star acted as a guide and beacon of hope for runaways. Martin said his mother had gone to bring it back for him so that his nights were never dark again. '*The star is far, so it may be a while before she returns, all right?*' Tears always filled his father's eyes when he told Corey the tale.

As he gazed at the star, pencil and pad in hand, doing his best to get along with the right words, he imagined he could see his mother's face amongst the twinkle. He pictured it while they were fleeing from the dogs with a vivid focus. It was the only reason he could unbolt himself from the lock of asthma.

The picture of his mother was the key.

Imagining his parents together was always a struggle and rarely materialized the way he wanted. On the floor, he fidgeted uncomfortably without anything to rest his head on, scribbling a few words down between long gazes at the North star and wistful reveries. Jeremiah's song was replaced by his snorted snore. Corey was a touch jealous.

"Come." Elizabeth patted her thigh. "I won't be getting much sleep tonight."

Corey shuffled over to lay on her lap. "Thank you"

"Thank *you*, Corey." She stroked his head with a maternal air. "You're very brave."

They hadn't even had the chance to reflect on the events that happened before they met their new company. It was even harder to perceive it all occurred under the same night. Speaking about it wouldn't help right now; instead, they left it to the wind. They knew what was what, and that was enough.

"What are you writing?"

"A poem."

"Really?" The back of the pad gave Elizabeth a red stare. "Can I read it?"

"Nope." Corey penned in a few words.

Her faced dropped. "What if I say *please*?"

"That's a better try. Still no." A cheeky grin spread across his lips.

"You little—" She playfully tussled with him, and they laughed.

"When it's done you can read it."

"Okay, okay," Elizabeth looked down at him from the corner of her eye, and when he wasn't expecting it, snatched the pad from his hand. She read, "The Co—"

Corey was quick. It was back in his hand before she even got the second word out. "You can read it. When it's all done."

An Ink Black

FAMILY WAS A WORD that occasioned those of like minds and kindred blood to feel a sense of belonging. As tradition would have it, a patriarch often governed the regulations the said family lived by. A loving matriarch would offset the stoic predisposition of the alpha and display qualities in which her kin could seek solace. An unspoken code of sorts.

What happens when the matriarch is lost in the past? Battling trauma and plights of devilish degrees, unable to buffer the prosaic deficiencies of the man's stipulation. What happens when there is no one to question the alpha?

What happens when *hate* is the only regulation?

Flo and Arthur simmered in the lounge room having evening tea, shooting the breeze and awaiting the alpha's broody descent from his room. His wife had called him. A dark arrival was on the horizon.

They ignored Loretta, who perched by the window sipping from a cocktail—when she remembered she was holding it—of lemon, vinegar, and soda water. A product of her inordinate superstitions.

"You see, darling," Flo began after Arthur had asked how she acquired such a home. It was strange it had taken him this long to inquire. "Many people have different talents. Some sing like songbirds, others can make you believe they are someone they're not, and I, my love," she stepped towards the mirror and squirted her neck with perfume, "have the talent of intoxication."

Arthur laughed. "So you throw good parties?" He sipped his tea that was too hot and ate more of the cake he baked. It was the first night in a while he put down the newspaper. Still it lay folded next to his plate.

"No, silly," she shooed away his joke. "I can make almost any man I meet hand over his heart. Nine out of ten anyway." That one fat cat from New York was annoyingly loyal to his wedding vows.

"You're telling me you got all this from swindling some rich fool?"

"More or less."

"Nonsense."

"You don't believe me?" She screwed him through the reflection in the mirror. "Would you like me to show you how it's done, honey?"

"Please. I'd quite like a house like this for myself."

Pink lips, swinging hips, and eyes that sent men begging. She hunkered down beside him, threw her leg over his lap and hand around the nape of his neck. Her bottom lip brushed his earlobe as she pressed her bosom against his chest. Warm breath trickled over and down his ear as she whispered something promiscuous, something about the cramp in his toes once she was finished.

Arthur didn't flinch. Not even a peek at her busty cleavage, which was dusted with some shimmery stuff and smelled of plum rose.

Flo looked half hurt and half impressed at his resistance as she shuffled away. "Well, like I said, nine out of ten."

"Sorry to be the ten." Arthur saw the mild irritation on her face in the form of pursed lips.

Flo ate a forkful of cake—red velvet was her favorite because of its opulent flavor and societal implications. A Los Angeles hotel had served it to her by mistake instead of the King Cake she ordered—King Cake on the menu had her overjoyed, as growing up in New Orleans, she developed a warm predilection for the colorful dessert. Red velvet was the best mistake she ever tasted.

The infamous New Orleans dessert was where she and her sister took their surname: *King*. They dropped the name 'Brown' in favor of the regal title. Their parents didn't want them, so they didn't want their name.

After the years of dismal days she and Loretta spent hopping from home to home, saloon to saloon, earning their keep through free labor for just a single meal a day, such a lifestyle made her crave the bliss of a lavish liberty. Despite being younger, Flo always had a penchant for leading and whipping the reins. A plan materialized for their lives to change.

Flo formed an art around making the carnal hearts of perverted elder men skip more than a single beat. Most of them weren't fit enough to survive such a palpitation, as their bodies were fueled by rich caviar, richer cigarette smoke, and the fine aged wines they had more of in their veins than blood. They risked perishing at the mere sight of her florid beauty. New foppery became a habit, and she was indigenous to the allure of novelty. Everything new made her feel reborn, fanciful, and lucent. Especially when Indian silk dripped from her milky skin.

She got herself into the finest circles and her name on the richest lips. Her goal was to marry an unreasonably wealthy man, old enough so that death was just down the street, then take everything he left her to share with her sister. It worked. But somewhere between it all, Loretta found love with a young Southern man while Flo moved to Chicago on her own.

On those nights of duplicitous persuasion in New Orleans, white wine delivered her sensibilities to a coercive purpose. Tonight, she swapped the white for red, and the specific brand of Claret dulled her to feel a touch lascivious. She told Arthur of it all while she finished her cake.

"Must have been lonely," Arthur sympathized.

"A little at times. She poured herself more wine. "But Bo came round on occasion to break it up."

"At least you're stuck with us now," he simpered.

"I got no problem being stuck with y'all, but your damn brother needs to lighten up some. Always so heavy about everything."

"He's been through a lot."

"Honey, we've *all* been through things. That's what family is for. How can I recognize that, and I ain't ever had one?"

Arthur went silent. He didn't have the answer to his brother's deluded position of autocracy. Jerry wasn't always this way, he thought. It was as if the more black people he saw, the darker he became. The further he thought of his daughter's death, pieces of himself were killed in the process. The pieces no one saw.

The pieces regulated by *love*.

Flo switched the topic; she asked about who Arthur was and he expounded his affinity for aviation. They conversed about that for a while, and then Flo spoke about her dreams of being a fashion designer, like that young French lady by the name of Gabrielle Bonheur Chanel who was making waves across the pond. Many knew her as 'Coco' and Flo lionized the woman for popularizing a new feminine standard of sporty and casual chic. Coco had a revolutionary spirit.

Arthur always complimented her, and Flo always let him.

They handled a sibling-like affection for each other, perhaps because they looked so similar, and of course, Flo was highly fond of the pictures mirrors framed. Although she had many more curves and was often covered in her best furs and make-up, they both had the same milky skin, emerald green eyes, full pink lips, and gold hair that yelled in the summertime and whispered in winter.

The stairs thumped with gloomy steps.

Jerry entered the room in a heap and glanced over at his wife. Unblinking and transfixed on nothing, she was locked in a thousand-yard stare. Opium had taken her mind to weightless places.

"Jerry," she called from someplace far. Long strawy hair tumbled down over her strangled blue gown. "Where's Rose?"

Jerry sighed with closed eyes. "In the past."

"Let's go..."

"I've been there all evening." He turned his attention to the others, as a conversation with Loretta would loop in esoteric and painful circles. "Anything new?" he asked Arthur.

"Nope, nothing. But I made a few calls to the authorities. They said if they hear anything fitting, they'll inform—"

"Where's Bo?" Jerry asked Flo.

"Honey, I am not the boy's mother. He's probably out doing what orphans do." By that, she meant picking people's pockets. "Can't we just have tea, and wine, and cake tonight?"

Jerry got closer so the light above them cast him in silhouette. "There ain't no time for tea, and wine, and cakes when we got niggers running around looking for guns. When that's done, you can drink and eat yourself into a coma if you like."

"Mississippi...then St. Louis. That'd be nice don't ya think Jerry?" Loretta mumbled, her gaze fixed now upon the newspaper that no one noticed.

Jerry agreed to placate her, waving a dismissive hand. He sat, and the phone went off in another room. Arthur went to get it.

The sound of the front door closing perked Jerry up to a foreign arrival. Bo came in with the spare key Flo had cut for him and settled straight into thorough questioning from Jerry. "Where have you been? You found anything out yet?"

"Not yet," Bo responded in a childish tone.

"The hell you been doing out there?" Jerry didn't want an answer; he just wanted to disperse his displeasure.

Arthur came back in the room with bright eyes and an air of good news. "They've been spotted!"

Jerry shot up and paced the length of the long couch. "Where?"

"A hotel owner in Louisiana claims he saw a black boy and white woman in a hurry to get gone. Says they looked like they were headed east."

"Louisiana? East?" Jerry paused, his brow screwed in the shape of suspicion. "That don't make no sense. Why wouldn't they be headed north? Coming back here?" The information baffled him, and he took a seat again.

"Can we go on a boat in Mississippi, Jerry?" Loretta's rambling received the same agreement and dismissive wave.

The room fell into silence. Only the occasional gulp from Flo broke the stillness. Jerry flitted his gaze between the remnants of red crumbs on the table, a random newspaper, and the juxtaposing image of teapots and wine glasses that jarred his nerves. Then he went back to the paper. "They're heading east, you said?"

"Right." Arthur confirmed. "According to the hotel owner."

Jerry scooped up the newspaper and flapped it. The title, for the first time, wasn't about riots; instead, the bold black ink read: *STEAMBOATS & STREAMS!*

"What's the chances they're headed for one of these?" Jerry's bony finger tapped at the image of a steamboat.

Arthur narrowed his eyes. "Slim, but not impossible."

A smile crept upon Jerry's face for the first time that night. "More possible than our mother driving the distance back."

"Actually—"

"With no money," Jerry cut his brother off in his excitement. "And all them miles to cover."

"That means—"

"They're likely headed up the Mississippi."

"It's a long shot," Arthur interjected. "But it's the only one we've got to take. If they're scared to take the train, perhaps a boat is just as good."

"If that's the case they'll get off at St. Louis," Flo recalled the first time she rode up the Mississippi. Fifteen hours doped up, riding other things. "It's the most northern stop on the ride."

"You two," Jerry's fingers darted over Flo and Arthur. "Get whatever you need and head to St. Louis. Arthur, keep in touch with that contact."

"What about the guns? What do we do while they are gone?" Bo asked.

Jerry pulled Corey's photo from his breast pocket, flipping it to glare down at the address on the back. A smile spread wide across his face, and his eyes grew dark. "Make some noise."

An Ash White

ONE. TWO. THREE. FOUR... Seven was the final tally when he finished counting the cupboard full of white bricks.

Two was enough to buy three more. Four meant another six months of food on the table. Seven gave him room to breathe, and enough snow for the fiends to sneeze.

Kat barged into his office with a listless air. Martin shot up, kicked the door to his cupboard almost closed and feigned fixing himself a drink, scratching the back of his head as he did.

"You ever used a gun before?" Kat refrained from the pleasantry of a simple greeting and charged by Martin to pour herself a glass two fingers taller than her usual—her choice of Prince H. De Polignac was especially strong and in order tonight. It had been a few days since Nina passed, and the details of her death abetted her to switch the tune of her prior song in antipodal degrees. Peace stood far from her heart.

"Twice," he said.

Once when he was fourteen and frail in his adolescence, still a walking riot of hormones. The Colt .45 was kept on his father's side of his parents' bedroom, underneath the floorboard. Martin always wondered why that specific plank was bulged and squeaked with the sound of a mother's cry. It favored the tools used in those western tales he had come across; cold, heavy, and greening at the hilt, it had a beak like a woodpecker. He wondered if it shot as fast. Then he wondered if there were any black cowboys. Whether the white man was frugal enough to remove the metal from their wrists and allow it in their palms—it was an opaque thought. When his father took him to shoot one of the chickens from his produce, the gun was heavy and off-balance, undulating in strained waves as he peered down the rocky iron sights. Arms no thicker than the chicken's legs. Remorse riddled his body as he watched the bird bleed out. 'You ever have to use that against a man, shoot first," his father once said. "I promise he won't hesitate to do the same."

The second time was after Cora died. He asked Nina for a connection to a man who sold bullets. Pointy ones at that. Claimed it was to put down a friend's sick horse and she had no reason to disbelieve him. He returned to that same floorboard. Sly accompanied him as they rolled around looking for any white person who even looked like they had an acrobatic selection of defamatory opinions about his people. They settled on a known sex offender. The gun did not feel heavy this time; instead, its sights were still and true—a weight his hand was missing. Truth be told, nothing came of the man's death. Martin was arrested but was let go by the sheriff when he reached the precinct. The sheriff's daughter had fallen victim to the murdered man's violations and took her life earlier that year. He applied impunity to Martin, swore his officers to silence, and strangely thanked him. Some things were more poetically pressing than the minute factor of race.

"Good, you're gonna need to teach me," Kat demanded. Freckles spangled across her nose like a brown constellation.

Martin recoiled. "I thought you—"

"Things changed." She took a hearty sip from her drink. "One of them killed my sister."

"No problem," Martin shelled out the twenties from his blazer pocket to retrieve the scrap of white paper. He was silent about the white they were truly stained with. "This is it," he slid the address across the counter. "Right under our noses the whole time." Like his father's hidden firearm, these guns were close by in an abandoned warehouse a few streets from the shop. Now all they needed were the trucks.

"Who would have thought." Kat copied down the address when he wasn't looking. She didn't trust his diligence when he was excited.

Martin tucked the money and address back into his outer coat pocket before he fiddled with the paisley silk ribbon around her wrist. "You still wear this, huh?" He hid a grin behind a sip of his drink.

"You know I'm sentimental. I still have the microscope Cora gave me when we first met. It's in a drawer at home."

Martin gifted Kat with the ribbon when they met some fifteen years ago. It was even before he met Cora. Vivian, his mother, ran a league of young nurses from their home, and Martin was always around. It was a present to Kat before she embarked on a retreat to Boston. He and Cora were acquainted soon after her departure. "But you *still* wear it."

"I know you're not hard of hearing. I'm sentimental." She cringed at the soppy thought.

"So, why don't you still use that microscope?"

"Because I don't need a microscope anymore."

"But you need this ribbon?"

"No." She hadn't questioned herself as to why she wore it every day since. "I-I don't know."

"Maybe you just can't leave it in the past."

Their eyes met as if for the first time. Butterflies flapped big wings in her stomach—he could tell by the way her pupils dilated and pushed the honey of her eyes to its edges. Martin stepped closer, sure not to break eye contact. Kat swallowed on nothing. Something about the moment felt new, blinding, and it overwhelmed them with impulse. She stepped towards him, licking her lips as she rested her drink down.

A wild noise ran up the stairs and scattered along the mahogany floor like metal mice, snapping them from their trance.

Martin cleared his throat and pulled back. "I better go check if Joe's all right."

"Yeah." She held up his empty glass. "When you get back, another for the past?"

"Make it two for the future."

*

OIL MURDERED THE ROOM with an acrid odor. Joe had just finished changing the licorice-looking fluid when Martin entered the garage.

"Joe," he called. "Everything all right?"

The man was cowered behind one of the trucks, flinching even at the snap of Martin's steps. "M-Martin, s-s-" His words stuck at the tip of his tongue. "Something going on out there." The man wagged a murky finger over the door which led to the shopfront.

"What do you—"

The sound of glass shattering made Martin jump, his brow chewed up in confusion.

Joe started into a frenzy.

"I-I can't go back, don't make me go back!" He sped off towards the noise, and Martin pursued the lanky man.

They dashed through the damp stone corridor that led left towards the delivery bay and right towards the shopfront. When they burst into the shop, Martin saw the riot ensuing outside.

In his hysteria, Joe didn't.

"NO!" Martin cried. But Joe could only hear the drum of his traumatized heart.

As Joe stepped out the doors, a brick crashed into the side of his skull. Blood exploded from his face, and he fell lifelessly to the ground. Martin stood stunned, eyes wide on his nonplussed face.

Joe was dead.

Outside, his head spun as fire filled the mouths of storefronts that dotted down the street. A white swarm of around two dozen men stormed towards his shop chanting and slamming the air with racial invective, the hatred putridly discernible. Eyes glazed over, they marched with a sway of intoxication in their step, yet they were still thirsty. Not for the devil's nectar.

For blood.

The white men had fashioned bottles into fireballs that they launched across the street with indiscriminate aim. Any building was subject to slaughter. Between them, leading the pack was a tall man with his arms spread wide, carrying the swagger of the South. Smiling a sardonic smile, like the chaos, in some essence, had delivered him harmony. Martin had seen that same smile days ago when he rescued Corey from his end.

They locked eyes for a long while. A battle of gazes. A riot between their sights.

Joe's blood began to pool around Martin's feet, alerting him back to his killer. He scanned where the brick had been thrown, and peeking from around the side of the building, was a child. No older than Corey from what he could make out.

The boy was rabid-eyed and grinning. It was the boy that hurled that disparaging abuse at him after he met Joe that day.

The boy with the vitiligo.

Martin gave chase after the child, ducking a shower of red rain. Fire and blood waltzed through the air in a macabre dance. A white man baring cheese teeth and beetroot cheeks approached him with brutal intent, swinging a nasty piece of wood his way. Martin sidestepped the strike, planted a foot on the lumber and jabbed the man in the throat with a big fist. He made a sound that rung like grating car gears, and his whole face flushed red. Martin grasped his arm, hoisted the man over his shoulder, and slammed him into the curb. With the shuddering snap that played when the man hit the ground, Martin knew he wasn't getting up.

Further down the street in pursuit of the boy, a burly fellow twice his size in width, appeared with a malevolent objection to Martin's path. The man was beefy, with muscle that was grotesque and disproportioned by the habit of lifting old iron. The odds weren't great, but he had no choice but to take him. They charged at one another, but before they collided, a jagged brick met the side of the man's face, hissing red over Martin and rendering the brute twitching on the ground. Too bad he couldn't train his temples.

Violent breaths ragged Martin's lungs as he wiped the blood from his face, confused. When he turned to meet the person with the fast arm, he saw Earn's pale face. The man nodded; Martin nodded back. From somewhere, half of Earn's Alley filled the road with a less than equal offence, but some offence was better than none.

A shop exploded down the street, vomiting charred clumps of furniture through the splintered remains of glass teeth. *Chester's Table.* The restaurant had been there for as long as Martin could remember; his father used to take him there for lunch every Saturday to exemplify the agency of growing one's community and stimulating the economy. Chester's son, Tony, took over when his father had had enough. Tony changed things, erased all the nostalgia and warped the aesthetic with a crude display of tires and hub caps and other things the white mob fashioned eclectic weapons from. *Tony's Table,* he called it. Now there wasn't a table to set.

Martin chopped through the musk of burnt rubber, hacking his way through the haze to reach the alley. It was cooler, quieter and darker—the entrance only kissed by the rage of red flames.

Pools of pungent refuse sprawled across the ground from the guts of tipped trash cans that were splayed in intrusive patterns. There was hardly any space for his feet. Monstrous-looking rodents scampered for safety from the bricks and hurled bottles.

Martin took his time, creeping through with caution and careful eyes. A few rats ruffled his attention. He went further, desperate to catch the boy's pale face. A sigh escaped him, and he hooked his hands on his hips when he realized the boy was nowhere to be seen.

The faintest tug pulled on his jacket, and from the corner of his eye, he caught a little white hand shooting back into the only standing trash can. Martin flipped the lid and hoisted the boy against the wall, palm like a bear paw.

"Why'd you have to do that!" Martin screamed, spit whizzing from his lips as tears dared his eyes. "You killed him!"

The boy couldn't speak, he couldn't even breathe. In Martin's rage, he couldn't curb the strength of his grasp. The child kicked out futilely for release, eyes squinted and watering. Martin barraged him with rhetorical questions the boy had no answer for.

When the boy's fight dwindled and limbs grew limp, Martin snapped back.

This was someone's son. It could easily be his. The boy was no older than Corey.

He released his grip and the child fell into heavy gasps before he took off into the night. Martin pressed his hands to his knees and collected himself, shaking the tears from his face.

The tears were perhaps not all for Joe. Some were for Oscar, some for his father, some for Jewels. Some for all the other black men that got taken without reason.

He slumped down and gazed into space for longer than he could count. The riot went on without him. Trauma had trapped his mind.

After the streets had settled, and the madness was purged from the pavement, Martin emerged from the alley to gaze at the chaos with regretful eyes. He did not recognize a single face. They were all battled and bloodied, sculpted by violent white hands into busts of fear.

One. Two. Three. Four... Seven corpses spread across the street; limbs flayed in impossible angles. Two were beaten featureless. Four had their clothes fused to their skin like burnt armor. All seven of them were his brethren. Though their bodies had fallen, their spirits put up an eternal fight.

The scene was amok in ash white.

A Ribbon Red

NIGHTTIME IN NEW ORLEANS was the exemplary setting for a celebration.

Mardi Gras was that setting with added adrenaline.

Between the breaks in the broody clouds, the sky was stained drips of starlight and bliss. Their inner ears tingled with the dulled thrum of jubilee that sent waves of elation down through eager knees and buzzed to the ends of their toes.

Jimbo, their bearded driver, pulled into a low concrete gully that was so deep they couldn't be seen from any roads that ran alongside it. Corey and Elizabeth followed Jeremiah and his son out the truck.

"Y'all gon' have fun!" Jeremiah buzzed with a bowling-pin grin.

They could hear the festivities but couldn't see it. Perhaps they were dreaming, under a heavy slumber still miles from New Orleans. The night had that lucid air to it. But Corey's head thumped, and Elizabeth's lip stung.

They were very much awake.

Glancing around, Elizabeth saw nothing but the dusted stone walls of the gully and a large pipe protruding from the trenches end. "Where are we headed?"

A buff finger darted towards the pipe. "Right there," Jimbo said with the smile and snigger of Cheshire Cat. "I'll see y'all on the other side. Jeremiah, all the stuff is in the truck." With that, he saluted them and ducked into the tunnel.

"It's...through the pipe" Elizabeth asked, nonplussed.

"Yep." Jeremiah ambled over to the passenger's side. "Mardi Gras ain't supposed to be happening this year, on account of the war and all. So, couple folks decided they's gon' do it anyway, just in the summer and away from others."

"What if the authorities find out?"

"Well," Jeremiah hiccupped with a slight simper, "then we gon' be in trouble. But don't worry 'bout that. Don't know one know but everyone who's been told."

Corey looked baffled by the man's sentence, but from an abstruse angle, it made a modicum of sense.

"Look here," Jeremiah called them over as he rummaged through the car. "Here it is." He pulled a creaky wooden box from the vehicle that shocked Corey to his strength despite his bony frame. "This is for you." He handed Elizabeth a frilly blue dress that dripped with dazzling sequins. "And this is for you two." He passed the boys silky brown shorts and white shirts—the New Orleans night was heavy with humidity—but he only had one tie. "Corey, you can have this; Isaac don't know how to tie no tie."

Corey swallowed hard.

When they were all changed and headed toward the pipe, Elizabeth noticed Corey struggling with his tie. "Corey, you all right there?"

"Uh-huh." he lied.

His chin tucked into his chest to pin down one of the tie arms as he made aimless loops. A mangled knot formed when he pulled it tight.

"Are you sure?"

He sighed. "I..." He dropped the tie. "No one taught me how to do one before..."

"Not even your father?"

"No. He promised he would but is always too busy."

Elizabeth knelt to him and took the blades of the tie in hand. "I'll show you, then you can keep doing it until you get it, okay?"

"Okay." Corey watched with the focus of a hunting wolf.

"You go loop." She swung the thinner blade around. "D'loop," Another revolution. "Go round then through the hoop," she finished.

Corey looked as though he just saw how magic worked. "Loop d'loop, go round then through the hoop?"

155

"That's the best way to remember it, I find. It's how I recall Henry teaching our boys."

Corey tried a few times, mumbling the mantra as he went. The first ones turned out as dreadlocks. His face fell sour.

"Take your time. You've got this," Elizabeth encouraged.

He went for another attempt, this time double-checking each stage with calculated scrutiny. The 'loop' was good, the 'd'loop' impressed even Elizabeth, and the 'hoop' could represent with pride if there was such a thing as a Suit Olympics.

His face lit up, and Elizabeth threw up a playful gasp as they laughed. She squeezed his arm. "I told you."

When the four of them reached the pipe, the cacophony of festival was amplified through the hole. Jeremiah and Isaac went first.

"Corey, go before me." Elizabeth was not going to let a repeat happen of the fence situation.

There was no argument on his side, but he froze for a moment as he gazed into the void of the tunnel.

A portal to a secret paradise. Or to a second hell.

Darkness wasn't Corey's most acquainted of elements; it often cradled things that loathed light, and that concept alone was unsettling. Still, he thought of what his father told him about his mother, took a glance at the North star, and proceeded on his hands and knees. His palm sapped in some bilious liquid that made it itch after a time—just his luck to place a hand in that spot—the blackness crowded around his shoulders like little beasts.

Light from the other side painted the tunnel with an ethereal gleam. That's when he saw it.

A web of daunting proportions. The owner was home.

"M-Miss Elizabeth..."

The catch in his pallid tone was alarming. "Corey." she shuffled a couple yards closer behind him. "What's wrong?"

"There's—" His chest wheezed when he went to breathe. "There's a spider," he whispered.

"Stay calm—"

It was too late; the wheezing duplicated in intensity. The hyperventilation was in motion.

In an instant, she grabbed hold of his back and shoved him through and past the spider, forcing him through to the other side. The cramped space wasn't a friend to the lungs.

They burst out of the tunnel, tumbling to the ground in their hurry as Corey battled for breath. Jeremiah and Isaac rushed towards them, but Elizabeth halted them with a prohibiting palm.

She clasped Corey's face in her hands and stared dead into his wide eyes. "Copy my breathing. Take your time."

First, nothing changed, his chest still ached, and breaths were still rabid. When Elizabeth continued with a maintained patience and unbroken eye contact, the strain began to lift. Slowly, with each breath they took together, tranquility washed over Corey. For the last few breaths of the ordeal, he closed his eyes and inhaled through his nose.

It was over.

"You all right?"

"I'm all right."

The only thing that had ever calmed an attack before was the picture of his mother.

*

UNDER DRAPED FACES, flocks of bright smiles ticked to the raindrop rhythm of pianos and trumpet songs. They were mostly black, save for Elizabeth and a few young girls ill with terrible cases of jungle fever—so their fathers would say.

Purple, gold, and green beads littered the ground like strings of fallen plum leaves on a daffodil-speckled meadow. They watched their step to save turning an ankle.

Colored buntings, and beads, and garlands, and ribbons, and frills, and frivolities festooned the festival with a mazy decor. Bands frolicked along the street tuning indiscernible instruments, readying them for bass-bright performances.

Something was liberating about the revelers: They could be free under gaunt masks, make merry and masquerade in plain sight, be unjudged for but a day. Elizabeth plucked a fallen red ribbon from the ground and tied her hair away from her face.

The city held close the beats of early Spanish and French culture. The latter to sacrosanct degrees. Perhaps it was more of a Caribbean city than a Southern one.

Ornate works of iron grill cast the burly buildings in gritted fashion. Gaudy shapes twisted in flamboyant curls between the metal. Open courts surrounded by palm and tropical trees—the Cycads had a particular verve and showy attitude—sat in the bosom of those buildings, alive with untamed vegetation. Young spruce planted in cracked clay pots scattered around the fountains that were as excited as the air above it.

The Crescent City.

It surely didn't own a special edition of the moon, although tonight, it played a full show to an audience of applauding stars, each twinkle a cosmic clap. New Orleans was named such because its original design was cradled by the crescent shape the Mississippi River commanded.

Elizabeth had heard from Flo on several occasions about the panache of the floats and their desultory design. Some were amassed with white horses and paper lion heads poking from wooden windows. Others sailed by the crowd in the form of gilt boats with shimmery palm trees for masts, spangled with inordinate amounts of bling. Gold men and women riding on the backs of inanimate elephants and encrusted camels were always a sight, arms jiving the crowd as they sent out a rain of vibrant beads. It seemed animals were a bizarre yet happened theme. Apropos to a point, it suited the feral energy.

"What's that smell?" little Isaac asked his father.

"Heaven, child."

One wind blew spicy meats and molten cheese brews that tempted them to cartoon-like levitation. Another harassed them with sour belches and bad breath. The man who sat, dazed, in a food coma, drooling on his collar with a beer perched on his belly like an oxpecker, Corey decided, was the source.

When they got deeper into the crowd, the air whispered to the night a lascivious rumor. One that would make Corey's cheeks go red if he were fairer. Dancers popped their hips in promiscuous patterns, their desirables kept hidden only by the cover of glitter, sequins, and rhinestone. He ducked to see whenever Elizabeth covered his eyes. The bigger men and wilier women took down alcohol in pernicious intervals, without care or consideration for their livers and squealing kidneys.

"Y'all hungry?" Jeremiah asked. He knew a guy.

"I could eat," Corey said.

"I'm fine, thank you." Elizabeth declined, but her stomach betrayed her with a low growl that anyone who spoke the tongue of poverty heard as 'Foooood.'

They reached a stand blown out by the fame of new aromas. The chef was a large-ish bald gentleman with a sweat-peppered scalp and arms with casino-scale bingo wings. He had a stomach so grand it denied a view of his toes.

"How you doing, Leroy?" Jeremiah gave a courteous bow.

"Jeremiah!" He threw his arms out as if to hug him but the counter was in the way. His voice was the same as the lowest note of a cello. "What can I do for you, brother?"

"I got some good peoples here that wish to be blessed with your cu-cu-culi-"

"Culinary?" Corey asked with a pursed grin.

"Boy, am I glad for you. Mama Esther would love you." Jeremiah hiccupped and patted Corey on the back. "*Culinary* wonders."

"So, what can I get y'all then?" Leroy had a real lazy eye and a mole on his shiny nose the size of a blackcurrant. "We got all sorts. Best on the whole darn street! Matta o' fact, best in New Orleans!"

Jeremiah caught sight of some jolly cohorts, and with a jingled exchange of a few 'Ayyyyy's, he and Isaac disappeared with them. Said they'd be back before they got to the desserts.

"What's on the menu?" Elizabeth asked.

Leroy cleared his throat. "We got Crawfish Boil, ahh—" He shuffled to peel back foil to expose a steaming tray. "Shrimp and Grits, Crab Cakes, Crab Chowder, ahh—" He turned, watching that his gut didn't bounce one of the bands of deep pots that played a bubbly song. "Dirty Rice, Red Beans and Rice, all kinds of poutine, and we can Cajun just about anything."

The list dizzied her. "That's...diverse."

"Oh fo' I forget!" Leroy's creole twang came out thick in his excitement. "Fo' sweets, we got pancakes topped with frosting and sprinkles, heavenly beignets good enough for a Queen to eat that were made by my daughter who's just as sweet, and of course, King Cake."

"What's in that pot?" She pointed to a scaly cauldron. Flame-formed tongues licked at the pot from below, churning the broth to infuse it with puissant pork and prawn flavors.

"That there's gumbo."

"What's that?"

Corey and Leroy recoiled, looking her up and down as if she was a stranger. She was, to this culture at least.

"You've never had gumbo?" Corey was confused. He'd never been to Louisiana before, but his grandmother hailed from New Orleans, and along with her other infamous foods, when Christmas came, so did a little of the city.

Elizabeth flitted her eyes between them, cheeks blooming red. "What's in it?"

Corey and Leroy looked at each other. "Everything."

"Is it good?" she asked her umpteenth question to Corey.

"The best."

"Then I'll have a bowl."

With blithesome and sloppy manners, the first spoonful tingled her mind to oblivescence. All the plights of their journey reduced to dregs with the scoop of each spoon. The pork sausage in the beany broth snapped in an explosion of salt and Southern spice, the juice pooling under her tongue in a fountain of flavor. The crunch from the bread on the side ladled the moisture and dissolved into a sea of smoky paprika, garlic, dried onion, and a scrummage of green herbs.

Next came the shrimp, seared and golden with red tails like two-toned tulips. Every bite sweet and meaty, so delicate you almost felt bad that they tasted so good.

Corey and Elizabeth tried a little of everything: the Dirty Rice, several jambalayas, more varieties of gumbo Leroy had stashed away, and certainly, the grits—Corey hadn't had any since the last time he saw his grandmother, and the chef's were much better than Oscar Jr. ever made, so he dealt with them accordingly. Desserts got vanquished faster than the mains. The beignets, they imagined, were the same as biting into shrunken sugary clouds. The King Cake they tried was full of chocolate and almond filling, not nuts and spiced fruit like some of the other stands advertised.

Leroy grinned from ear to ear as he watched the glee drip from their lips. "How about some Milk Punch to wash it down?"

"Wass en bhat?" Elizabeth said with her mouth full.

"Milk, of course, sugar, vanilla," the chef searched for the final ingredient under the counter. "And bourbon."

"No. Thank you." Her faced dropped and she placed down the remainder of the food.

Jeremiah and Isaac still weren't back.

"Miss Elizabeth, can I go look for Isaac?"

Elizabeth couldn't shake the thought of the two boys somehow finding their way to the top of a float and looking like they were supposed to be there. The crowd was dense and a little perturbing, but the night strummed euphoric strings; there was no point in denying him the chance to be a boy after everything they had endured. He deserved it.

"All right. Don't be too long; we don't know when we're gonna be leaving, and I don't want you lost. I'll be right here waiting."

"Really?!"

"Really, but before you go," Elizabeth untied the red ribbon from her hair and put it around Corey's wrist. "This is the only condition. If you *do* get lost, wave, and I'll find you. Fair?"

"Fair!" He squeezed her with a tight hug. "Thank you."

*

THE FESTIVAL THINNED OUT into an eerie backwater. Only a few lustful stragglers were this far out. They were posted against brick walls, doing their best to stay upright and licking the fuzz from each other's faces, staggered by an entrenchment of alcohol.

Corey ignored them as he scanned the bleak street for Isaac. He called his name a few times, but under his breath and cautioned, careful not to disrupt the quiet.

The buildings here, without all the effusive partygoers, stood like the cold stone statements he was used to in Chicago, whistling wind and the murmur of an autumn chorus. The craters of the moon turned it to a milky skull.

Corey wondered how Claude McKay would describe the night, exemplify his journey with wordy expertise. Most work from the *Constab Ballads* and *Songs of Jamaica* were written with the heavy impression of Jamaican patois— Claude was mindful enough to include a translation glossary for those of foreign origins. And although somewhere down the line—before the grim carousel of slavery spun his roots from history—Corey hailed from that same heritage. Plus, his grandmother crept into those tones and inflections when he wouldn't listen or expressed jovial transgressions.

Scarce can I believe my eyes,
Yet before me there it lies,
Precious paper granting me
Quick release from misery.

It was about McKay's admission into America from Jamaica. It seemed to bring him so much glee it was worthy of a poem.

The little peoples of the troubled earth,
the little nations that are weak and white:
For them the glory of another birth.
For them the lifting of the veil of night.

This opening section of "The Little Peoples," Corey assumed, was a metaphor for blacks and their racial plights. Despite the mention of the word 'white.' In fact, the mention of the word made him believe it was about his people even more. White was used to demonstrate the colorless liberty that they existed in. Yet, they were still waiting for the veil to be lifted from the night.

A passage of a more recent work of the poet's stuck with him on quiet nights as of late. One he read that morning his father let him play outside. The day he met Elizabeth.

The day he met Jerry.

If we must die, let it not be like hogs
Hunted and penned in an inglorious spot,
While round us bark the mad and hungry dogs,
Making their mock at our accursèd lot.
If we must die, O let us nobly die,
So that our precious blood may not be shed
In vain; then even the monsters we defy
Shall be constrained to honor us though dead!
O, kinsmen! we must meet the common foe!
Though far outnumbered let us show us brave,
And for their thousand blows deal one death-blow!
What though before us lies the open grave?
Like men, we'll face the murderous, cowardly pack.
Pressed to the wall, dying, but fighting back!

A humane demand or a gentle threat? Corey wasn't sure yet, but it sounded like something his father would endear.

Further out, he thought he had gone too far; even the last dregs of people dissolved into the lights of the festival when he turned back. Maybe it was time to do the same.

"Boy!"

A loud crack jumped his nerves, and Corey locked onto the source. From an alley across the road that was scrutinized by a harsh streetlight, two police officers took turns in the barbaric bruising of a black man.

Corey slipped into the alcove of a shopfront to remain out of sight.

One was meaty, with pounds of beef for palms. He had the habit of making sure all his buttons were still done on his trench coat after each blow he dealt. The second was thinner, fidgety, and staring with lunacy alive in his lidless eyes. He had a nasty cackle that rivalled the laugh of a Spotted hyena.

"We can have some fun now huh, John?" the thin one said, head nodding and nightstick wagging like a painful tail.

"Looks like you're right, my friend." The burly one pulled up his belt and fixed his hat lower. He had the accent of a man born of old money, like his current profession was only to placate his appetite for dominion.

"Please—"

One of them cracked the black man in his forehead with the hilt of his baton, while the other swept his legs from underneath him. It happened so fast, Corey didn't even see who had done what.

"It'd do you good to speak when spoken to." The one who looked in charge crouched down and slapped the man's cheek lightly. "You hear?"

The black man hiccupped. Corey threw his hands over his mouth to suppress a gasp.

It was Jeremiah.

"You jingled there, boy?" the pinguid cop screwed.

164

"No, sir, I'm not drunk." Jeremiah lowered his head in submission. "I gots a nervous fidget that's all."

"You lying to me, boy?" the bigger officer blessed him with the back of his hand, disappointment on his face that Jeremiah hadn't been trained on how to speak to his superiors.

"No, officer." Jeremiah remained on one knee, his subconscious defiant. "I'm just looking for my son, I swear."

The thin one with wild eyes and the frail face of a whippet struck Jeremiah across the face with his nightstick. Blood burst from his lips, teeth surfing a red wave. Jeremiah slumped to the ground, and with all his strength, managed to clamber to one knee, panting and aching with a shattered jaw. His eyes cried, 'please,' but his trembling mouth strained to speak. "I just want my boy..." Tears flashed in his eyes.

The big officer sighed and rubbed patience from his brow. "I told you to speak when spoken to." He pulled a gun from his side holster.

"Let me do it, let me do it," the weevil one buzzed.

"No, I gotta teach this maggot a little lesson in manners."

Jeremiah reached for his pocket. "Please, I have a picture—"

The bullet crashed between Jeremiah's eyes, turning his tears crimson. It echoed down the street, but in Corey's mind, the sound didn't fade. It persisted in torturous intervals.

Limp and lifeless, Jeremiah slumped to the ground.

"Now why'd he have to go and do that for, huh? We were all having a fun time, and the nigger had to make me go on and shoot him." The fat officer holstered his gun and turned Jeremiah's face with his muddy boot. "No matter. There's plenty mo' of these spooks out here tonight. Let's go round up the boys and tear this parade down."

The men disappeared down the alley.

When Corey got closer to the festival again, pandemonium replaced the sound of music. Screams took the stage of strings.

The police had arrived.

As he fled, what Claude McKay said during the summer looped through Corey's mind like a poetic premonition.

'If we must die, let it not be like hogs.'

*

AMIDST THE TERROR, Corey found Elizabeth panicked and rattled by the riot.

"Miss Elizabeth..."

"Oh, Corey!" She squeezed him tight, relieved. Worry took over when she spotted the tears brimming in his eyes.

"Jeremiah...he's dead."

A lump clotted her throat. "W-what?"

He explained in his shaken haste what he saw, but before Elizabeth could react a pop of smoke filled the air.

Tear gas.

Throngs of frightened people stampeded for escape from the scourge. In the frenzy, Corey and Elizabeth were swarmed. Stands fell victim to trample; beads, tarnished cloth, powder, sugar, and streams of scolding stew were sent flying into the air. Cutlery flashing in violent torchlight.

White walls of tear-jerking smoke scattered the crowd as some gallant revelers punted the seeping cans back at the oncoming police force.

In the madness, Corey slipped into the rush.

"Corey!" Elizabeth shoved by people, looking for him, but he was nowhere to be seen. "Corey!" She grossly imagined him somewhere with little space, battling for air, while elbows chinked his cheeks. Flustered by the idea, she revolved time and time again looking for his face. From within the mob a few yards away, a small black hand emerged, tied with a red ribbon.

Corey.

Elizabeth squeezed through the swarm, her back weathering a few shoulder blows, and pulled Corey from the crowd. "Stay close!"

166

They broke to escape the crowd, avoiding the best they could the cruelty of tear gas and nightsticks. Ducking the monsters in their leather masks, the eyes of which were ever staring like portholes. Trench coats flared like demon wings.

They darted by Leroy's toppled stand. Four officers ruined him with their nightsticks as he threw his arms up in surrender. It mattered not. The men remained unrelenting despite the ceded gesture.

At the edge of the horde, near the pipe no one seemed to know of, Jimbo stood scanning the crowd. "Where the hell is Jeremiah?!" Corey went to speak, but the bearded man was too frazzled to care. "Doesn't matter, if y'all ain't at the truck in two minutes I'm leaving ya asses." He took off down the tunnel.

"Corey, let's go." Elizabeth tugged at his arm.

"No!" he snapped back. "We can't leave. We have to find Isaac. He's probably somewhere out there looking for his dad!"

"Corey, we can't do anything about that. Jeremiah is gone." She paused, but there was no way to cushion the words. "Isaac is probably dead too. If we go back in there we'll die!"

"Isaac is probably dead too..." He repeated it a few times to himself, face grimaced and made up with injustice.

"I'm sorry, but we can't help him now. We need to leave or we're going to get left."

Corey turned to Elizabeth with low red eyes. "Why'd they kill him?! H-he was on his knees—" He slapped away unfallen tears. "Why'd they have to kill him...?" He broke down, his voice but a whimper.

She scooped him in her arms and wept with him.

Corey couldn't understand why. He had known Jeremiah for a mere few hours, but the pain of his death weighed heavily on his soul. Jeremiah could have been his father, or his cousin, or uncle, or any relative of his. The officers' execution seemed discordant with and unconscious to the

167

man's human actuality. The only issue was, they never saw Jeremiah as human.

"He's probably left by now, but it's no use sticking around." Elizabeth half-hoped Jimbo hadn't departed.

Corey agreed and went through the pipe first.

"Miss Elizabeth, the spider is still here." His voice was level and almost dispassionate.

"All right dear, stay calm—"

"It's all right. I don't think I'm scared of them anymore."

A Burnt Black

NINE MONTHS AGO, Jerry and his wife were cold and frost-toed, not getting any sleep in the back of a ramshackle saloon on a supperless winter night. War had brought a winter like none other. For weeks he scoured the paper for jobs with the mazy rebuke that he had to seek one so soon. Shedding blood on foreign soil in service of pride and patriotism only delivered traumatic reparations, not the monetary ones vital for modern survival.

Nine months later, he and his wife were hot-collared, worlds apart in a fantastic mansion on a burning summer night.

Fatigued, Jerry stumbled into the house, back from the riot and the burnt-black scenes of the distant streets. Not from exhaustion, but from the distaste of lingering with the demotic. Drunken men weren't friends. They were tools.

As he entered the house, his wife was pacing through the lobby, eyes mauled with tears. "Honey, are you all right—"

"Where. Is. Rose!" she snapped, eyes wide and veiny, trembling with balled fists.

"Honey—"

"No!" she ran her black stiletto nails through her straggly hair. They crawled like spiders across the matted web of her graying mane. "I don't want to hear it. I want to see my daughter!"

Jerry's brow knitted together; he couldn't understand the frazzled display of her passion. The satin of her dress was dull, her feet raw from the pacing. A pair of rose earrings danced under chandelier light, and shakes rocked her body like she had been worrying for hours.

It hit him.

Loretta only ever wore those earrings on one day.

Rose's birthday.

In all his hurry to find order through chaos, he declined to notice the date. Loretta roared and rushed to him with a fist. He slipped the strike, restraining her with a bear hug. The wrinkles around her crying and scorn-lit eyes were the map to their daughter's demise. Her pupils traced him in hate.

"This is your fault!" Loretta wriggled free enough to slash a scratch across his neck. Blood trickled out, but it wasn't serious enough to cause him alarm. "We should have *never* left the farm!"

Jerry released her, and she stormed up the stairs, stumbling with the dysrhythmia of withdrawal. She needed the numb of her drugs. She stabbed a condemning finger at him before she disappeared.

He slumped down into a fancy chair by the door and dabbed his neck with his sleeve—there was more of others' blood on it than his own.

Before the farm got sold—in fact, much further back than that— Jerry had no real need for money or its sinful sway. As a boy, a ranch had all the space to play and all the food you could eat. Money adopted the blessed position of being a matter of trifle. Fishermen never worried about the price of cattle because he had a fishing pole. A duck never worried about bathing because it lived in a lake. It was the same for Jerry.

'Money is the root of all evil,' his father said, before he taught him to be a man of God.

'The love *of money is the root of all evil,'* Clinton expanded, before he taught him to be a man of vindication.

A man of purity.

Everything had changed. Those anachronistic ways would reduce him to levels he thought himself higher than if he didn't take action against his destitution.

Blacks practice criminality. Whites practice superiority.

This was the simple effect of his version of some societal natural selection. Something Clinton learned him young.

Despite latter scriptures in the Good Book depicting Jesus with "hair like wool and feet like bronze"—perhaps he was subject to the tanning qualities of the sun during his apotheosis—Henry read bible verses to Jerry and Arthur on a nightly basis. Expressing with insipid interpretations that they were the chosen ones. All else lived wherever they pleased beneath them.

So when God said, '*Thou shalt not kill,*' Jerry asked, '*Why?*'

Translations shifted the perspective on the explicit 5th commandment. The Hebrew doctrine explained that one killing an innocent is considered sacrilege. But murder to preserve one's life from the threat of an aggressor cuddled with divine immunity. Who decided who was innocent? And who decided the aggressor?

It was a gray area in which immoral men made their homes.

Now Jerry shed blood in service of money. *Sacred circumstances,* he reasoned, but how far was he from holy absolution?

Answers came in the form of a doorbell.

Bo came in panting like he ran his way back.

"Did you get in?" Jerry asked.

Bo shook his head. "When I got to the door, one nigger in an apron came running out. Socked him real good in the side of the face. He ain't waking up no how."

"Why didn't you go in after he was down?"

'You see, I was about to, but another one came out and chased me. Tall fellow, low hair, thin stache, and a nice brown suit." Bo puffed air out the side of his mouth. "Looked like he was doing better than most."

Jerry seethed after Bo's closing comment and snarled at the thought of a black man experiencing affluence. Then he paused, "You say tall, low hair, stache, and a brown suit?"

"Sure did."

Jerry's eyes thinned. "A flat cap and squinted eyes like he were up to something?"

171

"Mm-hmm."

Jerry chuckled. "Martin."

Bo pulled a wad of fives from his pocket. "I couldn't help myself."

Jerry took the cash from him, shelled one out to Bo, and went to tuck the rest in his breast pocket. A piece of paper fell out. He scooped it up and in poor handwriting, an address was inked. "Where'd you get this?"

"From the spook that chased me." Bo scratched his head. "Don't know why but he let me go."

"*Martin...*"

This could only be one location, the only location either of them sought.

The guns.

With them, he could design his own rules. Decree his own commandments. Create a reality where purity is objectivity.

The 1st commandment God gave was, '*I am the Lord thy God.*'

'*No,*' Jerry thought, '*I am.*'

A River Red

THE SUN CAME ON LITTLE WINGS, dipping and diving through beaten, ready-to-cry clouds in a silent morning flight.

The Mississippi River sparkled in the dawn light like a million mirrors, rivaling even the shine of the pearls that hung from Elizabeth's neck. Grace's pearls were the only thing she had left of value in her pit of mental and material debility. As for Corey, Skip—wherever the charlatan was—still owed him a fair amount of cash he'd likely never get back.

They ambled down the waterfront that docked a huge boat being loaded with eclectic goods. Instruments followed paintings led by vegetables chasing garments.

"What does S.S mean?" Corey cocked his head to read the name on the side of the boat: *S.S Sydney.*

"Steam Ship, dear."

"Makes sense."

Sydney puffed black smoke from her top like she had a bad habit.

Deckhands, merchants, and men of maritime filled the morning with haggles and laughter and drunken chatter that clanked with the creak of wooden wheels on the long drawbridge. Rowdy seagulls chirped to the hush of ebbing river water. Horses, mules, carts and carriages, buckets, barrels, and bales of hay littered the shoreline in an untidy display.

Clad in pressed black suits, a band of negroes waltzed up the drawbridge whistling and snapping their fingers. Corey wondered who they were, but whatever tune they harmonized in the distance was infectious. His head started bobbing, fingers snapping, but he couldn't whistle. So he poked his lips out to pretend the talent.

"How are we gonna get on?" Corey asked.

"We're probably not."

The truth was harsh. They had no money. Jimbo, wherever he had fled to, was their only way in and Jeremiah...well, they opted to leave that memory in the prior night.

A wind blew a fresh clap of salty air in their faces, so raw they could taste it in the back of their throats. "Maybe we'll get lucky." Corey spotted that the handler of the boat was black and hoped for the allowance of bias.

"You ever been on a boat before?" Elizabeth twirled the pearls on her neck.

"Nope." Corey tapped his finger on his chin. "But I have read about one."

"Really?"

"Yeah, Moby Dick. Longest book I ever read. I felt seasick afterwards." Herman Melville's classic contained enough maritime travel to satisfy even a sailor.

Elizabeth had never been on one herself, yet she had an assumption about the sailing sensation. Although the memory was faint and a decade old, she imagined it felt like the sway of drunkenness. She likely wouldn't find out today if that comparison was true. When she asked Grace, all those years ago, if she had sailed before, Grace said, *'No sah,'* in her Georgian Ebonics. *'Black folk don't do water. The last time was a disaster.'* Elizabeth never laughed whenever Grace dug into her bag of dark humor.

"You remember what that place was called Jeremiah told us about?" Corey asked, searching between the hotel and riot-clouded memories. "The place he said he was headed?" Corey kicked himself that he hadn't written it down. He wrote everything down. Why not that?

"Ahh..." Elizabeth drew a blank. She was more focused on staying alive than the nuances of Jeremiah's plan. "I got nothing."

They sighed in unison.

A squat Asian man hollered at them from the left, nestled in one of those cupboard-like stands often found in antique shops. "You buy," he called, and he wasn't asking.

Corey and Elizabeth moseyed over to humor him. What more did they have to lose?

Chinaware filled the stand, gold trim catching the light of the rising sun. The man shuffled about, arms like snake strikes as he picked up every item possible to show them. Polished porcelain plates, saucers, teapots that had spectacular hand-crafted lids and handles, teacups with a range of koi fish designs, and those itty-bitty silver spoons fancy folk used for dessert—Flo had many in her house, so Elizabeth knew. Stunning Jade pieces were locked away behind a glass cabinet, along with a pristine collection of pearl jewelry. He wasn't in a hurry to show those. Too precious for the regular.

"You see, pretty like you." He gestured to Elizabeth, disingenuous. The man had squinted eyes, full tan lips, and a neck as wide as his plump face.

"Thank you, but no, we're just looking."

He plucked one of the plates from the back and shoved it in her face. "You buy now."

"No, thank you. We don't have any money."

"No money," he dragged out the last syllable in shock. "You go."

"Okay..." They backed away from his arrogance.

As Elizabeth turned to leave with Corey, the sunlight glinted off her pearls.

The merchant didn't miss it.

"Wait!" He hurried them back. "I sorry." The man's eyes were alight as he tapped his neck. "I buy."

"Excuse me?" Elizabeth frowned at his excitement. "Buy what?"

"Pearls." He darted a stout finger at her neck. "I buy."

"Ohh," she chuckled. "These aren't for sale, unfortunately."

"You make mistake, no let me buy. I gi' you good price. Mikimoto Method make your pearls real 'spensive."

"They're invaluable." Elizabeth pinched Corey on the arm. "Come on, let's go."

The merchant mumbled something likely unsavory in mandarin.

"What now?" Corey asked when they were far enough.

Elizabeth looked at the man guarding the drawbridge. "Guess there's no harm in asking, right?"

"Right."

The man at the drawbridge was strapping and even taller than how she remembered the ephemeral glimpse of Corey's father. A cream linen kaftan was glued onto his body, showing the cuts of his physique, and tucked into black pants. Biceps and pecs built from iron and cornbread. No-nonsense stained on his face.

Grace told Elizabeth about her son once, and only once, the topic was too sore for any more than that. He was young when Grace had to leave him, and she opted to be a mother—almost—to someone else's child while strangers raised hers. Either she stayed with him and risked him falling victim to the plights of hate—fifty years ago, death was more likely than life for a black man in America —or let him go to London in the hopes he'd live a better life. Even if the odds were disparate.

England was ruled by white men, but it wasn't built by the blood of slaves. At least not directly.

'Letting things go that you love is the true test of one's strength.' Though her voice made her fuzzy on the inside, Elizabeth felt embarrassed when Grace told her that, as, at that age, she couldn't even let go of her favorite doll for more than an hour, let alone someone she loved.

Save for the austerity on the man's face, Elizabeth imagined he was a facsimile of what Grace pictured her son would be when he grew up.

"Hello—" Elizabeth said wimpishly.

"You got tickets?" The man cut her off before she began.

"No, but please just listen for a moment."

First, she told the man about their reason for being in Louisiana before she explained they were from Chicago. How they had to flee from a mad man trying to kill them—

she failed to mention it was her son. The hotel, the riot, the affliction they'd suffered. Even about how Skip robbed Corey, who she made clear at multiple points throughout her story was "just a child." Anything to inspire pity in the man.

"$1.70 for adults, $1.20 for kids," he repeated when Elizabeth finished. The look in his eyes told her he wasn't going to be swayed. "Either pay or go away."

They went away.

A bale of hay served as seating for them to rest in a dismal slump. "What are—"

"I don't know, dear," Elizabeth answered the only question he could be asking. She played with her pearls, thinking of any way to get on the boat. They could sneak on, slip behind a flock of barrels or a wagon if they timed it right. But Corey would disapprove, go on about how dignity was a virtue they should always maintain. Elizabeth was sure that that was his father speaking. They could ask someone to lend them the money, promise to pay them back as soon as they could, but $2.90 was a lot, especially for the sort that populated the shore, and Elizabeth wasn't fond of lying. There was no way she could pay them back.

So, they sat there, Corey swung his legs, head down, feeling sorry for himself while Elizabeth toyed with her pearls and did the same.

The sound of porcelain smashing drew eyes from around the embankment. It was the oriental merchant. He had dropped a plate and was cursing aloud in his language. Elizabeth's heart sank as she glared at the man. In that moment, she knew how to get on the boat. She glanced at her pearls, then to Corey, then to the merchant.

'Letting things go that you love is the true test of one's strength.' Grace once said.

For Corey's sake, it was time to let Grace go.

*

SOON AFTER BOARDING, with only hunger for luggage, the first port of call was to ingratiate their stomachs. Elizabeth had enough left over from selling Grace's pearls to get them lunch, dinner, a room, and see them through to St. Louis. And if the universe willed it, *home.*

For the first time in the last few days, things didn't feel like they were battling against attrition.

"I wonder where the kitchen is." Corey clutched his belly to suppress its growls.

Elizabeth gazed through listless eyes, rubbing the ghost of Grace's pearls as the pair ambled down the white-washed hallway.

"Miss Elizabeth." He tapped her arm.

"Huh?" She snapped from her trance. "What did you say, dear?"

"I'm sorry about your pearls."

"Oh, don't be silly." She soothed the back of his neck. "I'm sure Grace would much rather our safety than me clinging onto some token of her. I have her memories. They're priceless."

"How does Grace feel about us eating?"

Elizabeth chuckled. "She'd be fuming that we aren't already full." She pulled a key from her dress pocket. "Let's find our room first."

There was no real point in going to their room yet; they had nothing to drop off. But Elizabeth insisted they best find it before anything else. The last few days had forged her thoughts with caution—she wanted to be sure.

Room 58.

Corey was surprised the ship had that many rooms, but he was sure it wouldn't be anything fancy.

Two beds, with cold itchy sheets and deflated pillows. All white —save for the off-purple carpet scuffed from rubber abuse—with fist-sized bolts bulging in the corners of the room, a porthole window, and a table in the corner with no chair. Everything was nailed down.

They looked at the interior, then at each other.

"Food?"

"Food."

In the dining region, tables were filled with a wealth of upper-class patrons dressed to the nines in sable tuxedos with long tails and silky evening dresses. Corey did up his top button to not feel out of place. Laughter bounced off the walls as they told rich tales of investment and their affluent increments. All the aristocrats didn't even seem to notice the odd pair of Corey and Elizabeth. Perhaps they were too rich—or drunk—to care.

One thin man on his third glass of champagne bragged about how he met John D. Rockefeller in New York the past July at his birthday. A second man scoffed as he arranged a short trip for the whiskey to reach his lips. He claimed he owned a portion of Standard Oil—albeit minute as Rockefeller kept the divvying of his company to a minimum—before it was dismantled by the Supreme Court. Another gentleman, who stuffed his face with a medley of hors d'oeuvres and had more grease in his hair than on the plate, boasted he once saw Andrew Carnegie across the road from his printing company. The others on the table glanced at one another and burst out laughing.

The one-up game didn't seem to end, so Corey stopped listening. It put his father's success into perspective. A black man could only dream of speaking in circles like these. Not because he wasn't perfectly capable or highly qualified, but simply because they wouldn't let him. He'd have to have invented money itself to even be considered a seat.

Propped on a small stage near the rear of the long room that opened up to show the glitter of the Mississippi, a black man blessed the room with the drips of piano keys. Corey wondered where the band he saw enter earlier was; their equipment was set up around the grand piano, but they were nowhere to be seen.

"There's a free table over there." Corey pointed out.

When they sat, a dark peppy man came dressed in a waistcoat and half-apron to give them menus. They thanked him, and he said he'd be back soon.

They might have needed longer judging by all the words Corey didn't recognize.

Elizabeth looked at him with *I-don't-know* eyes.

Wiltshire bacon—smoked—Vienna bread, Yarmouth bloaters, fried cerealine fritters with maple syrup, Epicurean ox tongue—it made Corey gag at the thought of the smell of it—and broiled Finnan haddie. A far cry from grandma's cooking. Eggs were the only thing they recognized on the menu.

They got eggs.

After they had finished their breakfast, the band came out and replaced the pianist. A shiny, bug-eyed black boy with a smile as bright as the morning took to the mic.

"How'd you do everyone, my name's Louis, and if I could have your attention for just a moment, please," he continued as the room grew quiet. "Our lead singer has fallen ill. We believe he ate some ox tongue that didn't agree with him. And we need a new voice."

Corey feigned wiping sweat, thankful they ate the eggs.

The room of fat cats went back to their drinks and laughter. Louis looked annoyed.

An idea lit up in Corey's mind, and he shot his hand into the air.

"Little fellow with the waving hand," Louis called. "Can you sing?"

"No." He pointed at Elizabeth. "But she can!"

"What?!" Elizabeth spun around in an attempt to hush him. "Corey, what are you doing?"

"Miss Elizabeth, you love to sing, and you're a great singer. After everything, don't you want to have just a little fun?"

She knew he was right but couldn't muster the courage to admit it. Fun wasn't something she felt she deserved. It wasn't for her to decide.

The musician boy appeared by them with his toothy smile. "C'mon lady, show us what you got!"

"Cor-"

Before she could object, Louis whisked her on stage. Corey began the applauds—he even tried to whistle.

"Give it up everybody for—" Louis put the mic to her mouth.

"Elizabeth. Elizabeth Glass." She used her father's name like in her stage days.

The band started after the drummer kicked it off with, "Ah one, two, one, two, three!" Louis blew the trumpet like it was part of his body. He was sweet with it too.

The sound was foreign to Elizabeth, and she hadn't a clue of where to come in. Between the brass hits and horn melodies, it was all very strange.

"Satch, she gon' sing?" one of the bandmates asked.

"C'mon lady, you got this." Louis tried to encourage her by singing some himself. His voice visceral and deep, with a rumbling aged tone. An ancestral pitch rang through his husky cadence.

Elizabeth had only heard something similar from an old record her neighbor gave her before they moved years ago. "King of the Bungaloos" by Gene Greene. At a point in the record, the singer began to sway from lyrics and resorted to a function of zesty sound effects from 'Bodabo' and 'Patadee'—her neighbor said it'd never catch on.

Here she was about to try it. First, a light head bop got her in the rhythm, then a shimmy of the shoulders filled her with song. Elizabeth broke out with *scits* and *scats* as the crowd jived to the music. Louis was smiling behind his trumpet, joining in on occasion to offset the flowery quality of Elizabeth's soft voice.

As she sang, eyes closed and toe-tapping, Corey worked on his poem.

Thirty minutes later, Elizabeth returned to the table with Louis, who was beaming. "Oooooooweeee, lady." Louis plonked into a chair, out of breath. "You can't sing. You can sangggg."

"Oh, it's nothing really." Her red cheeks betrayed her modesty.

"Waiter," Louis called over the boy about his age. "Could we get a drink for the lady? On me."

"No, thank you, I don't drink."

"Oh, excuse me." He waved the boy away. "So, where y'all headed?"

"Chicago," Corey replied.

"Chicago?" Louis cocked his head back. "What's there?"

"Home," Elizabeth added.

Between the two of them, they explained how they ended up in the South. It was a tale that caused Louis to puff his cheeks in awe at the regretful segments.

"We're on our way to St. Louis." Elizabeth fixed a lock of hair behind her ear. "See if we can somehow get back from there."

"Well, you best go see Old Blind Griff."

"Old Blind who?"

"Griff," Louis sighed through his smile, "is the coldest man the world don't know about. He runs this place up in St. Louis. Real secret. *Only those that need to know, know.* It's a bar, a club, a hotel. You name it, Griff's got it."

"Really?" Elizabeth looked impressed.

"Sure thing, him and his grandson, Monty, got half the city in their pocket. Not through drugs or violence. Just favors and good deeds. People tend to owe them much more than money. Loyalty is the only payment I've seen the man take. If anyone can get y'all home, it'd be Griff all right."

Corey and Elizabeth glanced at each other with auspicious smiles.

"What's the place called?" she asked.

Louis leaned in, glancing side to side, to make sure no one was listening when he spoke. "*The Bleach Barrel.*"

*

"WE'RE GOING HOME."

Dizzy with glee, Elizabeth flopped onto one of the beds in their room, arms wide and cheeks hot from grinning.

"Right after we find this Griff character." Corey loosened his top button. Night was falling and neither of them had slept in a bed since they left Chicago.

After they bathed and got ready to turn in, Corey flipped out his notepad and jotted the name and address of The Bleach Barrel down before he worked on his poem, satisfied his piece was coming together near its end.

Elizabeth hummed away to the sweet memories of Grace. The pearls she wore in her mind.

"Can I ask you something?" Corey laid his notepad down on his covers.

"Of course, dear." She was still humming with a smile on her face.

"How come you don't drink?"

Elizabeth ceased her tune and perked up in bed. "I just don't prefer it." Her smile had gone.

"Usually, people don't do, or do things for a reason. Like my dad drinks to remember my mother." he turned to her. "Do you not drink so that you can forget someone?"

The symmetric analysis sent Elizabeth to her thoughts. For long moments she said nothing. "Yes."

"Who? If you don't mind me asking."

"Myself."

Corey closed his pad and slipped it under his pillow. The somber in her tone required all his attention. "What happened?"

Elizabeth took a deep, shaky breath. "Years ago, when my career had dwindled due to a shift in the times, I met Henry, or rather I was suggested Henry by my mother. She thought it made sense for me to start a family, and after failing to truly fulfil my dream, I had no contention to the idea. So Henry it was. He was nice enough, made me feel comfortable and his efforts to woo me were something straight out of a farm girl's fantasy." Elizabeth puffed out a tired laugh. "But I was no farm girl. The world had shown me bright lights and showrooms, and despite what I told myself and my mother, I wasn't ready to let that go. I can't say it was love with Henry, because everything happened so quickly. Before I knew it, we were married and expecting within six months of knowing one another. After Arthur was born, I wanted to give my boys a better life, one away from the hate that hid in the South, so we moved to Chicago. In truth it was completely selfish. I just couldn't let go of that brief feeling of fame...of success. I tried and failed for years, left Henry to raise our boys while chasing a dream that kept picking up speed as I slowed down. When I finally looked up, my boys had grown up, and there was little of them in my mind when I recalled the years. Henry was teaching them things I just—" She took a breath to collect herself. "I just couldn't believe in." She wasn't specific, but Corey had met Jerry, and it was easy to assume Henry's teachings. "Not only had I failed as a singer, but as a mother too. I started drinking a lot, equally for both of my failures and twice as much as I should have. Henry didn't like it, and before long, he took my sons away from me and back south. Jerry was only your age when they went. It was the worst day of my life." This was the dark, cracked jewelry that tangled in her mind. "I'm a terrible mother."

Corey hopped out of bed, shuffled over and embraced her. "You're not a terrible mother. You just made a mistake; we all make mistakes."

His hold stopped any influence of tears and briefly removed any more of the bleak memories. "I stopped drinking that day, but ever since then, Jerry has resented me for leaving him and his brother. When he grew up and started a family of his own, he let me see my granddaughter before she died—" She paused, her chest heavy and tight like she wore a lead bra. "That was the last day I drank. Ten years ago."

Corey kept quiet, unsure of what to say until the words of his mother came to mind. "My mother wrote something in the back of her favorite book. I think I've read it more times than the actual story. I thought I understood it, but meeting you made me better digest it."

"What did she say?"

"Family isn't flesh and blood. It's time and love."

A Royal Red

IT TOOK AN HOUR once they reached St. Louis to find the place. They asked a few people about it, but no one seemed to know its location or even have heard of it before.

'Only those that need to know, know.' Louis's mention of the sequestered haven rolled through Corey's head. They needed to know, and the directions he offered were royally abstruse.

One sleazy-looking man with a straggled stache and wet upper lip—he wore a special suggestion of greasiness under the pale moonlight—informed them of a place not too far that could be what they were looking for. But when they reached, it was clear licentious temptation had ruined the man's mind. It was an establishment of corsets and groans.

They took their time to decipher Louis' directions after that surprise.

In a building with no face, on a street with no name, tousled on the outside but glimmer at its center, The Bleach Barrel opened up like a ruby geode.

The air was electric.

It tingled over their skin in a rhythm of elation. At the center of the long oval room, a mahogany bar varnished to reflective standards stood as a bastion for well-dressed folk to fuel their night with cocktails bewitched to dark scarlets. The carpet was more a vermilion, shaded and stainless; cushioned highchairs held a fortune of pretty people, gilded with joy and drunkenness. Indian silk curtains tumbled like crimson locks down windowless walls, while waiters dressed in red waistcoats zipped across the floor in an urgency for service, hoisting rounds of drinks overhead. Gold lined every edge of furniture and glinted under the shimmer of chandeliers.

Everything was red and gold. Everything was royal.

It viewed like Griff, whoever he was, was the wizard of this hidden ruby city. Unlike Oz from Corey's favorite book, this place existed in real life and not the emerald expanse of his imagination. He wondered what type of wishes Griff granted.

He, like Dorothy, simply wanted to go home.

Propped up on a beautifully laid estrade to their left, a curly-haired singer awash with creamy velvet, sang some mellifluous tune that had Corey enchanted. Her eyes were slanted and sultry and hot with red blush. She winked at him when she caught him staring.

A man in a tight suit and white gloves began the applause as the lady floated off stage. "Madame Bean, everyone!" The room clapped her off as a jazz band took the stage.

"This is nice, huh?" Elizabeth's eyes twinkled the pattern of gold leaf.

"Uh-huh..."

Elizabeth looked down at Corey gawking at the lady. "Corey."

"Huh?" He snapped back from his stare. "Yeah?"

"The sooner we find Griff, the better."

"Right."

"I wonder if that guy knows anything." Elizabeth gestured to a gent just ahead of them whose tuxedo tails licked the ground. The man was poised behind a black lectern, thumbing through a pile of papers as thin and dangly as himself.

"Excuse me," Elizabeth greeted when they reached him.

The concierge graced them with a cordial smile and pressed his round glasses up onto his face. 'Welcome to The Bleach Barrel, how may I help?' Long neat dreadlocks fell between his sharp shoulder blades. They were well-greased and seemed almost glued to his head as they pulled back into a ponytail. His skin was shiny and taut like shrink-wrapped leather.

"Yes, we were wondering if we could see Old Blind Griff?"

"Of course," the concierge flicked out a pen, his voice eloquent and sleepy. So flat, it threatened to banalize the fresh energy. "Your passage, please?"

"Passage?" Elizabeth looked perplexed as she repeated the words. "What's that?"

The concierge slid his pen back in his pocket and clasped his hands behind his back. "I'm afraid if you do not have passage, it will be entirely impossible to see Mr. Cook."

"But we weren't told of any passage. We were told Griff could get us back to Chicago if we asked him for a favor."

"True. Mr. Cook is a man of many miracles. I can vouch for his favors myself. But," the man continued. "If you do not have passage, then you do not have permission to ask a favor."

"How do we get *passage*?"

"Only those that need to know, know."

The concierge went back to his work as Corey and Elizabeth stepped away from his stand.

"What now, Miss—"

"Corey?" It wasn't Elizabeth. The voice came from a man by the bar and the pair locked onto him. "Corey, that is you!?"

Incredulous as fortune was, the man came waddling towards them with a bowl belly and bell pepper features.

Donald.

Corey's eyes went wide with excitement. "Uncle Don!" He ran into his arms, and Donald swooped him up and spun him around.

"I can't believe you're here." Donald's speech was clear and coherent. "What are you doing here?"

"That's a long story." He let out a nervous chuckle, privy to the clarity of Donald's diction. "What are *you* doing here? Why'd you leave Chicago?"

Donald's face fell, befuddled. "Your father didn't tell you?"

"He only said you were going away for a while, didn't know when you were coming back."

"We'll leave it at that then."

Corey explained what he was doing in St. Louis. Made it seem like it was no big deal and they had everything together. Far from the truth, but his father taught him better than to show his wounds to people. Even those who were closest.

"Sounds like one hell of an adventure?" Donald dabbed sweat from his brow. "So who's this Elizabeth character?"

Embarrassed by his inattention, Corey dragged Donald over to Elizabeth who stood idly by the concierge. He introduced them and Donald was almost smitten after the greeting—he hadn't spoken to a woman past "I'll have the roast tonight" for some time. He thanked her for taking care of Corey.

"Y'all tryna see Griff to get home? I think I can help with that." Donald moseyed over to the concierge. "Good evening, Sidney,"

"Ah, Master Donald, how are you tonight?" Donald tucked something into the man's blazer pocket. "May I ask what that was for?" he added, smirking with a raised brow.

"Just killing some old habits."

"And burying them in my pocket," the concierge furthered.

"This here is family." Donald called Corey over. "I know they haven't got passage, but is it all right this one time to make an exception on behalf of myself?"

The concierge glanced over Corey and Elizabeth through the slits of his long eyes. "Why, of course. Mr. Cook has you on The Red List. Anything for you, Master Donald." Sidney was about Donald's age but carried a professionalism void from his burly brethren.

"Thank you." Donald squeezed Corey and told them both how to find Griff. He was in a building in the next lot— another decrepit-looking place with nothing but rusted iron for features. "Go on with the lovely lady here. I'll be right with you."

Elizabeth thanked him, and they skipped off and out the double doors from which they had come.

Donald found a phone in the hallway away from the madness of habitual weekend celebration. He dialed a number. Half relief, half panic plastered over his sweaty face. The line picked up.

"Kat. It's me, Donald. What's Corey doing in St. Louis?"

A Glass Green

ART, BY ITS DEFINITION, was the expression of human emotion and ideas into a tangible form. Many forms existed. Some made music to stimulate the ears and mend wounds of the soul. Others bent colors to their will to craft abstract and actual interpretations of the imagination. Some nurtured a penchant for words and the magic that only twenty-six letters could create infinite ends; they could take the pallid minds of dulled men and women to manifold worlds of wonder. There were many forms of art, too many to quantify without leaving room for disrespect of the styles forgotten.

Sly knew that well.

He once practiced a model of it that made one's pupils dilate because their brains simply wanted to see more of his stellar depictions. Cora always told him he could go to Paris, make something of himself, make the world know the name: Walters. He owed Chicago nothing, and the world owed him at least something. However, what he called art now still made pupils bloom, but he no longer used paint or paper.

People were his canvas. Drugs were his tools.

His work made them experience an expression of creation that was theirs and theirs alone. An art that made them feel all the effects of the many forms.

The ultimate form of art.

Art that remained untainted by opinion and perfect in the imagination.

Sly and Dumbo tiptoed through the carpet of fiends, swapping brown-stuffed green bottles for greenbacks—Sly had stickier methods of making money—occasionally ducking to avoid the fragments of plaster and hardboard that broke away from the ceiling. 'Abandoned' wasn't the apropos word to use for the building; 'abused' was. It was dingy with a darkness they felt on their shoulders; screams split the den in capricious interludes—they never knew when to prepare for a scare. Fat rats scurried over the people on the fringes, making dinner of leftover vomit and rotten fingers that were still attached, before they returned to their homes between the walls. The sole speck of hope in the room was a heavenly weave of falling moonlight that stitched over the exit coming up on their left.

The opium den was diminutive on all fronts; Sly had never seen one like it. Others had furniture, beds for one to experience their high with clean equipment, special pipes, and lamps. This one barely had flooring that would hold. Addicts crawled over each other to reach the only lamp and a handful of saliva-scarred pipes. Others who couldn't get hold of a pipe had to resort to chasing the dragon.

The Chinese man who owned the place didn't seem to care what the den looked like; as long as he got his ten percent of whatever was made, anything seemed to go.

A leaden aroma of fermented fish hung with the musk of medical smoke, bile, and the metallic tang of dried blood. Scabbed veins, bloodshot eyes, and dolorous faces were flayed in flamboyant ways like the vague essence of a renaissance piece. One came to Sly's mind.

The Barque of Dante by Eugène Delacroix.

The poet Dante with his poet partner, Virgil, sailed across the River Styx, which was teeming with tormented souls who clung to the boat with demented intent.

This scene was just the same.

"More," one of them called, latching onto the cuffs of Sly's pants. He shook the woman off and booted her in the face.

"I need, I need, I need—" Another washed in from an induced sleep, unable to finish his sentence before the opioid tide took him back out.

"This is beautiful..." another mumbled.

Sly looked to see a man gazing up at the solitary white light that poured from the only window in the cramped building, tranqullity alive in his eyes like he had seen the face of God. Sly hoped he had; it was the only thing that could save him.

The ogling man began to foam at the mouth, his body amok with violent shivers. He keeled over and after a few moments, stopped. Dumbo was rattled by the man's sudden switch from bliss, to panic, to nothing.

"S-S-Sly-" Dumbo stuttered.

"Don't look." He eased Dumbo's arm off his shoulder. "Bad karma watching a man die," he sighed. "Worse when you know why." Sly had seen someone go like that before, and one time was too many. He hoped his destination was on high and not akin to the depths of Dante's.

He shook one of the bottles before he sold it to their last customer. The opium rattled behind the green glass like clumps of melted dark chocolate, bitter and sweet to the psyche. When he asked Earn how it felt a few months ago—his first opium client—Earn swore he couldn't remember. The memories, he described, were like trying to grip syrup.

It was of little matter. Of those that bought his art, none ever complained. What difference did it make to know how it felt? The artist could never feel the same way.

"Dumbo, let's head out," Sly drew the big fellow back from his harrowed gaze at the dead man. "Martin's waiting."

*

SOUTH ILLINOIS provided a rural escape from the rush of the city. In a town where most streets were calm and nameless, Sly and Dumbo trudged for the municipality's only bar. There wasn't much in it but a sparse selection of half-drunk sailor types, likely on route to or from the Mississippi.

But there was a phone. Just like Martin said there would be.

Routine calls back to Chicago let Martin know where they were and any updates they had on Corey. They always ended in no news. No reason the next one wouldn't be the same.

Sly loosened his collar to let the heat escape, while Dumbo, slick with sweat, plodded alongside him.

"What we gon' tell Martin?"

"Nothing," Sly said. "We ain't heard nothing about Corey, so there's nothing to tell him but the usual."

The bartender didn't take too much convincing to let him use the phone once Sly showed the man some of his art.

He dialed Martin's office, and the line picked up before the first ring finished. "Um-hmm." Sly's brows jumped each time Martin spoke. "I can't believe he's still—" He caught himself from cursing. "We'll head straight there." They hung up, but Sly's face was pulled between an unsettling dichotomy.

There was news of someone he loved. There was also news of someone he hated.

"What? What happened?" Dumbo urged.

"He knows where Corey is." Sly stopped Dumbo from expressing a messy delight. "But gimme a sec, I gotta make another call real quick." He shooed Dumbo away for privacy.

The conversation lasted less than a minute, but judging from the smile on his face, one could only assume it occurred with leisure.

Dumbo had a childish grin turned on and rocked in a nosy sway. "Was that your sweetheart?"

"Why you so damn nosy?"

"Only 'cause you was speaking so loud."

Sly chuckled. "I put my hand over my mouth, especially for you not to hear." He slugged him playfully in the shoulder.

"So, was it?" Dumbo pressed.

"Something like that."

When they got outside, lightning bugs awoke in the clearing of twilight as mosquitoes buzzed, bloodthirsty, around the hum of streetlamps.

"Where we headed, Sly?"

"St. Louis." Sly smiled and tucked his hands in the pockets of his raven suit. "A place called The Bleach Barrel."

An Emerald Green

DONALD WAS HERE. Sly detested that truth. Martin knew the mention of their former family would send Sly seething, but he told him in spite of the fact. Better to tell him everything than leave such a surprise.

Sly gazed like a new fool at the interior of The Bleach Barrel. Gold dripped from the gushing scarlet ceiling, spinning his eyes with a reason of red. "Damn..."

The concierge met them with an upper-crust greeting. "Welcome to The Bleach Barrel, how may I help you gentlemen?"

Sly passed dissecting eyes over the thin man, his voice seemed to match the mellow bloom of a low cello in the distance. "I'd like a room please."

The lumps Dumbo called brows squished together. "A room? I thought we were here to—"

"Dumbo," Sly shushed. "Go get a drink or something while I talk to the fine man here." Sly stuffed ten dollars in his hand, and his companion waddled off to the bar with a wet grin. "Excuse me," he continued. "Like I was saying, could I have a room please?"

The concierge cleared his throat. "I'm afraid we have no rooms available, sir. I do apologize for the inconvenience."

He hid it well, but Sly suspected the man's accent was foreign; it showed itself in words that owned more vowels than consonants. Still, he couldn't place it. "That's a shame. I heard this was the best place to stay in St. Louis if you know about it."

"You're not mistaken." The concierge pushed up his glasses. "We are the finest and most prestigious establishment in all of the state. *Only those that need to know, know.*"

There it was.

England. London, by Sly's limited assumption.

It was faint, but Sly had an art teacher—the few times his mother could afford for him to go to school—that pronounced certain letters the same way as the preened concierge. The teacher claimed he hailed from Waterloo or Westminster or something by their famous river.

"I hear from one of my clients that there's a place in London just like this." Sly lied, opting for a reaction at the city's mention. "You ever been to London?"

The concierge perked his chin up and narrowed his eyes. "I was born in London, and no such place exists to my knowledge."

"Maybe it's the same as this place," Sly leaned an elbow on the man's lectern. "*Only those that need to know, know.*"

The concierge pursed a smile. "Well played, sir, but there are still no rooms available despite my appreciation for your wit. It cannot make guests disappear."

"Of course. I wouldn't dream of you putting people in the street for me." He threw his hands up in a languid surrender.

There had to be something else, Sly thought. Something that could turn even a statue's neck. Change the absolute of dried ink.

A little green bottle peeped from the concierge's pocket, the contents winking its brown eye. The caramel man noticed Sly notice and notably tucked it away.

"You have intrusive eyes," the concierge said.

"You should get better at hiding."

"Perhaps I wasn't trying to hide."

"But what if I was seeking?"

"Then you have found."

Sly was a tailor of the mind's toxic attire. Weaving men to Elysium while pressing the innate buttons that blossomed sinful thoughts. The man before him was no different; in fact, Sly assumed the concierge easier to read than those that opened the book of their dejections. The people intent on concealing themselves protected their purposes too well, squeezed too tight what they wished to hide. It always seeped through the gaps, and Sly had become adept at spotting the signs. A master at threading his ambition through the eye of their desire.

After they came to understand each other, and Sly's art was something the concierge was interested in, a room freed up on the third floor. The concierge indulged the offer with a smile and erudite air.

"So you prefer brown sugar with your tea?" Sly asked.

The concierge smiled. "Aye."

*

DRINKS SURROUNDED DUMBO as if they had him cornered for a crime. One he was unsure the nature of, judging by the confused look on his face as Sly joined him at the bar.

"S-Sly," Dumbo stammered. "I think I bought too many drinks. On accident, I swear."

Sly laughed as he perused the guard of cocktails and gins and wines and whiskeys and some fizzy beverage he didn't recognize. He took one of the gins and told the bartender to dish out the drinks to the folk that wanted them. A few patrons cheered when the free libations reached them.

"Nice place, ay?" Sly darted eyes over the opulent place, pinging them to the door ever so often.

"Real, real nice." Dumbo sipped gingerly from a wine. "Martin should do something like this back home."

"Maybe one day, but there's some important stuff we got to take care of first. One of them being finding Corey."

"Right." Dumbo picked at a coaster. "Why you get a room, Sly? Ain't we supposed to get Corey and go?"

"Yeah, we ain't staying the night. I just have to see someone before we do all that."

"Your sweetheart?"

Sly smiled and sipped his gin.

A pair of white people floated in and settled at the opposite end of the bar, out of place in an establishment like this. They occasioned raised brows and asking eyes, but none more than Sly's. The man was timid in stature; he wore a crisp white shirt under a blazer he was visibly uncomfortable in and chose to nurse a serving of orange juice when the bartender reached them. The lady dripped in a red gown that sparkled like the champagne she ordered. A fluffy white boa hugging her tight figure.

Focused, Sly looked on.

Milky skin, golden hair that rivaled the gleam of the chandeliers, full red lips, plump and perfect to kiss, and eyes that were emerald green.

"Sly, is that your sweetheart?" Dumbo goofily giggled darting his eyes between Sly and his enchanting target. The woman Dumbo viewed was gorgeous, so much so that she made that little hidden place behind your sternum panic at the glance of her beauty. "So, is it?"

Sly finished his drink, stuffed five dollars in Dumbo's pocket and said he'd be back soon. "Something like that."

*

UPSTAIRS IN THE HOTEL, the corridors were long and wide. Decorated still in red, but in shades of silent, broody burgundy. Nestled above each door bloomed electric green lamps, replacing the glitz of gold and granting bilious sight of iron numbers. At the end of the hallway, a chilled night breeze coursed through a cracked window, blowing the thin curtains like a widow's veil.

Sly's room was not that far down, and the concierge warned him that the room's door had a slight kink that required some additional force to shut.

The room was done in that Art Deco fashion so popular with the coming decade. *Staying ahead of the times is the only way to stay with it at all.* Sly read something like that in an art book Cora got him when they were young. The space was short and pinched at the ceiling's zenith like a big birdcage. The wallpaper hopscotched between a striped and flowery gold design, a pattern which every other piece of furniture adopted. Chests of drawers lined the walls near the door. Two high chairs sat by a marble table across from an unlit fireplace, which was guarded by a set of silver teeth—one of which had fallen away—and a double bed nestled under a wash of moonlight through a long, droopy window.

Sly lit the fireplace and shed the feathers of his raven suit, eager for his company's arrival.

The door knocked. Sly contained his excitement. He opened it and there they were. *Milky skin, golden hair that rivaled the gleam of the chandeliers, full red lips, plump and perfect to kiss, and eyes that were emerald green.*

His sweetheart.

"Sylvester," the voice said.

"Arthur."

*

"WHERE IN THE MASSACHUSETTS IS THAT MAN?"

Flo stormed up the flight of stairs with the hem of her dress in hand, heels clapping like applauds for her third-floor efforts. She had searched the two levels below, inquiring about a golden-haired man to one of the housekeepers, who had little words for her. The feeling of chasing a man was a foreign one. Worse, it was one who had no money or interest in her, though, despite her senile late husband, she preferred the stoic dark type. Not black, just dark. Though she had never considered the flavors of an African-American; even if she did, they were unfortunately illaudable by current society.

The third floor was the same as the previous two, but to her left a door split with a slither of flickering firelight. She couldn't help herself. Peeping through the crack in the door, she saw a naked black man locking lips with his white partner in bed, but their face was shielded by dark skin. When they turned, she stumbled back, throwing her hands over her mouth to prevent a scream.

Milky skin, golden hair, and eyes that were emerald green...

Arthur was here. Flo detested that truth.

A Rug Red

FIFTEEN SECONDS was all it took to take away his sight. Fifteen seconds...

At the door of the building beside The Bleach Barrel, Corey knocked, waiting with Elizabeth. "What you think he looks like?"

"Old," Elizabeth joked. "Blind."

A slot in the door opened and the bronze gaze of some huge man glared through. "Um-hmm?" he grunted.

"We're here to see Gri—"

Another of the man's grunts cut Elizabeth off, and she and Corey looked at each other, perplexed. "We're here to see—" she tried again.

The man grunted again at Elizabeth's attempt at conversation and cocked his head towards Corey. "Mhm."

Corey translated the grunt as 'you.' "Me?"

"Hmm."

"We're here to see Griff, please?"

The slot slammed shut. The swoosh and snaps of locks and bolts reminded Corey of his father's safety habits. He wondered what type of superfluous precautions he might adopt to keep Corey secure when he finally returned.

A piney rush of hashish hit them in the face as they entered the cabin-like room, hung with Native American décor. Dreamcatchers, medicine shields, which looked like large dreamcatchers, wolf pelts, and strings of colored feathers fluttering from the ceiling. A carved buffalo skull adorned the left wall while the ancient headdresses of past chieftains lined the back one. All glowing under crimson lamps like ancestral guardians.

Old wisdom slotted into the rows of a gargantuan bookcase on the right wall. It watered Corey's mental mouth. *Poems on Various Subjects, Religious and Moral* by Phillis Wheatley—the first black person to publish a book of poetry. She had to defend herself in court as whites couldn't grasp the concept of a nigger learning how to do anything but labor. "An Address to the Negroes of the State of New York" by Jupiter Hammon sat next to Phillis' work, much like their positions in the history of Black literature. *Up from Slavery* by Booker T. Washington, an autobiography that took the grand educational figure to the White House. *Clotel; or, The President's Daughter* by William Wells Brown, was considered the first novel by a black man and was based on the incessant rumor that President Thomas Jefferson fathered a mixed-race child. It would be proven true in the following century that Jefferson fathered *six*.

These were books Corey had never read.

All written from the roots of Slavery. Excuses for some, were motivation for others.

Between the native decorations and the masterpiece of a book collection, photos of sceneries and vistas from the Hudson River School of art tied in a theme of freedom. Green mountains wore laces of winding rivers, golden skies breaking through black clouds to bless lakes, and half a dozen others that yelled dramatic realism. It was almost unnerving how boldly and vibrantly they were rendered. Corey wondered if Griff had seen any of the places before his sight went.

Rufus, the brute who answered the door with grunts and no manners, rested on the trunk of a tree—engraved with the name of a loved one, Corey thought, judging by the heart whittled next to it. His arms were so large they could barely cross and were marred with a covering of obscure tattoos. His skin was like onyx.

Some men, when he was young, whistled at his sister. and he told them to stop. They cut out his tongue for his insurrection, then took his sister to a local woods. Too late to cut his sister loose that day, Rufus hunted down one of the culprits and committed him to an equal end. He proceeded to chop down the very tree they both died on. For three days he rolled that trunk—it might have been the start of his penchant for pumping iron—while evading the pursuit of maddened whites until he met Griff. Griff gave him food, water, shelter, and asked for nothing in return. He never did. And before Rufus knew it, he had been with Griff for six years.

Tick, a man of sweet features and a thin frame, stood by a door just left of the oak desk near the back wall, nodding his head to a tune only he could hear. A Native American hunting knife twirled through his fingers. The man's hands looked quick.

A rumble came from behind the door that sounded like the mess of men gambling. Loud laughter, beating tables, and chips shifting like shells on a high-stakes shoreline. Tick seemed to not notice the noise. Well, that was because he hadn't heard even the wind blow since '02. All anyone knew about the man was that he worked as a musician before he met Griff. Judging from his charred ears, the affliction that maimed him was hot. His hands were quick because they had to be, whether that involved slicing or signing a sentence.

In front of the spanning oak desk, atop a battered red rug, a wizened elder sat suppressing the tremors of Parkinson's in a wooden wheelchair. His stare held the milky vacancy of blindness. In the sixteen years Griff had his eyes, they witnessed disparate divisions of cruelty.

Thinning hair wrestled on his head like cobwebs across a boulder. His porcelain under-bite cleft was enough to shovel salt, leathery cheeks dotted with struggling shoots of grey nettle. Hi skin was pale and burnished, creased from the curse of time.

Griff looked historic.

Or prehistoric depending on the perspective.

Then there was Monty, Griff's grandson, who, upon sight of Elizabeth, rose from behind the desk with a hardened scowl to sit next to his grandfather near the edge of the table. Monty whispered something in his ear, and a smile took the place of the old man's crumpled lips.

"Donald sent them?" Griff confirmed. His voice as shaky and unsteady as his wheelchair.

"Yeah, pops." Monty was unconvinced.

"Well then, welcome." He paused to cough but it passed. "How can I help you?"

Corey cleared his throat. "Well, you see, me and Miss Elizabeth was told you could get us home to Chicago?"

"Of course, you're Donald's company, anything for him." Griff waved Rufus over. Each step he took shivered the ground. "Could we get some inconspicuous clothes for our guests, please?"

Rufus grunted and entered the ebullient room behind Tick. A burst of jingled laughter escaped the smoky room before he shut the door behind him.

Monty looked visibly unsettled, draped in anxiety as he glowered at Elizabeth, tapping his foot and chewing his bottom lip.

"How would you prefer to get home? Car? Carriage? Train? Or some other way?"

"Whichever is easiest for you," Elizabeth said. "Mr. Griff."

"Griff is fine." A wavy grin tweaked Griff's lips. "You have a wonderfully soft voice, ma'am."

"Thank you, I used to sing."

"You should resume it." Griff told Monty to call Tick over. "Tell him to ready a car for our guests."

"Will he be driving us?" Elizabeth asked.

"No, he'll give you an address in Chicago to drop it off, and one of our associates will return it."

"Oh," she swallowed hard. "In that case, can we take a train?" The thought of driving gave her undulating remembrances she'd rather not materialize any further. A car was off the cards.

"Fine." Griff motioned, and Monty signed the new orders to Tick. "Shouldn't be too long now; you'll be out of St. Louis before the morning comes."

"Thank you, Griff," Elizabeth let out a sigh of relief.

"So, tell me, how y'all know Donald?"

"He's my uncle, so to speak," Corey refrained from the details of their relationship. "Known him all my life. And Miss Elizabeth only met him today."

Griff's white gaze shrank as he turned over the thought. "Only today? I thought you were his people?" He shrugged it off. "Elizabeth, you must look as lovely as you sound then." Griff chuckled. "What's *your* name child?"

"Corey, sir."

"That's a good name. My son's name. It means *God's peace*."

Corey's cheeks grew high. "Umm, Griff," Corey approached the bookcase. "I don't mean to be rude, but why do you have all these fantastic books if you can't read them."

Griff burst out laughing and slapped his knee with a tremulous palm, "The truth is never rude, Corey. Check behind them."

Corey pulled a book from the case—*The Souls of Black Folks* by W. E. B. Du Bois—and behind it laid a book of equal size in a cream cover with a copy of the book's title in plain text. Inside the copy was a system of raised dots that ran rows down the page.

"Braille."

"Clever boy."

"How did you get all of these? I'm sure all the books you have couldn't have been published in Braille."

"You're right, they weren't. My grandson here is an expert at linguistics. He knows 6 languages, not including his proficiency for Sign and Body language," Griff chortled at his joke. "And for me, he learned Braille and translated every book that wasn't already so I could read them."

Corey looked over to Monty on the edge of the table. "Wow."

"You see, son, our abilities are only limited by our fear of change. I lost my eyes making a change for myself. Some would say it a tragedy, but I see it as a liberty. Without that change I may have never been able to do what I did here, find my purpose along this path. I learned as much as I could, as quick as I could so that I could pass on the torch of knowledge to the next." Griff's smile was almost ascendant as he tilted his head to the heavens. "I am not the first link in this chain, and I won't be the last. I only know I must be a strong link for the sake of not breaking the chain."

"So, these books are for—"

"The *next* link."

Corey flicked through the bookcase, and to his surprise, he found two works of Claude McKay on one of the lower shelves. While they waited for Tick, they conversed about books for a little while, sharing a laugh over common interests in the prose they had read. Griff took to Corey like a kite to the wind and a shine glossed over his eyes in a way they hadn't since Monty was a boy.

Elizabeth was quiet as she admired Corey's glee. And Monty still stared her down with a livid frown.

Tick returned with two tickets and handed them to Griff. "Here we are, two tickets for both of you."

"Thank you—"

"Pops," Monty interjected Elizabeth's gratitude. "I think you should know something before you hand them over."

"Hmm?"

"I know how grateful we are to Donald, and these are his *people*." He glanced over at Corey. "At least one of them is, but..."

"Speak up, Monty," Griff demanded, a touch annoyed.

"Elizabeth is a white woman."

Griff looked like he had been struck by lightning. The joy melted from the lines in his face, and his porcupine brows rummaged together. "Is this true?" the question was directed at Corey.

"Yes, is that a problem?"

"Yes." Griff tore up one of the tickets and tossed the shreds on the ground. "I do not give passage to white people."

Elizabeth looked sallow from the sudden shift in Griff's energy. Never in all her life had she felt the sting of bigotry. But here it was, gray and pale-skinned, scowling in a wooden chair.

"What? Why?" Corey asked, aghast.

"I don't have to explain the nuances of my reasoning, I just do not help white people. Now," Griff held a single ticket in the air, "you, my boy, are fine to go. You have a future of brightness before you. But I will not be helping her."

Elizabeth remained silent but shaken. This was the reason Monty watched her with eagle eyes; he was contemplating the passage his grandfather was to give them and wondered whether he should know all the factors of the accord. He made his decision.

"No. I'm not leaving without Miss Elizabeth. We left together; we'll go home together. I don't care if she's white. That doesn't define who she is; it doesn't make her the same as the people that blame us for our color." Corey was seething. A point of poignancy lingered in his intent.

"Let me show you something, Corey," Griff's voice was oddly calm as he asked his grandson to move him off the red rug.

Corey neared them and Monty pulled back the patch of scarlet carpet to reveal an iron hatch. Griff nodded for him to open it and as he did, a wind like Corey had never felt blared from the hole like the gasp of some black beast. He was unsure if it was his mind or the sensation was so surreal it didn't register with reality, but Corey was sure he could smell the stench of ripped flesh, hear the cries of hungry and hopeless children who would have to live a life of labor, and the cascade of waves against a ship's bow as the sound of some holy spiritual full of sanctity echoed below. Unheard by the ears. Digestible only by the soul.

Griff leaned close as Corey stared wide-eyed down the portal. "After I lost my eyes, I met this lady who took me to freedom. Her soul had the strength of a thousand lions and her heart the love of a thousand mothers. She risked everything, everything, to free slaves in the South to degrees no one ever dared. Her name was Harriet." Griff's words were ice. "She set up a network involving men and women of freedom, including myself, to lead those cuffed by hate to a land where love had a chance to roam." Griff pointed a wobbly finger down the chasm. "I hid thousands of people looking for a passage to freedom down here, in line with what Harriet envisioned. 'Every great dream begins with a dreamer.' I fancied myself a dreamer."

Corey stepped back from the hole and Monty closed the hatch, drawing the red rug back over it. It was here where Griff gained his influence; the loyalty people bestowed to him was not for simple favors. Every time Griff said 'yes' in the past to those mourned souls, he risked his freedom. And without his freedom, he could not be a link in the chain.

Only those that need to know, know.

It became clear to Corey that this was not just some playful mantra to add a sense of character to an establishment of entertainment. It defined who Griff was. What the Underground Railroad was.

What *freedom* was.

"One half of me tells me to be better than them, but the other half questions what better is. I do not yet have the answer. I may never." Griff asked his grandson to wheel him behind his desk. "I hope you find your way."

Corey walked with his head down back to Elizabeth, "Our abilities are only limited by our fear of change, right?" Corey quizzed Griff who sat quietly behind the desk. "I choose to change despite fear. Miss Elizabeth saved me when she didn't have to, chose to *protect* me when she had reason to *leave* me. She was willing to jump in front of a bullet to save someone she didn't know. I'll make sure my abilities are unlimited by always changing."

As they made for the exit, the door to the left of the desk burst open, and a man in a clean suit and freshly trimmed hair stumbled out. All eyes shot to him.

"I'm sorry, Griff." He tidied himself, voice hoggish. "You know how rowdy Rufus gets when he loses. Not too good with words but them fists speak loud."

"Skip?" Corey called.

"He-hey," Skip opened his arms out to greet them. "Asthma boy and train lady, how you been?"

"Broke," Elizabeth stated. "You said you'd pay Corey back, and you vanished with his money."

"I know, I apologize, poverty makes a man do some things. Let me make it up to the two of you." Skip shelled out a bundle of notes. "Fancy seeing you two in here, ay young blood?" He attempted to lighten the air, but it failed. "Will five dollars do?"

It was more than enough. Gambling had seemed to be where all his luck was hidden.

"Keep your money, the notebook you sold me is worth more to me," Corey demanded. "If you want to pay us back, instead just buy us tickets to get home."

Skip tapped his finger on his chin in thought. "Chicago, right?"

Corey nodded.

"When?"

"Tonight."

Skip grinned. "Y'all think you can meet me at the station in twenty minutes?"

"We'll be there," Corey agreed. "We just need to get one more person before we leave."

"Griff, is that cool?" Skip asked, fearing retribution.

"You can do whatever you like." Something in Griff had shifted slightly. Whether it was Corey's take on the man's mantra or the aura of Corey himself, the old blind man had a placated look on his face. "Corey,"

"Yes?"

"Take whatever book you like."

"What? I thought you said they were for the next link—" He looked over to the bookcase then back at Griff. "Me?"

"If not you, then who? If not now, then when?" Griff's words came from a ripple back in the chain.

"I thought you didn't agree with me?"

"I'm getting old...what do I know any more? Just because I am unable to be better, that does not stop you from doing so. Come back before I pass. We must speak again, and if you want, learn all that I have to teach."

A smile caught in Corey's cheeks, "T-Thank you."

"Promise you'll come back, for the sake of not breaking the chain."

"I promise."

*

GRIFF HAD THE BANE of growing up on a plantation in Macon. No father or mother to explain why he had to pick cotton and plough fields and get punished for it. The work was punishment enough. The white men above him, with their backbreaking and flagitious emissions, marched the porch of the big house like pale beasts.

Only nine when he got his first beating, Crookfoot—the crippled man who watched over him with his hobbled, pigeon rhythm—had been glad Griff had gone that long without his skin tasting the master's hand. It had been over a minor transgression: Griff only wanted water, as the sun was clutching at one hundred degrees. Master Rayne was having a bad day. Griff got ten on his back from a cat-o-nine-tails specially designed for deep cuts, two on each hand for wanting what wasn't his, and one firm one in the mouth to which Rayne asked, "Still thirsty?" Ironically, Griff had to drink his blood. He kept his head down after that, never asked for anything that he wanted, sang when they told him to sing, and made sure to clarify the height he should reach when they ordered him to jump. A nostrum settled in his mind. He was not Griff; he was simply an extension of the tools he used. Rayne's stock. And ideas were not for him to have, but for him to concede to.

He made friends, Everett and Sam. Two boys who Crookfoot—he never did find out the man's real name—also took care of in the absence of their slain parents. One wet night in April that year, Everett and Sam ignited a plan to run. Griff laughed and said they were crazy before the three nodded off in their bunks.

The next morning, siren bells rang like heaven's last call, and Griff awoke to find Everett and Sam missing. When the plantation gathered at the big house, Everett and Sam were battered and deluged with a luggage of creek water. Rayne made an example of what happens to runners that day, made sure Griff was front and center to see his friends die. Rayne drove hot spikes through their feet. The echo of their screams still woke him on rainy nights. Then he hung them, Everett by the neck and Sam with a meat hook through his rib cage. Griff had to watch his friend's take their last breaths, the fight fade from their spirits and the light leave their eyes.

Night fell and while everyone else had returned to their bunks, Griff was still watching.

If they were going to kill them anyway, what was the reason for the torture? They were only boys.

Crookfoot was killed the following week. Another of Rayne's bad days. He made his son do it this time, said he had had enough of Crookfoot doing nothing but eating and lounging in the workshop.

Rayne's intention was clear. He wanted to break Griff.

It worked.

When Rayne sent for Griff a week later, his intention became muddled in Griff's head again. His master thought to rebuild his broken property with the glue of good treatment. Execute a languid attempt at employing Stockholm Syndrome. Griff's body may have been shattered but his spirit had adhered to rebellion.

Gladys, one of Rayne's many maids, took handle of Griff and showed him around the house. She went around to the boring rooms first: kitchen, washroom, laundry room— where he'd be working—and lastly, the conservatory. "My favorite place," Gladys said with a twitchy smile. "It's like a little home. I'm the first one in the house in the morning and the last one out, ain't never bothered to lock the thing," she chuckled, and Griff took note. Then they arrived at the upper floor where a mass of bedrooms splayed across several intersecting white-washed hallways. Gladys showed him the one place that was forbidden, Rayne's collection room. Filled with the dreams of being a sailor, the room was canvassed with anchors, cartography maps, mask rope— which Griff was sure wasn't used for sailing—pictures of ships, and even models and other desultory chattels like compasses and a company of spyglasses. "Now, don't ever, I mean ever, come up in here unless you wanna end up like a trophy on one of them trees. Ya hear?"

Griff nodded but got ideas.

Little more than forty-eight hours later, Griff plotted his revenge.

In a sense, Rayne took his family, the only family he had. So Griff would take something of his. The decision to pick what to take was counter-balanced with the weight of circumstances. He wondered what could cause the most pain to Rayne and leave himself immune to wrath. Then he rationalized that he cared not for impunity as he had nothing left to lose.

He decided to take everything.

Griff chose to subject the man he viewed as hell-spawn to immolation. Cleanse the inborn sins of him and his kin. Sure he wouldn't be breathing tomorrow, Griff would do so with one final sin of his own. Metal would hold his lungs like it did Sam's, or rope would dress his neck like it did Everett's. Or, should he survive the blaze, Rayne might manifest some new brutal creation varnished with his cruelty.

Night came with a nervy swiftness. Sweat barreled down Griff's face as he collected the tinder and hay from the workshop before pressing towards the big house. Gladys, the maid with the twitchy smile, was leaving just like he expected, and he slipped in through the back door of the conservatory. It was unlocked. Just like he expected.

Between the first flight of stairs and the last, an ill-favored flicker of his conscience sparked second thoughts. He thought maybe to turn back, return to his place, and keep his head down going forward. It wasn't too late, the floorboards in the house were well laid and made no whingeing sound under his feet; he could sprint out the house and no one would hear. But was it too late for Sam, or Everett, or Crookfoot? They were taken for reasons only hate could explain.

The fire he planned to set wasn't one to burn the big house or tie a bow on the swathe of personal vengeance. It was a spark in the house of indignation. In the home of America. To kindle revolution in the unshakable mind of some young black man who had had enough of deranged despotism and slaughter. Add a flame to the bonfire of emancipation.

Griff lit the straw in the collectable room full of Rayne's maritime obsession. Right under the model of a British ship that held a prime position at the center of the room. It felt poetic in a way he wouldn't fully appreciate until he met Mrs. Tubman.

The house crumbled mostly by dawn while Griff was back in his bunk, not sleeping and a mess with new sweat. Rayne came for Griff that morning, devilment alive in his eyes. It was not a bad day for the man.

It was his worst day.

Rayne had already strung up eight of Griff's brethren before the blaze settled, and he was next on the list.

The night Everett and Sam chose to flee, Griff said they were crazy. Now it would be crazy if he didn't.

The chase lasted two days before Griff thought he lost Rayne and his posse. Two days without water, shoes, money, or help. He ran through the Georgian outback, following the North star and singing spirituals in hopes he could continue his swim against the waves of trepidation. To the sound of bloodhounds barking, he awoke in a barn without memory of even reaching the place. Creating distance was more imperative than the fantasy of whatever destination he had in mind.

Griff shot out the barn, dazzled by the rise of morning light and sway of spring leaves. The forest wall was a quarter mile ahead of him beyond a set of washing lines, white cloth, cleaning utensils, and a freshly picked berry field.

Rayne's voice was the loudest out of the bunch and Griff bolted under the washing lines before he saw the shadows of his undoing behind the masks of bedsheets. He wouldn't make it in time to the woods, the dogs may have been easy to outrun when he was fresh and full-bellied, but he was a far cry from that state.

There was a bundle of sheets he could hide in—the hounds would sniff him out in mere moments though—and there was a barrel of clear liquid he knew would quench him of his scent. With a deep breath, he plunged himself in and waited for their search to end.

Fifteen seconds was all it took to take away his sight. Fifteen seconds submerged in a barrel of bleach.

A Guilt Green

LIGHT FROM THE FIREPLACE clipped off as Sly left the room. Pants fixed, face washed, and raven suit back on, he was ready to take flight.

Cora told him about birds one time; she had a passion for ornithology that extended to boring him when they were growing up. How he would kill to hear his cousin ramble about birds now. For hours she'd go on about mating rituals that involved flamboyant choreography amongst the tropical sort. "Bright feathers and fancy footwork," she described.

Her favorites belonged to the Corvidae group of fowl. Also known as the Crow Family. Crows, ravens, rooks, jackdaws, jays, magpies and more. They were amongst some of the most intelligent species of bird, with their self-awareness and toolmaking. Sly didn't care, but Cora's round face lit up when she spoke about them. He recalled that the first thing she ever nursed back to health was a raven in an alley she heard cry for help when she was passing by.

Help was how Sly remembered her.

Even when she found out he was gay.

Cora helped him keep it secret from the rest of their family. He feared ridicule but she made him know that it didn't matter what he preferred; such a thing didn't define the fiber of his character.

Sly felt like the raven in the alley at times. Broken, flightless, and blending into the bleakness of desertion. Cora gave him his wings again, told him to fly, because the birds on the ground always envied those in the sky.

At her funeral, he wore the raven suit for the first time. Cora was survived by her son, Corey, who was named after her. At three-years-old, the boy was too young for the reality of their loss to truly settle in his little heart. All day in Sly's arms he asked where his mother was. Sly pointed to the sky. "She learned how to fly."

Corey said, "I want to fly too."

"When I learn, I'll teach you."

Martin gave a speech that was whole and heartfelt but faded in Sly's mind, erased over time by the peerless pathos of the day. Kat bawled rivers from her eyes that sailed with suffering. Oscar Jr. was quiet most of the day, and Donald...well, as of late, he expunged the man from that memory, especially given his root in Oscar's passing.

Sly wore the raven suit every day since. Not because he was still traumatized by her passing—although it left him torn for years—but because she said: *fly.*

Now he had to find Corey, so he could one day teach him to fly.

*

OUTSIDE IN THE HALLWAY, Sly spotted a figure trudging towards him in a blob of silhouette. *What time is it?* His watch was somewhere lost in his sheets. Judging from the intensity of the filtered moonlight at the end of the hallway, midnight wasn't far off.

The figure got closer. *Must be Dumbo.*

When the person fell into view under the haze of green lamplight, they were both frozen in time.

"Donald?" Sly mumbled, cold with surprise.

"Sly...? I-I didn't expect to see you here."

Sly noticed the clarity of his speech; it gave him a distinguished air. "I expected to see you."

"Right." Donald rubbed the back of his neck and simpered. "I guess Kat told you I was the one who made the call about Corey?"

"Doesn't matter how it got around to me." Sly's tone was sharp. "It got around to me is all that matters." He buttoned up his blazer. "Where is he?"

"Down to see Old Blind Griff. He runs this place and got a lot of pull in the city. Corey and some white lady he were with, Elizabeth, I think her name was, went to ask for transport to Chicago. I was just going to meet them."

"I see."

Arthur was looking for his mother; it was the reason Sly knew to come straight to The Bleach Barrel. Their contact had not been merely for the means of love.

"Say, Sly, I know you probably got some things you wanna say to me, huh? We should talk. Clear the air before we go get Corey. What do you say?" Donald looked wimpish in his request, he could barely retain eye contact.

"Fine."

"Is this your room?" Donald motioned for the door handle, but Sly stepped forward to block him.

"Yeah," he forced a smirk. "It's a mess though, how about we go to your room?"

Arthur was still inside.

"Of course, follow me."

The journey to Donald's room was plagued with a scourge of awkward silence. Sly watched the man's every move as they made their way. Every twitch of the cheek, sniff of the nose, and lick of the lips. Donald looked clean but Sly searched for any sign of his old behavior. There was none.

"Here we are." Donald unlocked the door, and the two entered.

The room wasn't as nice as Sly's—shorter ceilings, boxy in shape but it still held similar features. It had a large bed with more pillows than one man needed, a coffee table at its center, a vanity table by the door, and a fireplace baring the flicker of naked flames.

Donald sauntered over to sit on the bed while Sly maintained his distance, propping himself on the vanity table.

"So, where do I begin," Donald let out a nervous laugh. "That whole thing with Os...I feel guilty...real bad, but you know I ain't mean for any of that to happen, right?"

"But it did."

"Yes, but it was all an accident. That boy was like a son to me."

"You know the first memory I have of *my* father?" Sly found a set of toothpicks on the vanity table and tossed one in his mouth. He had deaf ears for whatever Donald was trying to rationalize. "Huh? Of course not, we've never really spoken. That's one reason you remind me of him so much. Anyway, the first memory was from when I was about eight; he was drunk or high in the sitting room—maybe both—and I went to hug and kiss him for his birthday. He slapped me so hard I saw blue. Said men don't kiss other men. My father didn't even want to kiss his own son. He left a bottle of whatever drink had caused him to pass out, and I drank it. I thought it might help with the pain. Looking back, that was probably his reason for drinking. To help with *his* pain, you know. I threw up all night, had my mother worried sick. She kicked my father out the next morning." Sly plucked the toothpick from his mouth and twirled it through his fingers. "The next time I saw him was seven years later. I had heard he tried to come back around, but I only got to see him on the side of the street begging money for food—the type of food that feeds the brain likely. *You* know what I'm talking about." Sly tapped his nose. "He told me to talk to my mother for him, tell her he's sorry and that he'd change." Sly started flexing the toothpick's center, slightly seething from his retelling. "I did what he asked because I wanted a father. But soon after he returned, he got right back into his old ways, and instead of beating me, he chose my mother. She went half-blind in her left eye from his savagery." He took a deep breath, recalling how he ran his father out the house that time thinking he'd never see him again. "The last time I saw him I was twenty. He didn't even recognize me. To be fair, I had changed, but that's no reason to forget your child, right? I sold him his 'food' and watched him take it there in an alley on W. Polk street. His eyes rolled back, foamed built in his mouth, and before I knew it, he was gone. I felt nothing watching my father die."

Donald was as quiet as a Brazilian wind. "I'm sorry to hear all that about your pops, but I ain't him. I swear it, I've changed—"

"*Change*?" The toothpick strained under the pressure of Sly's tense fingers, his jaw flexed like Donald's words were some poison. "You think you can *change*? Your inability to change got Oscar killed. Who's to say you won't go back and next time get Corey killed?" Sly's eyes grew hooded and dark.

"Nothing like that will happen. I promise I've changed."

"People don't change. They just get better at hiding who they truly are."

The toothpick snapped, and with his teeth gritted, Sly flew across the room like a shadow, charging towards Donald. He clocked him in the face with an elbow, and the crack sounded like it broke the man's nose. They tumbled to the ground. Sly mounted him and struck his face with sharp fists. Again. And again. And again. Blood spritzed from Donald's nose.

"Sly, please—"

Sly went to strike again, but Donald caught his arm and rolled him over so that his face was down and near the rage of the fireplace. He struggled. Donald was much heavier than him, and this close to the fire, he couldn't risk rash movements.

"I don't wanna fight you, boy," Donald panted, blood gushing from his broad nose. "This ain't what family do."

"Boy? Family?" Sly slammed an elbow into Donald's stomach. As the man was winded by the blow, Sly clambered to his knees. He dove for a pillow on the bed, and after a heel to Donald's face that knocked the man to the ground, he began to smother him.

Sly could hear his muffled cries and feel the desperation in Donald as the man's hands clawed at his suit. He flashed him off, wild-eyed and baring teeth, and he pressed all his weight into the pillow to stop the man breathing. Moments of sheer agony passed by for them both.

Then the fight went limp in Donald's arms; they went crashing to the ground.

Sly rose, wiped the spit from his lips, took some deep breaths to steady himself, and glared down at Donald's dead body. Flapping the wings of his suit, he retrieved a little green bottle from his pocket. He fixed the pillow back on the bed, sure to position the blood and saliva-marred side downward, before returning to Donald for one last look. It was the last vial of cocaine he had left, and a poetic sensation crawled through his body. He tipped it out and over Donald's nose and shirt, dropping the bottle near his hand by the fireplace that was ever reaching for the light.

"Pfft, change..."

A Dead Red

ROOM 33 OR ROOM 13? Corey wasn't sure of what number the concierge had told them Donald's room was. But Elizabeth trudged up and past the first-floor hallway, so she must have heard the former.

"We're close," Elizabeth said as the pair ascended the velvet steps.

"Skip was serious about paying me back." Corey smiled, feeling like he had made some omniscient decision back on that train. But it had all come down to the lambent factor of a 'Clean Heart Coincidence.' Despite the red Cletus was left dead in, there wasn't a time when Corey made room for the principle of disdain. Some part of his mind rationalized that decision of disposal as: *It was him or her.* And if Elizabeth had been disposed of, then Corey would have been next.

"I was wrong about Skip," Elizabeth rescinded her colorless judgement of the man. "If we hadn't bumped into him, I would have been stranded."

Griff's denial of aid to Elizabeth solely because of her skin color was a feeling she had never felt before. It hollowed her out, replaced all the blood and bone and veins, with knots and cords of hate that bounced to the beat of execration.

A feeling Corey would have to fight all his life.

A pain every black man and woman endured until their ends.

Even for the single moment that she shrunk in that room and had to look Corey in his eyes if he decided to leave her, she knew she never wanted to make anyone feel the same way. Not ever.

On the third-floor, Corey buzzed with excitement to see Donald and get on the road home. He counted the doors as they went. *31, 32, 33...* 33 was wide open, blaring the apricot haze of firelight.

"Why is his room open?" Corey looked up at Elizabeth with asking eyes.

"I have no idea..." Elizabeth crept beside him. Her nose scrunched. "What's that smell?"

Corey pushed open the door, and it creaked like the hull of a slave ship. "Uncle Don—" His eyes shot wide, pupils quivering at the sight as the scent of urine and feces polluted the air. Donald lay lifeless, covered in a sprinkle of white, blood-curdled clumps. Corey's nose fizzed with the test of tears, and an almighty pressure formed in his chest. Knees weak, he darted for the man's body. "Uncle Don!"

Elizabeth snatched him back before he got out of arm's reach, shielding his eyes from the abhorrent scene.

Corey lurched for him in her arms. "No...NO!"

"Corey, no!" She dragged him out of the room as he fought against her. "I'm sorry. I'm so sorry, but we can't be here!"

They vanished from the doorway.

Skip was waiting.

Donald was dead.

A Rail Red

SILENCE DRAPED BETWEEN THEM in the train carriage. The relief of arriving home was over-toned by the pathos of Donald's death. Not much could be done for the man, them being in the room caused more harm than good, and Elizabeth knew that well. So did Corey, but emotions on acute occasions cordoned off room for reason.

Corey hadn't turned his head from the window the entire journey. He just gazed at the silent movie of the city streets below. As they pulled into Chicago, he watched the stars dissolve into the blue wash of morning and the stone buildings become glazed by a rim of sunlight. Branded with an auburn tinge, the skyline dawned with the promise of an autumn mood.

Even when the stewardesses came by to offer refreshments—Skip had deep pockets now and used them to invest in life's luxuries—Corey didn't even flinch, though his stomach rumbled. Elizabeth ordered them both teas, a sandwich, and some biscuits. He only drank the tea.

All those days ago when they travelled in the back of that cargo train with only the service of engine smoke to feed on, the expectation wasn't to be cruising home at the front of a deluxe train, elevated from the ground. Above it all.

Skip buzzed from table to table, dishing out cards for businesses he didn't own and making promises he couldn't keep. "The best tailor in the state," he lied to a group of over-preened gentleman a couple of booths down. "Best couriers in the business. 'Say where, and you'll be there!'" Skip didn't know how to drive, and the whippy tagline was an obvious tact of its fraudulence. The white men took the cards with dismissive smiles, and Skip hopped to a few more tables before he settled back in the booth with Corey and Elizabeth. "A lot of good folk in here. You gonna eat that?" He scooped up the sandwich Corey had left and chomped away. Skip couldn't see those same 'good folk' were shredding his cards as soon as he turned his back.

"I just want to thank you again," Elizabeth said as she glanced out the window to view the city. "I don't know how we would have gotten back."

"That's all right," Skip took a bite and straightened his lapels. "The least I can do after my man here gave me a start-up. I would have still been on that train." He chuckled and sucked the mayonnaise from his thumb.

"How did you even get off the train? I thought you said it was a one-way to Dallas?"

"It was. I jumped."

Elizabeth was taken aback. "You jumped off the train?"

"Yep," he said so casually even Corey looked around with narrowed eyes. "When you've been homeless as long as I have, a certain regard for personal safety gets umm...dismissed in desperation. We were passing through St. Louis, and I knew about The Bleach Barrel, so while y'all was sleeping, the train slowed just enough for me to jump." Skip held up his gold pocket watch, tugged the collar of his Stanton double-breasted sack suit, and jingled his rings, which twinkled in the window's eerie reflection. "Talk about a leap of faith and *fortune*."

"We haven't had much of either." Corey spoke for the first time since St. Louis.

"It's true, it hasn't been easy..." Elizabeth tried to engage, but Corey turned his head back to the window.

Skip slowed his chewing and darted eyes between them. "Y'all been awful quiet the ride up here? Everything all right?"

"We're fine," Elizabeth claimed.

Corey was not so much mad at Elizabeth for pulling him away from Donald as he was about all the plights that riddled had their journey. He had seen Nina die, Jeremiah—he was sure Cletus was dead because of him—and now Donald. His heart was heavy with regret and insalubrious trauma. All those things, all those bad, bad, things he had seen, culminated to douse his fervent optimism. He wasn't angry at Elizabeth; every step of the way she was there to catch him if the world pushed him to fall.

"The trains about to pull in. We should get going." Skip finished the sandwich as the train slowed. When it halted, they rose, and with the bungle of rich people, they exited.

Throngs tumbled out and into Central Station, bouncing briefcases and suitcases and nutcases alike. The announcers chanted with gibberish linguistics only those who spoke conductor could understand—that was usually only conductors. Skip handled the papers as they battled through a sea of waving tickets and hurried men, around a few polished pillars that touched the distant ceiling, and through some gates before they reached the doors.

"Look like this is goodbye then." Skip had a small grin on. Men and women whisked past the three of them at the station's doors.

"Seems so." Corey was still distant and tired in tone. "Thanks."

Skip bent down to him. "Listen, son, take this." Skip handed him one of his business cards. "Ever need an old fleabag stranger like me, gimme a call."

Corey's eyes went wide when he saw Skip's name on the business card of a courier company. "Y-you have a company, b-but how? It's only been days since we met, how is that possible?"

Skip straightened Corey's collar and dusted off his shoulders. "It's fake. But the important thing is that you believed it, right?"

Corey nodded.

"That's because I believed it," Skip continued. "Ain't nobody gonna believe in you like *you* should, so make sure everything you do, you do it well. The white man ain't gonna give you nothing for free except a hard time. Hell, even some black folk gon' try to keep you down. The only way to be something is to believe you are something before it happens. A lion doesn't go around thinking it's a cat—"

"Lions *are* cats."

"Well...you know what I mean. A lion always knows it's a lion. You just have to know you're great *before* the greatness arrives."

223

"How'd you get all the money and stuff then?" Corey asked, confused by Skip's clean attire.

"This," he gestured over his suit and chuckled. "None of this is mine. At least it wasn't up until last night."

"What do you mean?"

Skip sighed, "Let's just say gambling is a desperate man's game. Up until last night, I *was* a desperate man." He winked, and they shook hands. "Take care of yourself, kid." Skip turned to Elizabeth. "Lady." He shook her hand all dainty like, and with that, fluttered into the crowd and vanished.

"We should find some way home," Elizabeth suggested.

They made their way down the road where the mob thinned out at the street corner. "Miss Elizabeth."

"Yes, dear." It was their first exchange in some time.

"Thank you."

"For what?"

"For not leaving me."

Elizabeth paused, thinking he had things confused; it was her that should be thanking him for that same sentiment. "I was never going to leave you, Corey. Not in Dallas or New Orleans or St. Louis."

"I'm not talking about those times. I'm talking about here, in Chicago... When I was on the train you could have stopped running, went back to your son and never had to go through all of this. But you pushed on for me when we didn't even know each other. So, thank you."

"I'd do it again," Elizabeth stated, a smile creeping onto her face. "Thank *you* for not leaving *me*."

"Long time no see kid," someone called from behind them.

Recognizing the voice, Corey turned to see a slender man in a raven suit followed by a big lump of a human. "Sylvester?" Corey sprinted into his arms for a tight hug. "How'd you know I was gonna be here?"

"That old blind guy told us." Sly rubbed his head.

"Griff?"

"Yep, we were in St. Louis all night looking for you. Turns out we just kept missing each other. It's all good; at least I got you now, ay?"

Corey's face dropped. "Did you see Donald...?"

Sly looked pale. "No, why? Was he there too?"

"Yeah, he was dead in his room with this white stuff all over his face." Corey looked down at the ground like he was looking at Donald's body all over again.

"Hey." Sly tipped his chin up. "Ain't nothing you could do about that. Some people just don't change." He glanced up to Elizabeth. "This must be Elizabeth?"

Elizabeth felt a thrum of anxiety play through her chest. "How'd you know my name—"

Sly snapped his fingers, and the big man next to him snatched her by the waist, covering her mouth to mute her screams. "Take her to the halfway house. I'll deal with her once I get Corey back home."

"Sylvester, no!" Corey lurched for Elizabeth, but Sly pinned him back.

Sylvester's hefty companion dragged her around the corner and Corey's heart thumped, sinking lower with each beat. A numbness fell over him as he watched her vanish. Parts of his body turned cold, the same parts that froze when he witnessed all the death throughout their journey. Close or afar, seeing the terror in Elizabeth's eyes as that man took her from him was a feeling he never thought he'd feel again.

Not after they had come this far.

Not after they had endured so much.

Reality settled in quickly to save him from losing his breath to an asthma attack.

Elizabeth was gone.

A Gut Green

"THE PEN IS MIGHTIER THAN THE SWORD," Sly quoted Cora as he and Corey cruised down a sun-stripped street towards his apartment. "I don't know what pen she knew about, but I'm pretty sure it must have been from one of the books she liked to read."

Corey flicked at the side curtains of Sly's car. The flexible plastic sheet hooked over the frame of the car to act as windows, just like Elizabeth's car had. It made a *gonk* sound whenever he hit it. "Why'd you take Miss Elizabeth...?" His voice was pale.

"You think that white woman is gonna treat you with fairness?" Sly explained his stance on what he liked to call the *Cracker Question,* contrary to the *Negro Question,* published by Thomas Carlyle, which advocated for the acceptability of slavery and the deranged examination of its perks for the negro. Sly had antithetical points. White people, to him, were set in stone. If they were slave masters once, they were slave masters always. Forgiving them, whatever that meant after such oppression and prolonged genocide, was the same to him as loving them for their hate. Even the one he loved. He kept that to himself, feeling torn slightly during his lecture. "The sooner you understand they hate you, the sooner you'll know to stay away from them." Sly added a comma to his discourse and continued. The only way to answer the *Cracker Question* was to remove 'cracker' from the question itself. His personalized division of dismal science was far from superlative. It offered the thought that adopting the methods of whites could promote the survival of blacks tenfold—not that he truly understood the delicate balance of socioeconomics. Being like them, he assumed, would mean becoming them and that would mean someone would have to take the place of the blacks as the oppressed. A conundrum he hadn't mulled over. Whatever question needed answering was likely too complex to assimilate solutions as elementary and hypocritical as extermination, or perhaps it was such a simple answer that complex minds refused to see it.

Love. A simple answer with complex applications.

"Miss Elizabeth isn't like any of that..."

"You don't know Elizabeth to be saying that."

"Neither do you."

Between his lectures, Sly slipped in ill-formed suggestions of the lady, adorning her with disgrace without any knowledge of the way her heart beat. Corey highlighted his hypocrisy. Sly heard none of it, instead embracing the do-as-I-say ethos that was so popular in the black community.

They pulled up to a building with a crumbling brick frontage and a peeling red door. Sly hopped out, but before he left, turned to Corey. "I'll be right back, just need to sort something before I take you home."

Corey acted like he didn't hear him.

"Listen," Sly said. "Maybe one day, in some time where black lives matter, the pen could be mightier than the sword. But the white man ain't giving *us* a pen, so, for now, I guess the sword will have to do."

The door shut and locked as he sauntered around the car and through the red door.

Corey tried the car door, but, of course, it didn't budge. He tried the driver's side, but the attempt was committed with futility. Slumped back, he pressed against the film-like window sheet with his finger, flexing the material before he got bored and took his notebook and pencil out. The lead had been ground to almost a stub, but there was still enough of a point for him to jot down the end of his poem.

The only halfway house Corey knew of was on W. Polk Street. The street he almost ran down when chasing his mother's photo all those days ago. Sly always said it's where his dad died but that was all Corey ever heard about his cousin's father. Through the falling ginger leaves of trees above, Corey spotted the street sign that read: *S. Bell Avenue.* His eyes went wide as the realization hit; W. Polk Street was just around the corner.

Which meant Elizabeth was just around the corner.

A white rush took hold of him and he barged the door with his little shoulders, but nothing came of it. He paused, poked the thin window sheet and gazed down at his pencil. An idea shrank his eyes. Corey thrust the pencil into the window, stressing the sheet with a point of pressure that turned the apex white. It was almost there, and he bit down on his lip for the fiction of extra force. He pulled a palm back and slammed it into the rear of the pencil. The window popped the sound of freedom as cool morning breeze flooded over his skin.

A defiant expression crossed his face as he climbed out of the window and bolted down the street for Elizabeth.

This time, the pen was indeed mightier than the sword.

*

ARTHUR PACED IN AN ANXIOUS JITTER in front of Sly's bed, turning his thumbs over each other in anticipation of his arrival. Arthur was startled when Sly jogged him from his sleep the previous night and instructed him to get up and catch a train back to the city. He only left him with, "I know where your mother is," and a set of keys to his apartment.

The wait had made him curious, and although he had been in the room before, he perused over the space hoping something new would pique his interest. Arthur always hated the green walls; they reminded him of bile. The only window was in the bathroom to his right, so the bedroom sweated like a hippo in high noon. The shelves on either side of the room held monuments of Sly's past—only a few of which Arthur knew about—the easel was obvious and the first one Sly ever explained. His cousin had gifted it to him on his sixteenth birthday with an engraving near the thumb hole that said: *Fly*. There was a letter addressed to him from Marion and Esther, his two sisters. They had moved to Los Angeles sometime before the war to pursue a career in showbiz. That was all Sly had told him. The rest of the objects: the clay Indian elephant, a piece of crystal cut like a marquise diamond, either a tube of lipstick or a bullet

228

case, Arthur wasn't too sure, and a copy of *The Wonderful Wizard of Oz*, all eclectic and desultory, served as part of the enigma that kept Arthur intrigued. Hopeful he'd find out each of their stories one day soon.

But in the back, peeping out from under the clay Indian elephant, was a wrinkled ticket from an art gallery that had faded some from overexposure to light.

A slight flutter tickled his stomach.

The day they met was the easiest he'd had in a long time. It was just after the war, and anything to remove his mind from the grasp of trauma was welcome. Arthur went to the gallery alone, hoping for nothing but a distraction, and Sylvester had done the same. Sly spoke about birds because he had Cora on his mind that day, and Arthur compared aviation to them as they trudged through the gallery peering at prudent pieces of art that he struggled to assimilate.

That was it, that artistic polish that Sylvester had about him reminded Arthur of his mother, or rather, reminded him that he barely knew her. The only thing he could recount about her in large was the fact that she put her art before her Art. The poetic irony was incising. Whether Sly could paint for him the missing parts of himself where his mother couldn't was still to be seen, but despite Sly's views on those of Arthur's hue, he felt comfort in being chosen. Being loved for the things so many had hated. At opposite ends of the same world, they found each other. Even if it might be brief, a sole firework in the long night of liberation, he'd cherish the lights.

He sat down on the bed, which wheezed under his weight, and tapped away at the bedside table, transferring his disquiet from his legs to his hands. Arthur slid open the drawer of the curvy four-legged stand, shocked to see the cold iron of a Colt Peacemaker asleep in the table. It looked like something out of one of the Western films that were playing all over theatres. He picked it up, and the weight took him by surprise, it felt off-balance in his hand. Before he could put it back, keys jingled in the lock outside, and he stuffed the gun under the bed, slamming the drawer shut.

"Sorry I took a while." Sly slipped off his black blazer and hooked it on a peg behind the door. "I got your mother."

"Where is she?"

"In a halfway house not far from here." He rolled the tension from his shoulders. "I'll drop you there as soon as I drop Corey off. I promise."

"So what are you doing here?"

"I just need to get something." Sly motioned for the drawer and turned cold when he found it empty. "What the—"

There was a knock at the door that shocked Sly more than his missing pistol. *Who the hell is that?*

Couldn't have been Corey; he was locked up in the car. It could have been Stella from upstairs, but it wasn't even midday yet, and there was no way she was up—opium had become an egregious pastime of hers, which Sly had a hand in. So who was it?

Sly moved for the door slowly with squinted eyes, and his head cocked to the side. Brass brushed his fingers, but as he turned to peek out the crack of the door, it blasted open, knocking him to the ground. Dazed, he tried to get to his feet, but a boot slugged him in his stomach, ridding his lungs of air. The assault didn't stop. The tall man with a wiry beard grabbed him by the collar and tore his face up with a series of cracking punches. The first blackened his right eye, the second burst his upper lip, the third, he felt something in his jaw pop, but by then the man had proceeded to stomp on the side of his head, sending cracks of pain pulsing through his skull.

"NO!" Arthur cried.

Sly heard Arthur call the person's name, but it was muffled as his ears had pooled with blood. He struggled for air as the ringing in his head turned the scene to some devilish pantomime.

"Jerry, he knows where our mother is!" Arthur screamed out as he held the gangly man back. "He's trying to help me."

"Shut up," Jerry snapped, a finger darting at Arthur's face. "If you weren't my brother, I'd beat you too." He turned his attention to Sly, who was battered and bloodied, face like ground meat. "Flo told me about y'all's little rendezvous." He emphasized the 'Vous', oddly calm in the wake of the brutality he had just decreed.

"Jerry, listen—"

"I ain't trying to hear a damn thing from you. The whole time your *contact* was this nigger? And on top of that, I hear y'all are real *friendly*." Jerry played with the knife on his belt as he turned to Sly. "Where's my mother?" he said, his whisper chilling.

"I ain't telling you shit." Blood sputtered from Sly's gritted teeth.

Jerry slammed a knee into Sly's mouth and spun him over, twisting his arm behind him. He had no time for threats. He snapped Sly's shoulder from its socket, and his scream ricocheted around the room. "You *are* going to tell me where my mother is or when I find that boy—you know who I'm talking about—I'll make sure I kill him nice and slow."

After the pain dimmed, Sly thought hard about all he had done to get Corey to safety. He wasn't going to let him die for a woman he didn't know. No matter his love for Arthur.

Corey came first.

He assumed Jerry had no idea Corey was in the car downstairs; otherwise, he would have gone to get him or already had him. In fact, how did Jerry not know Corey was outside? He had to pass the car to enter the building. Sly couldn't muse that thought, as his life was on the line, and if he didn't tell the man what he wanted to hear, Corey's would be too. "She's at a house," he said through swollen lips. "On W. Polk Street, just around the corner. Take her."

"I must say," Jerry smiled in his face and slapped Sly's puffy cheek before he rose to leave. "That's mighty wise of you. Perhaps I'll just kill the boy fast."

"NO! Please...: A black panic took hold of his heart, all the agony his body had endured paled in comparison to the mere thought of Corey dying by this man's hands.

Under his bed, not even the blood in his eyes could mistake what he saw.

His gun.

With his one good arm, he dragged himself closer to the bed. Jerry had turned his back to say something to Arthur. It appeared to be a hurl of execration. Sly managed to grab hold of the weapon, hoisted his back up against the bed frame, and aimed it at Jerry's back. It trembled in his palm, the weight he was used to seemed to weigh the weight of all the promises and pledges most sacred to him. *Fly. Find Corey.* Sly would die now if it meant keeping them all by killing this man.

Arthur's eyes went wide when he saw Sly over Jerry's shoulder. "Sly, NO—" The gunshot blared as he shoved his brother out the way. The bullet split his skin, shattered his sternum, and stopped his heart before he hit the ground.

They didn't even share a final word.

Arthur died in Jerry's arms.

Jerry unsheathed his blade, took a brisk step toward Sly, and punted the pistol from his hand. When he slid the blade into Sly's gut, he made sure to watch the life vanish from him as warm blood puddled around him.

Sly died by the hands of hate, hate his hands held too. In some sense, it was his time to fly.

The pen may be mightier than the sword, but the sword still stung.

A Wine Red

EVERY GLASS OF WINE she ever had materialized in lament echoes.

The first time was blurry because she was ignorant of the fact that she was drinking an expert blend of Pinot Noir and only recalled waking up in a strange room with strange people. The time that left her crawling in a stupor up her apartment stairs, passing out in her drool before she reached the top flight, formed pins and needles at her fingertips. In the summer of '95, she took down two bottles of wine, with several mind-flaying shots of rum that left her throwing up bile through her nose. It was the summer she lost her sons.

She recalled them in disparaging intervals. One after the other. The feculent intermissions of hazy nights induced by alcohol chopped her reveries into noxious chunks.

The last time she drank was when Rose died.

In her weakened state, Elizabeth held onto the bottle dearly like this was going to be the next time.

The couch she sat on was torn at the seams from overuse. Wrappers from old, half-eaten candy, wood splinters, and shredded newspaper littered the floor. It was a cornucopia for roaches and rodents. A slash of light cutting through the gap in the boarded windows provided the only illumination, highlighting thick dusk that carried the musty scent of mildew. All the crying had made her head light; she wasn't sure if the fat man who brought her here had left or if he was still in one of the back rooms. But the bottle of wine and pint glass he left behind on the makeshift coffee table, crafted from plywood and a few cinder blocks, was all she saw.

Everything was gone again. Corey stripped from her without even the semblance of a goodbye. Her will had gone with him. As she glared at the dark bottle with wetness in her eyes, she asked herself, *What was left?*

Nothing was the answer.
Hope left her heart.
Tears scarred her cheeks.
Wine filled the cup.

*

WITH HOPE, he ran.
With vigor, he ran.
With everything Corey had, he ran.

Eyes darted at him as he whizzed down the street in pursuit of Elizabeth. Corey skipped in front of cars that skidded to a halt, the drivers heckling him with invective for his carelessness. Some stranger told him to slow down as he bolted by in a brown blur, said that he'd hurt himself. If only they knew he was already hurting. Elizabeth was close but too far for him to take his time, even with the tightness that was forming in his chest.

So, with pain, he ran.

When the streets got busy, Corey slipped between two houses and readied himself to clear a weathered picket fence. He made it. Unlike days ago, when he chased after the picture of his mother and the hedge slashed at his legs, the fence didn't even clip the tips of his laces. He was stronger now, but one thing hadn't changed.

He still chased the picture of his mother.

A garden opened up before him, burn-barrels skirted the rim of the yard, and mounds of grass and dirt scattered the ground with muddy obstacles that looked like someone had trouble finding a burial site. A clothesline pinned with red sheets clapped in the firm wind, applauding his efforts and parting a path for Corey that led out onto the adjacent street.

Fewer people walked this road; it was darker, draped by browning canopies overhead that filtered down thousands of threads of light. He glimpsed above to the street sign: *W. Polk St.* He was close.

Rubble piled in grizzly heaps on the lawns of the detached homes. He ran past them, hunting for a house that looked unloved. Near the end of the road, where the shushing trees joined their twiggy fingers, a dilapidated bungalow frowned under the gloom of the shade. *This must be it.*

Corey bolted across the overgrown slab path and charged through the stained plywood door. "Miss Elizabeth?!" He squinted as his eyes adjusted to the darkness of the house, and through it, there she was. Teary-eyed and trembling with a glass of wine in her lap.

"C-Corey?"

He ran over to her, placed the glass on the table, and embraced her. The scent of wine was not on her.

Elizabeth wiped her tears. "How did you—Why did you— "She had many questions that wouldn't come out.

"I broke out of Sylvester's car," he panted. "I knew where this place was, so, I came."

Elizabeth hugged him tight again. "You're very brave. Thank you."

"We should go,"

With hope, everything seemed fine, calm in the regard that being back with each other ameliorated the stresses they'd braved. Corey helped Elizabeth to her feet, and as they made way for the door, it burst open holding the silhouette of a slender man with a Southern voice.

"Hello, Ma."

A Lie White

WHITE LIES WEREN'T SO BAD when told to embolden black truths. So Martin lied to himself. Told himself he didn't enjoy the tact of playing the piano, when in truth, the prudence of putting together an arrangement was something that pandered to the tender regions of his sensibilities.

Serendipity played a role in him discovering the hobby—along with endless encouragement from Cora after she saw him get lost in the keys the day they met. Martin was terrible, but a rawness poked through when he played. The duality of controlling high and low ends met his tuned dexterity in conformity with his talent to balance the thinking of two minds. One of higher ground and one of lower.

One hateful. One loving.

It was the only time he ever let down his guard, was dulled to the enormities around him and became delicate with his approaches. The pearly piano in the corner of his office was like a step to some forgotten haven. A haven he owned. One he visited no more.

These days, he supposed, there was no time for the things he liked. Corey was more important; family was imperative. The plights of his black brothers and sisters were ever pressing against his will to create change. So, ten years ago, he lied to himself, said that the piano was a waste of time when really, he needed it more than ever after Cora passed.

White lies weren't so bad. He was sure of it.

If he hadn't lied, he would have spent most of the season playing his grand piano to blanch the redness of the summer. Cool the fires in him that licked bone and disparity alike, instead of fighting what he thought was the good fight. Now, the keys he played with were for the truck, to collect the guns he had finally arranged.

Martin swapped the car keys for his whiskey, setting them on his desk beside the newspaper, which rustled lightly from the wind passing through from the window. It rocked the bar's door with a faint knock, which was lost behind the chuckle of giggly blinds. The mild scent of charring fluttered in on the night breeze.

"What's the plan?" Kat called from across the office. "We haven't exactly got the personnel to move however many crates of guns we're expecting, so how are we gonna do this?"

Martin took a sip of his drink. "I was hoping Sly would be back by now." He glanced at the clock as his brow furrowed with a modicum of concern. But Sylvester was Sylvester, always late but always arrived. "If he isn't back by nine, we'll take a truck each and go—" Martin dipped into his blazer pocket and went cold when he found his money missing. And the address with it.

"What's the matter?" Kat heard his sentence clip off.

"M-My money, it had the address coiled in it... It's gone." Martin's mind flickered back to the riot, the boy with the vitiligo and their encounter in the alley. "Dammit!"

Kat laughed as she dove into her blouse pocket. "Thank God for me then, ay?" She produced a scrap of paper with an address scribbled on it. "I knew you'd get careless in your excitement. Always premature with you guys."

"You copied it down? When?" Martin thawed.

"When you were careless and excited."

Embarrassment measured Martin with shame as he approached Kat who continued cleaning the bar counter— a habit she adopted for the times she spent waiting. "Thank you. I told you I needed you."

"Mh-hmm." Pride all over her tone.

She didn't relent from cleaning even when Martin took the address from her. Her efficiency with time was something Martin delighted in—not a second was spent idle.

"Remaining sentimental, I see." He flicked the silk ribbon on her wrist.

Kat took a weak breath. "Always."

"I wonder what things would have been like if you never left back then."

"Different."

"Corey wouldn't be here, and that thought I can't bear."

"No." Kat looked him dead in the eye. "Corey would be mine."

An intense stare held them together for an endless moment, one that tempted the echo of sweet nothings to tumble from their lips. Neither said a thing. A breeze rattled the frame of the blinds and severed their internal embrace.

"Cora," Kat spoke, reminding them with a contrived essence why they had never done the things they longed to do, "always used to hate the wind. It was about the only thing she didn't like."

Martin laughed. "Especially at night. It made her jump out of her sleep, which made me jump out of mine."

"I'd give anything for her and her quirks to be here." Kat looked at the ground before she turned from Martin. "Like when she always used to announce she was a nurse," she chuckled. "Always so proud. I loved it."

"You used to love nursing, what happened?"

Kat sighed, rubbing the back of her neck. "I still do, but things changed when Cora died. We all had to make certain sacrifices. Nursing isn't for me any more...at least not right now." A white lie of her own.

"You ever think you'll go back to it?"

"Well, I've been thinking about going to join your mother and the NACGN up in Boston recently, get back to healing people the way I started."

"After this is done, why don't you go?"

"You tryna get rid of me?" she asked playfully with raised brows.

"No, no, not at all, but I don't want you to feel trapped or pinned down by my ambitions. Just because I feel I need to do *this*, doesn't mean you have to share that obligation out of unjustified guilt. You have your own life to live, and no matter how much I love having you around, I refuse to stand in the way of you living it. You got more talents than pushing numbers for a failing grocer." There were little nerves in his laugh. "If you want to go, go." He finished with a smile.

Kat ruminated for a minute, clicking her nails together. A grin formed on her plump lips as she looked him in his eyes. "Okay. After this, I'm going to go."

Martin finished his drink, feeling the tug of ambivalence pull him closer to the prospect of saying goodbye. "That's what I'm talking about."

"Come with me. You and Corey."

The smile wiped from Martin's face. "What?"

"Ain't Chicago done enough to us? Ain't we suffered enough? We could move, all of us, even Sly if he wants to, and start again somewhere else. I know your mother would love that."

"I can't move, there's too much to do here." Martin shrugged off the idea.

"Why? Because of *the people*?"

"Precisely."

"The goal is to arm them, Martin. It doesn't mean you have to pull the trigger yourself."

"It'd be like abandoning them. All the intent I had on seeing our people in this city be able to fight would have been for nothing if I ain't there to fight with them."

"What's more important, fealty to your family or the people?"

Martin pondered in silence like he was weighing up each choice. In truth, he knew which one mattered more. Having Corey around guns and an environment that was conducive to trauma left him with the inability to justify the other option. The family was first. Always. "I'll think about it."

Kat did a little shimmy in celebration; it was much better than a straight 'no.' Martin was known for knowing exactly what he wanted; having him consider the move was a win.

"We could even visit Africa after a while. Go back to the motherland, you know. I know Nina would be proud of me for that."

Martin stepped back to his desk. "How come you wanna go back to Africa?"

"Well, that's where we're from. We're only here because of the slave trade. Why wouldn't you want to go back to a place you belong?"

"Because technically we don't come from there. *Technically*."

"What are you on about?" Kat poured herself a swig of brandy, expecting some esoteric opinion of Martin's to follow.

"What if I told you Slavery was a lie? Now I see your face." Martin caught the disdain in her stare. "But don't get me bent out of shape. The fact is that we were most certainly brutalized, raped, murdered, and owned for over three-hundred years—and counting. It's hard to prevent such things when you're caught off-guard, unorganized, and are armed only with assent. That fact remains, but I believe they lied about how we were enslaved."

"Go on." She took a hearty gulp from her drink. She needed it.

"The number sits around twelve million—the number of people they claim were slaves. Logically speaking, to load a ship with four, five, six hundred men and women at a time and carry them across the ocean seems absurd. As back then it usually took between two to three months—four if the seas were upset—to transport such cargo in such quantities, packed like sardines, without exercise, proper hygiene, food, or water while they pissed and shat on each other the whole way. To me, it doesn't sound very efficient to transit people that way or be conducive to serving the white man's business. The amount of disease and malnutrition on the ship would kill the strongest of them. Then, by the time they got across the Atlantic, they'd be mostly unfit for work, let alone sweltering labor. I think they flattered themselves with a more twisted agenda, one so subtle that most whites who are sheep—the insensible—believe the wolf skin they wear is truly theirs."

"I guess when you think of it like that, it is a bit impractical, but what has that got to do with Slavery being a lie? Twelve million is a lot of us, and three hundred years is a long time."

"Hold on, there's more." Martin grinned like he was about to blow her mind in the simplest way. "When Columbus came across—not discovered—America, he found himself confused by the sight of people. Many people. Native Americans. They called them Indians because they were looking for India and the colonial ploy didn't subscribe well to the sound of 'native.' He wrote, and I quote: 'The Indians are so naïve and free with their possessions,' and 'They would make fine servants. With fifty men we could subjugate them all and make them do whatever we want.'" Martin had this provocative collection of knowledge swimming around his head. "In Webster's 1828 American Dictionary—" Martin skipped around to his desk, pulled a drawer and found the old dictionary. He flipped to the page he wanted. "There is an excerpt under the word 'American' that describes them as 'native' and 'copper-colored.'" He shuffled for a coin in his pocket and flicked it to Kat. "Looks like black folk to me. Anyhow, back to slavery. This is just *my* thinking; you tell me if it makes sense. Twelve million slaves, let's say half make it to the middle passage from West Africa and the Slave Coast. Stored the way they were stored, for as long as the trip took, with all that I mentioned earlier considered, do you believe, from an entirely logical perspective, that that was a successful procedure for hundreds of years?"

Kat drank. With it broken down like that it was hard to see an angle to fight Martin's reasoning. "It does sound highly unlikely, given all that you mentioned, but what are you saying then? Slavery didn't happen?"

"Is the sky blue?" he joked. "Of course it happened, but as I said before, they just lied about how and who was enslaved. I think they did carry as many slaves from Africa as possible, but quickly realized it wasn't as feasible as they perceived. So, instead, they took those that survived the journey into America and the Caribbean and mixed all those resilient enough to brave the waves with the natives they already had in captivity. Bred them to produce a race that was immune to all the diseases the Europeans had brought with them and create what they called the *African-American*. By doing that, they create the strongest, most elite humans to be slaves. After genocide and slavery and hundreds of years of historical confusion, we no longer know who we are. In truth, us today, you and I, are Native American, African, Carib, and likely some more. True descendants of *this* land.'

"Why would they lie about something like that? They still have all the privilege regardless of the truth, so what difference does it make? We were still slaves." Kat couldn't find his point.

Martin took a deep breath through his wide nose. "Because the man that doesn't know where he comes from, doesn't know where to lay claim. You keep telling someone they're from somewhere other than where they currently are, they're gonna long to return to that place and not even think they are right where they belong. Hence *African-*American. It's years of subliminal nurturing and false guidance. I've never heard a single white person call themselves European-American."

A white lie on a massive scale, Martin believed, made all the difference between them.

"Wow." Kat was nonplussed; something so simple was under her nose the whole time. She had no idea if it was true in its entirety, but his simple deduction of the matter proved to be more food for thought than she first assumed. She found his point.

"It's just something I've been thinking about for a while, and each time I pass it through my mind, it never quite seemed to line up logically with what they told us." Martin glanced at the clock. It was nine already. "Anyhow, we should go, doesn't look like Sly's back yet."

"Right." Kat was still brewing all he had told her, but she finished her drink and readied herself to leave.

An excited wind blasted through the window and ruffled the bar's door, the newspaper, and the mess of files on Martin's desk. He patted down his pockets. "Could you help me find the keys real quick?"

"Sure."

Martin scoured his desk; he was sure he had left them somewhere amongst the wind-made mess. Kat suppressed her habit to clean the bar while she searched it.

"Got them." He found them under the newspaper after he sorted the rummage on his desk. There was no response. When he spun around to see if she was all right, he saw her kneeled by the bar. A white brick of fine powder in her hand. Some of the other keys he played with. "Kat, listen—"

"What's this?" Her face was a picture of disdain.

"Listen—"

"No." She didn't know where to look as she tossed it onto his desk, eyes darting over him like he was a stranger. "This is how the business has been staying afloat? Through *this* shit?"

"I didn't have a choice. It was either this or starve. I chose not to starve." Martin's voice was low and deliberate now.

"So, you're selling drugs? To who?"

"Anybody that wants them. Mainly, people we know, and it just grew from there."

"Why, Martin?" Kat shut her eyes and turned away, her steps weak. "You blamed Donald for what happened to Os..." The thought of Oscar snagged her words. "When you might as well have done it yourself..."

"*Why*?" Martin's face turned to stone. She had gone too far. "Because I'm a black man in a white world!" he roared, veins strained in his neck. "Why else would I risk everything just to gain a little something. Do you think they gonna give me a job? An opportunity or a fair fucking chance? Huh? The only chance I got is to roll these damn dice every day knowing full well they only land one way. *Their* way. And still, hope that I don't get fucked by a system specially designed to fuck me! I go out and pray that one of these crackers doesn't see me first when they're having a bad day, because it could mean my last." Tears brimmed in his livid eyes. "They have my brothers kill my brothers. Scar our kids with the repression of knowledge and taint the minds of our sisters with the rhetoric that niggas ain't but a goddamn thing! So that even in our own homes, instead of solace we find ourselves still fighting just to be who we are. You ask *why*? Because I'm a *black man*, that's why."

Kat remained quiet, trembling while tears wrecked her cheeks. She just shook her head, slapping the wetness away. She untied the silk ribbon and laid it on the desk beside the keys. "At least you've got a better devilment than your father. He stopped with vegetables. You started with drugs." Kat hurried out the room, face wet and salty.

A tear tumbled down Martin's cheek; he clenched his jaw tight, forbidding any more from falling. On the desk, he glanced over the ribbon and the keys. He could make amends, go after her, take Corey to Boston once he was back, leave all the madness behind. Or he could remain resolute in his conviction, realize himself as the crux of revolution and fight for the people he claimed meant more in the bigger picture.

For a long while, he looked at the desk, pondering the choices before him. Wiping his face, he took a shot of whiskey, which calmed him.

He snatched up the keys.

A Pitch Black

FULL MOONLIGHT FELL through the cracked ceiling, bouncing off wet metal and broken glass, casting the foundry in fantastic shadows. An anxious rain patted down into the black warehouse like little angel steps, resonating through the cold enclosure with a heavenly hush.

Jerry had waited for the cover of night to make his move.

On their way, when the boy asked where a man named 'Sylvester' was, Jerry said nothing. For whatever reason, the boy played with a hole in the car's plastic window on their way to the warehouse. When his mother asked where they were headed, Jerry said nothing. She had relinquished the honor of his conversation when she decided to mingle with the nigger child.

The pair trudged tentatively ahead of him, alert to the white noise of rain and the tick of foreign sounds. Jerry knew it was nothing but man-sized rodents and old metal squealing. Boxes were stacked in pyramids throughout the warehouse, some large like the rear of delivery trucks, others more manageable and cuboid in construction.

Perfect for holding rifles.

Ten Commandments were too many, he thought, left too much room for the lax of human interpretation. To elucidate his opinions amongst the demotic, he'd have to employ simpler strategies. Jerry always believed freewill was too high a grace. The honor should be preceded by a long rite of passage that proved one could be trusted with oneself. It was something he longed to ask the Lord. He wouldn't just arm people with guns, no, it was puerile to think that way. Yes, blood would spill, the blood of those he thought unworthy of freewill or even the right to earn it. But where would that leave him? Still indigent. Impoverished. Beggared.

A flagitious idea formed. Those who would see to follow him with the same hate draped across their hearts, would do anything to see blacks bleed. Instead of giving the guns away, he'd sell them, discounted and abundant. Two birds went down with the throw of a money-colored, bullet-sized stone.

That's why he had no intention of moving the guns.

As far as he knew, he was the only one with the location thanks to Bo's nippy fingers, and it was the perfect place to hide them. Abandoned building for abandoned goods.

With his ploy, he knew any lackey couldn't be trusted to govern the way they pointed their guns, but Ten Commandments were too many. Three would be enough. Simple rules for simple minds.

One: *Sympathizers die first, blacks second.*

There were few people worse than those who allowed negroes to feel worth. Like his mother, there was a bounty of them that he loathed who needed purifying via sharp ends.

Two: *Thou shalt not waste time on passion.*

Jerry understood, like most of his kin, the unexplainable passion that roused within when it came to afflicting a black man. How it mollified that tribal rage. They'd have to quell that fervor to maximize the efficiency of their executions.

Three: *Thou shalt not question ME.*

If all panned out the way he saw it, he'd be sitting at the peak of an ornery pile, dictating to those below the methods of their racial distillation. In that world, that plighted future, he was a god.

How long would it take to purify the city? Then the state? Was it possible to cure the entire country? Or even the world? All questions with answers in the foreboding future.

God created life; Jerry decided he could take it.

Jerry ordered the two of them to sit by a crate when they reached near the center of the warehouse next to a flutter of copper leaves, a half-broken whiskey bottle, and cloudy puddles writhe with furry sediment. The spot bathed in a stare of moonlight as a redolence of spoiled fish and wet metal punctured the air.

Some foreign sounds played from the pitch-black fringes. Jerry ignored them. More rats. He approached a crate a few feet away that was propped up on a large box, slipped his black blade between the crease, and pried it open with a loud crack. Puffs of hay burst from the rush of air, and Jerry peeled back straw to reveal the polished gunmetal. A maniacal smile drew across his lips.

Standard issue Springfield rifle. It felt the same as it did a year ago, cold, heavy and with a kick that rivaled a shocked mule. He peered down the sights, cocked back the bolt handle, and grinned at the clean chamber. "Beautiful."

He cracked open a few more crates in the glee of his findings: dozens of Colt M19's and Revolvers filled a few, Browning shotguns he recalled had a devilish bite, Enfield's, Remington's, and in one of the large containers, a Vickers machine gun stood readied on a tripod, decorated in strips of straw.

The time had come for him to predicate his principles on those of facile conscience, submit malleable disciples to live by his odious appraisal. One priced in gunshots and blood spray.

The sound of a door creaking rung from the pitch-black rim of the space. Jerry's smile dropped. He turned to his mother and the boy and told them not to move. Must have been a big rodent to move a door. Or perhaps not a rodent at all. As he edged slowly to get a look around the first crate he opened, a figure penetrated the darkness in a brown suit, with coffee-toned skin and a pencil stache.

A rodent. He was right.

"Dad!" The boy darted towards the stately man.

"Corey." The man knelt and squeezed his son, taking a deep breath as they embraced.

Jerry cleared his throat. "You must be Martin."

"And you shouldn't be here," Martin spat.

"Well," Jerry chuckled, his Southern twang aflutter in an echo. "My pop told me something about finders keepers when I was a boy, so here we are." He raised his arms as if presenting some grand stage.

Martin ushered Corey behind him. "I didn't think I was gonna see you again after we left your lawn. Then you decided to torch my place of business," he said, his teeth gritted.

"I told you I'd see y'all soon." Jerry played with his blade's hilt. "But you're partially correct; this is sooner than I'd have liked. You've only given me a mere moment to admire my guns." An acerbic smirk masked his face as he spun slowly with his arms wide.

"I think you mean *my* guns."

Jerry looked disappointed. "Now what would make you believe such a foolish thing?"

"Corey, stay here." Martin took a step forward to enter the circle of moonlight where Jerry patrolled. "I need to ask you something. I don't know how you know my name, and I don't care to know yours, because at the end of the day, it don't make no difference to me or you. But what I need to know is, why?"

"Why what? Why I want these guns? I heard you niggers been plotting some type of *takeover* if you will, and I won't stand by for that."

Martin flinched at the sound of the word nigger, a verbal bullet certain to pierce the toughest of skin when shot from the barrel of a white mouth. "Takeover? We just want to leave our homes and go about our day without the potential threat of death around the corner. All summer, hell, all our American existence you have fought tooth and nail to keep us down when you already placed us at the bottom. You know how many people I've lost this last week alone?" Martin took a flustered breath, a hardness taut in his unblinking eyes. "No. Why would you? It means about as much as any black life. *Nothing.* I don't want these guns." He stabbed a finger at Jerry. "But because of people like you, I *need* these guns."

They went back and forth for a moment, failing to exemplify each other's point of view. They thought themselves too different to understand. Jerry gave a brief statement about purification that Martin deemed heinous and deluded. Martin said that the summer was red with black blood, not white, although whites fell too, and he explained his motives as retaliation. *Fire with fire*, the man closed his argument.

They were not at opposite ends of a line that tilted from love to hate, but rather at opposite ends of a horseshoe. Two antipodal intents that were much closer to each other than they were to the middle.

The middle was compromise. Balance.

The middle was *progress*.

"Now what?" Martin asked.

Jerry thought he heard a flicker of peace in his tone. Like the man half considered an unreachable truce at this impasse. Jerry did not consider the same. He drew his blade and made his move.

Martin charged towards him knocking the knife from his hand. "Corey, stay back!" Martin cracked Jerry in the face, stumbling the man back, his hand a pound of pain. He got a few good hits in before Jerry caught his rhythm.

The Southern man ducked a swing for his head and jabbed Martin in the stomach, knocking the wind from him. He followed with an elbow across his face that echoed into the rafters and cut his cheek. A knee was next, and Martin tumbled to the ground.

Jerry bumbled over to where his blade had landed but as he went to collect it, Martin stomped on the back of his knee and clutched Jerry in a chokehold. He turned blue quickly. Martin seemed to have no plan of drawing out the altercation. Jerry's vision dimmed as he clawed at Martin's arms. The squeeze was becoming intolerable, but Jerry had plenty of experience from a long life with asthma. The lack of air would have shut the eyes of any other man at that point. With thin wet fingers, he jabbed Martin in the eyes, and the built man lumbered back, rubbing his face.

"Dad!"

The scrape of metal screeching against cold stone was overshadowed by Corey's harrowed cry. Martin opened his eyes to see if his son was okay, and when he turned back to his opponent, Jerry thrust the steel into his gut.

"*NO!*" Corey cried.

"No..." Elizabeth gasped by the crate.

Jerry pushed the knife to its hilt and clutched Martin by the back of the head to whisper in his ear. "My name is Jerry Lynch. Tell your wife."

A Rose Red

BLOOD. EVERYWHERE. On the floor, over his mind, and pouring from his father's gut.

A weightlessness ruined Corey's body with little ethereal knives. Air was now a foreign concept to the place where his lungs were. He couldn't breathe, and for the first time, it was due to a greater affliction than his asthma. It was like he viewed the scene from some phantom projection, with the silent figures of his mother, grandfather, and now his father, all watching with him. He watched himself rise, but the pain crippled his legs. Crawling was the only option. The cold stone and blood-blackened puddles were lost of their sensation. A tingle passed through Corey, one that spun his spine with vicious grades of grief. His brain raced to finish first in finding a reason why this was happening, why his father lay dead on the ground before him.

There was blood. Everywhere.

Corey crawled to his father's body, whose eyes held the gaze of the afterlife. Tears barreled unrelentingly down his face as he shoved his father a few times, hoping one would shake him back to life.

He was gone.

The rain grew heavier and doused Jerry as the man ambled over to Elizabeth, cleaning the blade of Martin's blood on his pants. Corey could overhear him uttering something disparaging.

"-Jerry you've gone too far..." A quiver rocked her voice.

"Ma, I'm just getting started. That spook was just the beginning. Many more will be purified along this path. Better get used to it." Jerry bent down to her and cocked his head toward the half-broken whiskey bottle. "Or drink up."

"She's nothing like you think!" Corey yelled, shaken but enraged. "She is strong, caring, and a mother if I ever knew one. No one's perfect, and if you think she is that same person she was when she lost you, you're wrong. She made a mistake." Water spritzed down his face, masking the tears. "We are all human, we bleed the same, we love the same, we hate the same. Still, we are all human."

Jerry rose and turned to him. "Looks like you got a little fan here, Ma." He sheathed his blade and took a nonchalant step towards Corey, bathing in rain and moonlight as he went. A dismal setting for a feigned apotheosis. "You think she's your mother or something, now do ya, boy?" The Southern man laughed like he knew more than them both. "I'm glad one of us got to feel whatever love she had to offer. I sure as hell didn't. My father taking me away from that *mess*," he snarled Elizabeth's way, "was the best thing that happened to me, second to my daughter. Coming back to her was the worst."

"If you had tried, she would have been a great mother."

Jerry chuckled and edged closer to Corey, rain droplets sparkling across his skin. "Silly boy, she's the reason *your* mother's dead."

Corey froze.

The words echoed through him, pernicious and unfathomable. They were a blow to his psyche. Speech struggled to leave his lips. "W-what? Why would you lie about that? My mother has been dead for ten years. That's not possible."

Jerry exhaled heavily through his nose like he was releasing a long, pent-up pressure as he crouched to Corey. "You see, boy," he dipped into his pocket and pulled out a photo. The photo of Corey, his mother, and a rose. "This is you, right?" Jerry tapped a blood-stained finger on Corey's three-year-old face. "And this is your mother?" He shifted to the honey-skinned woman.

"Y-yes-"

"See, about a decade ago, I met your mother on the worst day of my life. Every night I try to sleep, I see her face and hear her name at the start of the worst dream you could imagine." There was no expression on Jerry's face now. "*Cora Malcolm.*"

*

"DADDY," Rose called. Sat between her grandmother and father, she played with her blonde pigtails, voice like the calm of a summer breeze. *"When are we coming back to see grandma?"*

"I'm not sure, sugar bump, it might not be for a while." Jerry sat on the passenger's side of the car, stroking his daughter's head with a warmth Elizabeth didn't know Jerry had in him.

As Elizabeth drove, battered with sweat, she watched as the two sang songs, shared laughs, and spoke about adventures they hadn't had yet. Jerry tickled Rose until she was out of breath and even pretended to take her ear one time—the type of trick a seven-year-old could fall for.

Elizabeth blinked away the glaze of her eyes, too focused on driving to get involved. This was the first time she had met her granddaughter, and they got on like fuel and flame. Rose could sing well for her little years and owned a heart teeming with too much good for the evil of this world. A heart so pure it softened even Jerry's callous exterior to fluffy textures. Now they were headed to the train station on their way home before Elizabeth truly got a chance to know her granddaughter.

See, earlier that morning, she and Jerry had argued. About the past, about her not being there and being drunk all the time during his youth. He said some malicious things and topped it off by telling her she'd never see Rose again. The pain was lurid; just when she had the chance to make amends for all her past transgressions, Jerry stripped her of that chance like his father did all them years ago. Jerry left the house but returned later with Rose, who bawled to see her grandmother. It must have turned his heart tender because he couldn't deny her a goodbye. He agreed to let Elizabeth take them to the station.

The car swayed, and Elizabeth caught the steering wheel from running loose. *"Sorry."*

Jerry thought it was the person beside them who was at fault. He roared towards a grizzly black man in a tight suit. *"You dirty low life."*

253

Rose whacked him on the shoulder, frowning. "Daddy, that's not nice. I don't like when you're mean."

"You're right, sugar bump." He kissed her forehead. "I'm sorry."

Down the street, Elizabeth did her best to hide her flushed face, but the switch in attention proved calamitous. The car skidded left, then right, and before she knew it, it slammed into the front of another vehicle.

Everything went black.

When she awoke, her head was thumping and chin bleeding.

Rose was already dead.

A True Black

9-6-1-5. IT WAS WHAT HE SAW FIRST amidst the sour, burnt-black smoke and the sting of tinnitus before he caught sight of her body lying at the edge of life.

The world rendered an alarm to all his senses; he was at odds with balance. The ground was turbulent, as if walking through a rushing tide. Knees the consistency of jelly, he fought to stay upright. Fought for stolid strides. Fought to reach his daughter.

9-6-1-5. Four numbers that were the code to his past.

The first step was the hardest.

His legs were numb, and tendons clicked a brittle sound against bone. The last time his body felt this way was moments after he took his first life. Hunkered in a deep trench along the Western Front, when the guns went quiet and the stars were loud, a German soldier attempted an ambush on his platoon with nothing but a Stielhandgranate and madness in his mind. Jerry dealt him his end with a broken bottle and knee-jerk reflexes, disposing swiftly of the stick grenade. Nausea held him close that night.

He never thought the bottle would save his life, but he feared it may take hers.

Now, however, stars were exchanged for shattered glass, guts for car parts, but there was just as much blood. At least France had the decency to hide it in the mud.

The second step was accompanied by a new pain.

When he stumbled at the sight of smoke clearing from his daughter's face, agony in his arm sent him weak again. Blood gushed from a gash that ran the length of his forearm, dripping onto the hilt of his blade as he looked around for something to help his balance. Only his mother's unconscious and bleeding face, sat, in their ruined vehicle came into view. A rancorous feeling spread in his chest. "Illness is more than physical symptoms," he recalled Clinton saying when being taught the man's illusory opinions on purification. He knew his mother needed purification from her undertow of illness.

After the third step, he was used to the ache. The moment before he reached his daughter, a black, bloodied hand reached through the smoke—the devil coming to collect her, he thought.

"I'm a nurse," they said. "My name's Cora Malcolm."

"I'm a curse," he heard.

Panic sequestered his rationale in morbid hollows as he lunged for her through the haze. Drawing his blade, he thrust it in her gut and watched the shock explode onto her face. "Don't touch my daughter!" The same shock was mirrored in his own when he saw it was not the devil, but the face of a woman.

Flustered. Disoriented.

Jerry scooped up his daughter and called for help.

A Blood Red

THE FACE OF FATE hung in front of Corey, emotionless and a mess with rain. Believing what Jerry had just told him was something he found arduous, but the man's eyes were not lying. What reason did he have to lie?

"B-But, why? How?" Corey struggled, mind festooned with new images of his mother dying the same way his father did, and by the same man no less.

"I ask myself the same thing every night." Jerry's tone was somber, sincere like he was talking for that brief moment to someone he cared for. "But the fact remains, that *great mother* over there," he flapped the photo Elizabeth's way, "was drunk the day she drove me and my Rose to the train station. If she wasn't, my daughter would still be alive. So would your mother, as we would have never collided in that crash, and our families never would have met.'

"Miss Elizabeth... Is that true?" Corey wiped his face of rain and tears.

"Yes..." Elizabeth sobbed. "I was drunk, but it was an accident. When he left the first time that day, I was so sad. It reminded me of when Henry took my boys from me. So I drank. I just wanted to see Rose one last time. And when he came back, I was overjoyed. I didn't mean for any of that to happen."

"It was the last time for both of us," Jerry stated.

Corey sat confused, fighting the feeling of hate. If Elizabeth hadn't made her first mistake, losing her sons because of a long dance with alcohol, Jerry might have been different. Stayed North with Elizabeth and grown into a man of compassion and love. All the potential of a better man tarnished by corrupt nurturing. Then her second mistake was being too proud to say she was drunk when Jerry offered to let her to take them to the station. Both created the man that killed his father, his mother—Nina even—and caused more pain than he thought he could know. If she hadn't made those mistakes, his mother would still be alive.

"I'm sorry," Elizabeth wept.

No. All the love came flooding back to wash away the embers of hate. The desperation in her eyes when she chased the train for him, how she shielded him from Henry's enmity in Dallas, what he did to save her life and dignity back in Louisiana, even something as small as teaching him to tie a tie, the way she tussled through riot to reach him while staring at uncertainty, sold her precious pearls to get them closer to home, and did her best to make sure he was never alone. How she did all that and would likely do it again.

How she cared for him.

It wasn't her fault, and Corey knew it. "Miss Elizabeth, it's okay. I don't blame you for what happened. We all make mistakes." Corey was to grant her another chance to make amends. Correct all the wrongs of her past by living a future right. It was the least he could do after all she had done for him.

Jerry stood straight and trudged back to the center of the warehouse directly under the moonlight. He unsheathed his blade. "Now you know the truth, it's best to send you to your parents."

Corey's eyes widened as he shuffled back, scathing his palms on the concrete's imperfections, knocking stray glass from his path.

"Jerry, no!" Elizabeth went to stand, but her legs were weak from the ordeal. "Leave. Him. *Alone.*"

"You see, boy, I once learned a lesson about ablution. It came from a wise man with clear ideas of purification." Jerry twirled his blade as he approached Corey once more. "He told me that *darkness* is a disease, one intent on afflicting a pure mind." He stood over Corey now." And before that disease festers and breeds, becomes beyond your control, you must cut it out. I was young back then and didn't truly understand what he meant." Jerry drew back his blade. "I do *now.*"

There was a scrape of glass against concrete, and as Corey closed his eyes to accept his end, he heard flesh burst and felt warm blood spray across his face. When he looked up expecting pain, Jerry was wide-eyed, choking on his blood with a whiskey bottle bulging from his neck. He fell to the ground, leg twitching, guzzling claret.

In his place, Elizabeth stood shaken, blood on her hands as she panted for air to calm her nerves.

There was blood. Everywhere.

Fate deemed it not theirs.

A Love Red

LOVE HAD BEEN HIDDEN for weeks, while hate culminated into the eruptions of riots and indignation that stripped them of their families.

Corey had lost his cousin and father, while Elizabeth her sons.

They had come through a shadowy valley to reach home, and despite all the regrettable loss, there were things they gained. The people they met, the moments they had, but most of all, the fact that they had found one another.

A new day was dawning. They hadn't been entirely sure how long they had walked since they left the warehouse, but what was sure is that they said nothing to each other. They were silent on their way home as the sun rose to bloom golden petals. The hum of the city stirring filled the air as they took a long road north towards Elizabeth's. Before long, they split into a clearing that was bordered by bold buildings stretching far into the sky with gray fingers, only a dusty train track beneath them. Corey tied his shoelace halfway up the track, then stopped.

Where did he go now? Home? Where was home? After all that he'd lost, there was no simple solution. His grandmother lived in Boston, but she was none the wiser to the events that had occurred. He could go there after things settled, but what about Elizabeth? She'd be alone. The days they spent together felt like a lifetime. It wasn't as easy as just leaving, however irrational the idea.

They had laughed together, fled together, fought together, and lost together.

Martin monopolized the ambient regions of Corey's mind, his essence echoing in the hollow space that had permanently formed within him. He was gone, and although it hadn't fully sunken in yet, it would be a long road before he could accept that fact.

All the lessons he had learned from his father would need to be the foundation upon which he built his life.

Leadership.

Family.

Progression.

Though these lessons were never taught from textbooks like the subjects he salivated over, he learned them from looking. Seeing his father lead a fight for causes that would reap no acclaim. How everyone was family, those who had much and especially those who had nothing. And progress didn't mean fancy evening wear, big businesses, or elegant enterprises—it meant a full cowling of institutional and cultural consideration. Fairness that each person be given the same opportunities and aid to be who they wanted to be. The type of progress that can only proceed in the absence of greed.

Corey assumed his father wasn't perfect—no one was. But as he thought longingly about him, he decided he didn't need him to be.

He was too tired for any more tears. Exhaustion had left him only wanting to sleep, hoping that when he awoke, the mist of this nightmare would vanish the way it did in so many books he had read. Corey knew that wasn't going to happen, but being unsure about what was next, sleep was the only thing he was sure about.

Elizabeth smiled when she looked back and saw his eyes closed, taking deep breaths, bathing in the last of the summer rays. She joined him. For a long while, they just stood there. Together.

It was a summer the world would not forget, one *they* couldn't. How many other people suffered pain worse than theirs? How many people didn't make it home? No one would ever know. Their tales were locked in the miserable microcosm of the past summer. Laid to rest under blood and hate.

Corey and Elizabeth continued on their way, trailing the train track for some time before they slipped back in the gut of the city. Elizabeth recognized a shop and knew they weren't far.

They reached her street, and the crunch of green lawn underfoot thawed them, along with the help of the morning sun. Corey's eyes dipped low, and he kept yapping his mouth; tiredness had also come home. The minute they reached the porch, he simmered into Elizabeth's rocking chair while she sat on the step, her head resting against the balustrade.

Elizabeth wandered through floaty thoughts. They seemed to rise and not go anywhere. She thought loosely about Arthur and all she couldn't do for him. Some about Martin and how desperately similar he and Jerry were in their ambitions. A lot about how she had to take her son's life in order to save Corey; her hands still trembled at its ends as she clenched tight to stop the shaking and hide the dried blood that crumbled between her joints.

She asked herself if there was another way. Could she have redeemed him if she had tried? The short answer was no. The long one was yes.

Hindsight tended to be a master of analysis with an almighty perspective.

Perhaps if she was present throughout his childhood, more caring and comforting like she was capable of, taught him the things she knew were right, perhaps then he would have been a different man. He and Martin could have been friends, grown together and merged their symmetric energy to change the world from the inside and out. But Jerry was drawn in ink; no amount of erasing could change the lines his world had painted him in.

He was only her son by blood and not bond. The boy she had birthed was a far cry from the man she ended. Still, that reasoning would not be enough to purge all that pain.

Most of all she thought about Corey, and even though they had met just days ago, she worried he'd be alone.

"Corey," she turned to see him drooling and drawing deep snores. She entered her home to search for a blanket that was cream in color with a wobbly red heart knitted at its center—it was intended for Rose many years ago.

Corey's notepad tumbled out his pocket when she drew the sheet over him. She scooped it up and sat back on the step. A slight sensation of guilt ran through her. She was going to read it without him knowing, but he did say, *"When it's all done."* As far as Elizabeth could see, things were done. For now, at least, the lingering tribulation thought to take a break.

She opened it up and read the title of his poem: *The Color Within.*

We bleed at the setting of day
We bleed at the dawn of night
It is too black to know the way
And where it is white it shines plight
In shadow we remain waited
Darkness before a dance with light
If we loved as much as we hated
Then the mad dogs could sleep at night
That love would reach to a time beyond
To a place where black lives matter
A place pain is feeble and joy strong
Where there is no bullet or dagger
We war over the color of skin
And forget about the color within

Elizabeth cried till she was tired, and when the tears dried on her blouse, she read it again and cried some more. Sleep took her as the sun was in full rise.

There were still plights in the world, woes that manifested themselves in ugly minds and horrid agendas. Things that couldn't be cured entirely by words or golden doctrines. If even a single heart could be changed, rewritten in the language of love, the red that colored the summer could be viewed as the sharing of affection and not the spilling of blood. A lesson that whatever is *without* cannot take from what is *within*. There will be days to come, days that 'their' kind —the people who choose love—will have to embark on journeys just as, or far more, perilous to reach a destination of ethical parity. Wherever that journey terminated, if it would ever end, could breed an era of amity practiced innately by all creeds. As Corey and Elizabeth slept, they slept not knowing that they had love, and their Red Summer had come to an end.

Love was, and always will be, a simple answer with complex applications.

From the soils of South London, K. A. M./Kam developed a love for storytelling and writing when neither were prominent persuasions. Life pulled him in many directions from comic art, to game development and even more mundane professions such as currency trading but words and their infinite way of expression ultimately won the war. Seven years later, writing deludedly without assistance from pristine Ivy league halls, he honed the craft to present the world his debut novel The Color Within.

K. A. M./Kam is currently planning a Science Fiction novel he hopes can provide a new perspective on our little lives on Earth.

If he is not roaming his own mind, reading with red wine or enjoying olives, he can be found at the places below:
Twitter & Instagram: @kamlashley

Lightning Source UK Ltd.
Milton Keynes UK
UKHW012328070121
376448UK00001B/13